THE PROVING
THE SCEPTIC'S HANDBOOK SERIES

MERLIN GOLDMAN

Miracle Fish

ALSO BY MERLIN GOLDMAN

Pieces: Plays 1

The Carpenter and The Goat Herder

Want Do Get: A Screenwriters Manual

CHAPTER 1

Warren Stance studied the Bristol Post, slouched in his father's rust-coloured armchair. It was the only item Warren had taken after his death. The chair sat like a benign mole on the cream carpet. As a child, he'd sit on an arm and watch his father tackle the Telegraph's cryptic crossword, pushing each letter of each answer deep into the paper's fibres. It was the closest he'd ever felt to him.

Most people dismissed their local newspaper as a source of serious information. It was something you read if you wanted to buy a house, car, or baby buggy but not if you wanted to know the state of the nation. Warren disagreed. Hidden between supermarket openings and missed refuse collections, traps were being set for the gullible or unwary. In black and white and repeated online, were the Faustian pacts presented as simple slogans: Earn £250 a day from home, Order the next revolution in skincare, Learn the secrets of the rich. Human fallibility ready for exploitation by cheats, con artists, and liars.

Warren's mobile phone shook on the metal side table. He folded the paper and balanced it on his lap. It was a text message: Help me. Portland. They'd hidden their number and he didn't know anyone called Portland. He tapped out a reply: Who is this? He waited, his gaze drifting outside, at the branches flexing on the single oak tree blocking most of his view of the park. The window frames rattled.

Warren returned to the paper, open at the horoscopes. A housemate at Uni had written them for the Oxford Gazette. She'd been studying finance and knew nothing about astrology. But she'd been dating the editor and he'd needed someone urgently. She created a database using previous predictions and then randomly assigned them each week. The arrangement was still going when he graduated two years later. He wondered what she was doing now.

Warren squinted as the sun emerged from behind a large bank of clouds. His phone rang, vibrating in his hand. He snapped it to his ear. 'Portland?'

'What?'

'Who is this?'

'It's Harris. I need you to come into the office.' Harris was the senior journalist on the magazine: The Sceptic's Handbook. He got first pick of any new lead.

'On a Sunday?' said Warren. 'You're there already, aren't you?'

'Anna's bridesmaids came over to discuss...never mind. I thought I'd give them some space.'

'How kind of you.'

'Too right,' said Harris. 'Bring coffee.'

———

Warren paused on the pavement and glanced up at his building, still chewing a cooling slice of toast. His mother remained upset he'd bought a top floor flat. The communal door clicked shut. He'd take the direct route: walking from Cotham, he'd go through the University, across Clifton triangle and down Park Street. He'd pick up the coffees on the Harbourside close to the office.

Stood at the north-west corner of Queen Square, and holding two flat whites, Warren took in the city. The dark, elegant birch trees stood like mourners around its perimeter. The office was on the far side, it's single window an amber beacon. Two gravel paths ran corner to corner, meeting at a statue of William III astride a horse. During the summer, the square hosted various events. Last week, they'd held a comedy show in a red and white tent. Much of the grass was now mud

In his first month, (had it really been two years), Harris had asked Warren to drive to Swindon to photograph a pond of misshapen tadpoles. This had meant negotiating The Magic Roundabout, a ring of five small roundabouts orbiting a single, much larger one. It collected accidents like merit badges. Harris had told him, 'Aim for your exit, close your eyes and put your foot down.' It was worth a try.

Warren pushed open the office door with his hip, trying not to spill any more of the coffee. The folded magazine keeping it open, flipped face up. It was the crying statues issue, his only cover story. He kicked it inside. The door shut with a loud clunk. Harris's eyes appeared briefly above his computer screen before disappearing, leaving only his ragged, caramel hair.

Warren took off his coat and flung it onto the coat stand. The open plan office had six white Formica desks with computers on each. Four were in pairs and the remaining two were at the back, near the small kitchen. The boss, Professor Miriam Stanzen, sat there alongside an occasional intern. Miriam was a full-time academic and part-time magazine editor. You didn't do this type of journalism for the money. She'd sat him opposite Harris. 'So, I can keep an eye on you,' Harris would tease. Warren set the coffees down on his desk.

Harris pressed forward, curling his arm around the back-to-back monitors to pick up his. 'There no biscuits by the way.'

'I could be somewhere else, you know. Like church?'

Harris harrumphed. 'After seeing this, you might just choose to become religious.'

'Says the lapsed Catholic.' Warren used his arms and legs to wheel his chair along his then Harris's desk, the surface of long since hidden by layers of newspaper cuttings, copies of the magazine and food wrappers. Harris rotated his monitor so Warren could see. 'You know your desk is a …' Warren tried to complete the sentence, but his mouth refused to move. An image of a baby filled the screen. It was male, naked, and lying on its back. The eyes were open, but it was unquestionably dead. Warren turned away, feeling bile rise in his throat.

'I know,' said Harris. 'It's not something you'd ever expect to have to see.'

'Is it real?'

'It could be a doll, but it looks pretty real.' Harris turned the screen back. 'It was in the general email folder. Didn't you see it?'

Warren looked at the floor. 'I don't check work emails at the weekend.'

'Well, anyway, I tried replying but it bounced back and the address is just a jumble of letters.' Warren eased his chair next to Harris. The first time he'd seen his nephew Peter, his sister Faith was holding him in her arms in John Radcliffe Hospital's maternity unit. He was pink and wrinkled, warm inside a blanket. He looked again - this baby was blue.

'What about the image file – anything?'

'Only that's a month old, taken with an old phone. Not much to go on.' Harris straightened one of the smaller towers.

'The text message,' said Warren, searching through his pockets, causing their chairs to clash together as he stood.

'What text message?'

Warren pulled out his phone, his hand shaking. There'd been another text. He read it then turned the screen towards Harris.

'DT5 1BW,' said Warren.

'Number plate?'

'Check it.'

Harris opened the Gov.uk website and entered the sequence. It was a relief to obscure the image. Harris pasted it into a Google search bar: Portland.

'Not a name, a place. Where is it?'

'Blow in,' said Harris. 'It's in Dorset. It's an island, sort of, joined to the mainland by Chesil Beach. It's an odd place – feels like you're at the mercy of the sea, even indoors.' Harris minimised the window, revealing the baby once more.

'Anything at that location?'

Harris scanned the map. 'Guest house, petrol station and a quarry – which is to be expected.'

Warren slid the phone into a gap on Harris's desk, clasped his hands together and tried to look anywhere but the image. Harris had served in the army, maybe he was used to this sort of thing.

'I've checked news sites, even blogs and forums.'

'Local papers?'

'Dorset Echo, Dorset Live. Nothing.'

Warren pushed back his chair, cradling his head in his hands, and breathed out. 'What about the dark net?'

'I've not got the stomach for that today. Perhaps, tomorrow. I could take Glade on a trip to the dark side.' Glade Korza was this year's intern: an American researching any correlations between public data and social behaviour.

'You might want to check with the Prof first. The Uni's got rules about what you can and can't do with interns.' Warren stood up, shaking out his arms. He stood behind Harris. 'What's it lying on?' Harris zoomed in. 'Some sort of clothing?'

'Looks like a swaddling blanket. Standard hospital issue when you have a baby. Or so I've been told.' Harris scrolled across the enlarged image.

Warren rocked. 'I don't understand why'd they want us involved. If it was stillborn, they wouldn't be allowed to take it home. If it died at home, why take a picture?' Harris shrugged. 'Or maybe it was healthy but unwanted. You know the kind of thing. The mother was young, distraught, alone… and didn't know what to do. She left it somewhere. Perhaps she took the photos as a keepsake. But if someone else took it, why contact us?' Warren folded his arms. 'And why send *us* the picture, this isn't something we deal in?'

Warren swung his seat in a circle then stopped. 'So, all we have is a picture of a dead baby, taken by someone and sent to us. Along with a text message, which may or may not be related, of some remote part of Portland. And why send to us and not the police? A sick joke? Maybe it's just a doll. Or maybe someone wants to make us think that down in deepest Dorset there's a sinister cult operating, and this is some sort of sick ritual. That would be up our street. My money's on some bastard playing us for a bunch of idiots. Then again, dare we ignore it?'

'Not much to go on. I guess we should notify the police anyway.'

'Would they be interested with so little to go on. Let's do a bit of digging first. Bring in some outside help if needed.'

'Warren?'

'I think we should keep it to ourselves for a bit. At the moment, I don't think we have a good enough reason why we were sent this stuff.'

Harris poked at the screen. 'Maybe this is why.'

Warren gripped the desk, pitching forward. The baby was missing the index finger on its right hand.

CHAPTER 2

Warren opened his front door to find his sister, Faith, busy in his kitchen. Closing the door, he watched as she transferred multiple small, white bottles from a cardboard box onto his work surface with quiet efficiency.

'I thought you were giving me back the spare key?'

'You know Mum likes me to keep an eye on you,' she said without stopping.

'She wasn't like this when Dad was alive,' said Warren, crossing the lounge and collapsing into the armchair.

Faith closed the box's lid and slid it along the polished floor towards the front door. 'It keeps her occupied,' she said, striding into the lounge and leaning on the back of the chair. 'I think you'll really like those.'

'What are they?'

'You know you didn't give the last ones a chance.' She ruffled his hair. 'These are different; you'll feel great after a few weeks.'

'I feel fine now.' Warren peered around the armchair. 'Pete not with you?'

'Peter's trampolining with Gerry.'

'I hope his wig falls off.'

'Be nice,' she said, straightening upl. 'Some things aren't meant to last forever. There's a natural cycle to life.'

'Gerry cheated on you,' said Warren, pushing himself out of the chair. 'Thank god you've got your own place now, so I don't have to see him when I'm coming to see Pete.'

'And me?' she said, skipping around him to perch on the curved windowsill. 'You don't mind me helping you, do you?'

'Some might say experiment on.'

She swung up an arm, revealing one of the bottles. She shook it between her thumb and forefinger. 'Drink this.'

'Will it make me bigger or smaller?'

'Just drink it, you might like it.'

He snatched it from her. 'I doubt it.' Warren read the label: Energises and sustains. Made with nature's cure: Beech sap. He frowned. 'You've got to be joking?'

Faith snatched the bottle, shook it, unscrewed the top and handed it back to him. 'It's like a cross between a jelly and a smoothie.'

Warren got up and carried the bottle at arm's length in front of him to the kitchen. 'So, when are you going back to work?'

'I might not need to, I sold three units today,' she said, following him. 'If you bought a box, I'd only need another five to hit my target for the month.'

'It's a con,' said Warren, surveying the collection on the black granite work surface. He placed the open one by the others, before turning and opening the fridge. He took out a can of beer.

'Beech sap is great for detox,' said Faith, leaning against the galley kitchen's door frame. 'And hangovers.' She smiled, pointing at the open bottle.

Warren sighed, then picked it up. Faith glared at him the

same way their mother did when morning spoonsful of cod liver oil were compulsory.

He drank it in a single gulp. 'Jesus,' he said, shaking his head, He opened the can with a hiss and gulped several mouthfuls of beer letting foam splash onto the floor.

'Warren!'

'Don't worry, the cat will drink it.' He turned on the oven. 'Care to stay for dinner?'

'What are you making?' Faith pulled the bottle from Warren's grip and checked inside.

'Hawaiian pizza.' Warren drank again. 'You could pick off the ham.'

'No, thanks.' Faith threw the bottle in the bin. 'So where were you, morning run?'

'Funny.'

'I found the paper on the floor; did you find something interesting?'

Warren selected a pizza from the freezer. 'Something found us.'

'Go on.'

'Someone sent the office a picture of a dead baby.'

'My god, I've not seen anything on the news.'

'I don't think it's been reported.' Warren ripped off the cardboard.

'Are you sure it was dead?' He nodded. 'So, you reported it?'

'Not yet.'

Faith put her hands on her hips. 'Warren, you've got to?' Warren tore at the clear packaging with his teeth. 'Warren!'

'Look, if it turns out not to be a hoax, which it probably will be, we'll call the police in Portland.'

'Give that to me,' she said grabbing the pizza. 'Portland?'

'I got a couple of texts.'

'What texts?'

'The second one gave us a postcode in Portland, Dorset.'

Faith searched through the kitchen's drawers. 'And you think they're linked?'

'Maybe.'

'What are you going to do?'

'We're going down there.'

'Here we are,' she said, pulling out a pair of scissors.

'Do you want to come?'

She cut neatly around the pizza's edge then pulled off the plastic. 'Here you go,' she said, handing it to him. 'I don't think I'm ready and, in any case, I don't think it's allowed.'

He bent over, sliding the pizza into the oven. 'They don't have to know.'

'You should wait till it's at temperature.'

'Well?'

'I can't. I'd like to help but…I don't think I could trust myself if things become difficult.'

'I'm not expecting them to,' said Warren shrugging, 'but fair enough.'

'I could make a call to the office, see if anyone's heard anything.' Faith looked at the oven's fascia. 'Is that the correct time?'

'I've never set it.'

Faith kissed him on the cheek. 'I'd better be off.' She headed for the door. 'Peter's getting dropped soon.'

Warren swept his hand towards the bottles. 'Thanks for these delicacies. The police force's loss is network selling's gain.'

Faith scooped up the half-empty box, keeping the door open with her elbow as she slid out. 'Let me know when you finish them, and I'll bring more over.' He raised his beer as the door closed.

Warren stood in the bay window, observing Faith position the box into her car's boot next to several others. He hoped Pete wasn't having to drink them. His phone rang. He examined the screen, returning to the kitchen to find the beer can. 'What do you want now?'

'Fancy a pint?' said Harris

Warren lifted the can to his lips. 'I've already got one.'

'A real one.'

————

The Hare on the Hill was their regular haunt by the simple fact it was equidistant between them. It was on a corner, leaning down towards Stoke's Croft. A thick belt of green tiles ran around it.

Warren entered as an ensconced Harris rammed a large handful of pork scratchings into his mouth. Harris's soft pink cheeks rotated while his arm felt for his pint. The part of the sleeve below his wrist of his amber jacket was darker than the rest of it. He'd always wondered if Harris's had ever noticed. Of if he cared.

'Pig,' said Warren, approaching.

'Lovely,' mumbled Harris, standing up. 'What do you want to drink?'

Warren surveyed the row of taps and the chalk board behind them. He switched his attention to Harris's half-finished pint. 'What've you got?'

'Bishop's Kiss,' he said, swallowing. 'A hoppy aroma with a delicate finish of inappropriate behaviour.'

Kelly, the barman, gripped two of the beer pumps. His thick, red beard hid the tight slit of his mouth.

'I'll stick with my usual, the IPA,' said Warren. Kelly nodded, grabbed a glass, and began to pour.

'I have some news,' said Harris.

'You've joined the gym again.' Warren took out his wallet.

'We're having a kid.'

Warren shook the wallet at him. 'You kept that quiet.

Shouldn't you have asked me first? We're not even living together?'

'Funny.'

Kelly handed Warren his pint which he jutted towards Harris. 'Congratulations.'

Their glasses met. Harris drank the rest of his beer like a pelican swallowing a small fish. 'I'll get his and another for me.'

'Yours is on me,' said Kelly, pouring Harris a fresh pint. 'Comhghairdeas.'

Warren listened politely as Harris unburdened himself of weeks of secrecy. Harris had never been good at keeping things private from the moment they'd been introduced. When Warren had first started, it had been a rapid introduction to the magazine – its history of owners, investors, volunteers, and cases. But along with it came all of Harris's stories of his time in the army, the off-on relationship with his wife and him winding up as chief reporter. While Warren accepted the bargain he'd inadvertently struck, there where times when he wished Harris didn't take silence as encouragement. Warren recognised Harris had finished when he stopped gesticulating and melted back over the low bar stool. Warren wondered if Harris would make a good father. Undoubtedly.

'You don't mind the dog, do you?' said Kelly. He'd been circling the bar collecting empties and was now stood with his back to the door. His posture neatly framed him within its stained-glass inlay. He pointed down to Warren's feet, the glasses clinking together.

Warren dropped his head. A golden mass of canine flesh was splayed over his left foot. The dog lifted its head and stared at him with large, brown globes beneath inquisitiveness eyebrows. 'It's no problem.'

When Kelly was back behind the bar, Warren slid his incubated foot gently backwards. The dog remained unmoved.

'How's the crop circle story coming along?' Warren said to Harris.

'I've not got any pictures yet, but I'll get some next week, and rehash the text from some previous articles,' said Harris. 'Easy-peasy. Job done.'

Warren shifted on his stool. 'Is that allowed?' He'd been there for less than a year. Harris was meant to show him the ropes. Sometimes it felt like Warren was teaching Harris how to tie the right knot.

'A crop circle is a crop circle is a crop circle. It's either bored old men or pissed Physics students. But our readers love 'em. They don't *really* want anything new. The subscriptions never passed three thousand.' Harris opened his arms, aiming the white buttons on his tightening lilac shirt at Warren. 'People don't want their beliefs challenged. You've not been here long enough to understand that.' Harris rubbed the back of his neck. 'I think we'll be lucky to still be here in a year.' He offered Warren the bag of pork scratchings again.

Warren felt queasy and shook his head. 'Do you really think so?'

Harris drunk half his pint in a single drag and wiped his mouth with the back of his other hand, gripping the small bag tightly. 'Advertising's moving online. The owners don't have the money to make the transition. You've seen the website, it's pathetic. Even if they did, most of our readers are too ancient to migrate across.'

Harris emptied the remaining rinds into his mouth. His eyes darted towards Kelly. He held up the packet. 'Another,' he mumbled. Warren shot him a look. 'What? I'm celebrating.'

Harris ambled back to Montpelier while Warren began his ascent to Cotham. Everything is on a hill in Bristol. If you weren't on top of one, you were on the side of one. Often, it felt as if you were at the bottom of a completely new one. If you ever found yourself on a flat piece of paving, it was inevitably just a short respite before a concrete mountain reared up in front of you.

Warren stood outside his building, listening to the bass drum of his heart. He could see the top edge of his television in the bay window. The sandstone facade's sharp edges had softened like soap. He took a deep breath, entered through the communal entrance, and climbed the two flights of narrow stairs to his top-floor flat.

Once inside, he turned on the television and gripped the corner, as if he might feel it filling with electrons. He gazed drunkenly over the glittering city, from the tower blocks stood like sentries in Montpelier and St Paul's, over the underground tunnels of the Bearpit, down into Bristol's sprawling city centre and the boats moored at the Harbourside.

The city's apparent stillness was at odds with his own thoughts. He considered those beneath the rooftops: their mistaken beliefs and superstitious practices. Each one able to infect someone else with a misheard news story or an old wives' tale. What was it that made us all so gullible? And what drove those who took advantage? He imagined this damaging dynamic being played out: sirens, bloodsuckers, and vultures circling above, their screeches inaudible to those sleeping below. But not to him.

He shut the curtains and turned his back, stepping into the cocoon of his photon-bathed living room.

CHAPTER 3

arren's suitcase lay open his bed. Beside it, everything that he needed to pack was arranged in a grid pattern. It had taken half an hour. Each object would now be added one by one to fill it. He'd unpack in the same way. It was meditative. There was a name for it, but he'd long forgotten it. Something Scandinavian.

He checked his watch. Harris should've been here by now to pick him up. He checked his phone. Nothing.

He waited ten minutes then called him. 'Running late?'

'Look, I'm sorry, but I can't come. I need to be at home. Can you get there on your own?'

Warren paused, turning towards his window. 'How?'

'Train?'

'Then what?' Warren snapped. 'Hike about on foot?'

'Hold on.' Silence was followed by a door shutting. 'As soon as I told Anna why we were going, she got upset. I know it's only a coincidence. Babies. I said you'd understand.'

'I don't, but there's nothing I can do about it now. It seems you've got your mind made up.' Warren turned back to his bed. 'Look, I'd better get going if I want to get there at all.'

'I'm sorry.'

Warren surveyed the items for the trip: mostly clothes but also a DSLR camera, small torch, and an old laptop. The cat jumped on the bed. 'Hold on. Could you feed the cat, I forgot to ask Faith and can't get hold of her?' It tiptoed between his rolled-up socks and folded underwear.

'Sure.'

'There's a spare set of keys in the bottom drawer of my desk at work.'

The journey was in two stages, the first fast and the second much slower as he approached Weymouth. The train was sparsely occupied, students and families making day trips or returning to their studies. He felt disdain for their mundanity of their lives as his gaze shifting from the blurry countryside to each of them. This was neither fair nor generous, but he couldn't help it. Couldn't he be satisfied with something less disturbing than the potential death of a baby? No, and that's just how it was going to have to be.

The Fairview Hotel was near the beach according to his phone. Warren watched the blue dot move as the taxi drove him to it. He was surprised Harris had found somewhere this close on their budget. There had been little accommodation available in Portland. In any case, sometimes a bit of distance helped, particularly if his presence wasn't welcome.

As Warren hauled himself from the taxi, he cursed Harris. A flight of steps led up to entrance of the hotel: . Behind him was the esplanade in front of a long sandy beach. He began to climb.

A young female receptionist stood behind a wide, walnut-coloured reception desk. Her tight, short-sleeved milk white shirt mostly covered the rose tattoo runing from her upper arm across her shoulder. She pulled her collar closer as he approached. He signed the book, something that could only be their attempt at appearing quaint to tourists. He smiled at the round dab of moisture he'd left behind. His own wax seal.

His case bounced twice on the double bed before it settled. The room had two tall, narrow windows with a close view of the building next door. The bathroom had a single window with a view of the sea. If he leant out. He struggled to close it. He returned to his suitcase. It would take at least thirty minutes to unpack using the system. His stomach made up his mind. He'd unpack later.

Warren ordered fish and chips without deliberation in a busy restaurant overlooking the main strip in front of the beach. When halfway through, he surveyed the clientele. It was mostly families, the nuclear option, along with several retired couples. Was there anything more exciting to a child than chips - the glee on their faces as piles of yellow sticks were placed in front of them. One boy picked up a single fat chip and encouraged by his mother, gave it several cooling blows. Warren thought of the picture again. If it was real, how many breaths it taken before its life had ended.

As Warren held a single thick chip, tipped with tomato ketchup to his mouth, an image of the baby's hand flashed in his head like a struck match. He finished his meal quickly.

After unpacking, he slept with the bedroom window ajar. When woken by the angry cries of seagulls, he shut it and returned to bed.

———

You could take a direct bus from Weymouth to Portland. A second taxi would be pushing the Prof's tolerance. Warren sat near the front. He wiped the early morning condensation from the window as it drove down Chesil Road, a dead straight road acting as a soft bridge between the mainland and what would be an island without it.

Portland rose from the sea like setting toffee pulled from a pan of cooling sugar. Vegetation, houses, and a single snaking road clung to its light grey landward side. The bus growled as it began their ascent. Warren dug his fingers into the window's rubber seal and looked over his shoulder. No one looked perturbed. The bus slowed as the driver found a lower gear. His hands formed fists. The smell of burning oil penetrated the cabin and he closed his eyes.

At the summit, the bus turned inward, the incline gone. The engine noise softened, and they moved up through the gears. Warren breathed out.

He got off at the first stop he figured lay in the postcode in the text message. Harris had reviewed satellite images of the location but found nothing significant: a row of small houses, a quarry, a crescent beach, and the road that Warren now stood on, by himself.

The bus drove away. A girl pressed her face against the rear window. When Warren could no longer see her, he put his hands in his pockets and swept the surroundings. He realised he was a less than a hundred metres from the sea. Small trees and shrubs hid his view of it. Further up he could see a car park, protected by a metal barrier. Then further two houses. Despite the presence of man-made infrastructure, it felt cold, desolate and somehow inhuman, primitive.

On the other side of the road ran a long expanse of wispy, xanthous yellow grass, spreading back for a few metres, at which point it stopped abruptly. In the middle of it, nearly facing him, stood two thick white stone slabs, like bouncers outside a nightclub. Warren thought he'd try the houses first – at least there might be someone there he could talk to. Reaching them, he realised it was a wasted effort. Both were boarded up. He turned back and headed for the standing stones.

Warren rested his palm against the first; at shoulder height this was halfway up. It felt soft initially, then his hand grew cold. He gave it a push - it didn't budge. *Looks like I'm not getting in.* A chill crept up his arm and he pulled away. His skin had a film of white: limestone from the quarry below.

He moved past the obelisks and stood on the edge. He peered into the bleached abyss. It was six to seven hundred meters in diameter with steep, sloping sides. This was open cast mining: they cut blocks straight out of the ground.

On the far side, there was a solitary road leading out of the basin. At the bottom of this slipway stood a pale blue cabin. A light was on inside. There was no other way down. If he wanted to get to it, he'd have to walk around the perimeter. As he prepared himself for the hike, he thought he might as well take some pictures. His vantage point was good. Could see the whole quarry. The articles always needed pictures. He framed a shot and began.

Barking startled him and he lowered the camera, turning on his heel. A dog was bounding towards him, followed by a man gesticulating wildly and shouting at the hound. The dog bashed into Warren's legs with such force, he stumbled backwards, stepping onto loose earth and stone a the quarry's edge. He fell.

The dog's head appeared over the precipice as Warren frantically tried to grab something to break his fall. He slid, scraped, spun and tumbled, turning over and over. His view flipped between white and blue, quarry, sky, quarry, sky…

Then silence and Warren was on his back, winded. He did an internal scan of his body: his back felt okay, as did his arms and legs. But his shoulders and chest throbbed. His brain whined like a rescue cat.

Trying to inhale deeply, he was thrown upright by a fit of heavy coughing. A mist of white dust particles, sparkling like diamonds, surrounded him. He drew his coat over his mouth and slowed his breathing. Specks of chalk settled on him like ash.

Warren checked his pockets. His phone, wallet and a torch were still there. But the camera had been thrown clear. The lens had separated from the body and lay next to his left leg.

Warren reattached his prosthesis. The sock and shoe were still attached but like everything else, slick with white icing.

He tried standing and immediately retched, white sputum dribbling over his chin. He gathered up the camera and tried to reattach the two parts. They wouldn't engage and something inside the lens rattled. He placed the two halves in an empty pocket.

Looking up towards the rim of the quarry, a head appeared then drew back. *Thanks for the help.* He'd fallen a long way. If it hadn't been for the softness of limestone, he'd have been seriously injured, he reckoned. Dead even. He thought of the picture of the baby, finger missing. He imagined a picture of himself, a dead man, limb missing. He laughed uncontrollably and realised he was shaking. *All this is beyond my pay grade.* He orientated himself towards the cabin. There were two trucks and a car outside it. Tall, spindly floodlights surrounded them like insects.

Warren brushed himself down and headed for the cabin. Halfway he felt dizzy and stopped. He braced his hands on his thighs and dropped his head to his elbows. He breathed slowly. The space around him grew brighter and he felt faint. He pushed himself upright and was blinded by a light. He held his hand in front of his face, but it grew brighter, before splitting in two. Something behind it growled. An engine.

A truck headed towards him, its giant wheels floating on the soft surface. He waved his hands, but it continued unabated. He dived to his left and the light dissipated.

He was prostrate on his front and turned his head towards the vehicle. It had stopped beside him, it's front right wheel inches from his head. Even straining his neck, he could only briefly look up to the voice from the cab. 'Bloody hell. What are you doing in here?'

'Birdwatching?'

The truck driver assisted Warren to the cabin, his walk unsteady. The building's exterior looked like a sponge cake dusted with icing sugar. Underneath the frosting it was navy blue. There was a company logo too, but Warren was too disorientated to make it out as he was hauled up the wooden steps.

'I'm Geoff, by the way. Yeah, I know, place is filthy. Dust gets everywhere,' said Geoff, helping Warren inside. 'Like sand from the beach,'

There were two desks back-to-back and a small kitchen area in the far corner. A small fan heater ticked over in the other. Warren took off his coat and draped it over his legs as Geoff made tea. Warren tried to answer the man's questions as best he could. *What happened? What made you fall? What are you doing here, anyway?*

When brewed, Geoff handed Warren him a mug. It said "I love cats" on the side.

'Do you?' said Warren.

'What?' Warren lifted his drink. 'Oh, cats. Can't stand the things. My missus wants one. Keeps giving me things with cats on, hoping I'll change my mind. If you drop it, you'll be doing me a favour.' Geoff scratched his cheek. 'So why would someone writing for...'

'The Sceptic's Handbook.'

'Be wandering on top of a quarry's edge.'

'We got sent a post code that matches this location along with a photograph, that may or may not be related. We're based in Bristol, so it seemed worth checking out. Have you found anything in the quarry that shouldn't be here?'

'We get the odd bicycle and shopping trolley. Even had a car once. What sort of thing?'

'I'd prefer not to say at this moment. Do you normally work alone?'

'No. Health and safety and all that. Barry's on his way

back from a drop-off.' He picked up a walkie talkie. 'We've these things too, just in case.'

'I guess you only work during the day.' Geoff nodded. 'Would Barry have found anything?'

'I've been here longer than him. He's my little brother. Family business, you see. It may seem like a big place, but you got to remember, it's all white. Anything out of place sticks out like a sore thumb.'

Warren pushed himself out of the chair. 'I think I should go; I could do with a shower.'

'I'll give you a lift. I'll just let Baz know.'

As Geoff talked to his brother on the radio, Warren shuffled outside. He rubbed his back and surveyed the crater. He imagined a meteor crashing into earth, tossing each man-made object through the air like toys from a pram.

In the truck, Warren shifted his feet between the chocolate bar wrappers and empty drinks bottles. On the dashboard was a photo of Geoff, with what must be his family in one of those unsolicited rollercoaster pictures. He didn't think anyone bought those. There were three kids, two boys and a girl.

'Where would someone go round here if they needed help with a baby they didn't want?'

'Jesus, I wouldn't have a clue.' Geoff's shook his head. 'Who wouldn't want their own baby?'

They didn't speak for the rest of the journey.

———

Warren approached the reception desk, head down. The same receptionist was behind it, talking on the phone while twisting her hair. When she saw him, her head remained steady, but her eyes tracked him. He paused, smiled briefly then quickened his pace towards the stairs and ascended. She leant over the desk and saw a line of white footprints along the maroon carpet.

Warren pressed his palms against the green tiles of the shower, letting the water run down his back. It flowed past his right foot like single cream.

When the lower half of his leg was removed, he'd wake in the morning and forget it was gone. He still had those moments. Yet staring at it like this, there was no doubting its absence. He was due a blood test soon.

Warren sat on the end of the bed, watching television as he dried himself. He then fell back, sensing the blood pulsed thickly through him. He stared at the ceiling; two brown stains in the shape of Sicily and Malta. He let the remaining water droplets evaporate from his chest.

He chose to have dinner in the Raj. It was the first restaurant he'd found in Weymouth that wasn't serving fish and chips. It was less royal than its name suggested but it was busy, and the food was palatable. And he'd wasted a day. Achieved nothing. No new leads. He wondered if Geoff might have been more helpful if he'd revealed more about why he was there. Shock tactics. A dead baby, possibly in his quarry. It might have caught him off-guard. He might have let something slip … if he had anything to slip, that is. Warren sighed, realising he was going to have to give a bit more away to get something back. The waitress held the payment machine as he presented his bank card.

'Are you local?'

'I live in Portland.'

'I was there today, looking for information about a baby.'

She frowned.

'Would you know where someone might get help about a pregnancy they'd didn't plan or if they wanted to keep it secret?'

'Well, ...erm,... I dunno...There was this girl at my school. She got pregnant and had to leave before term finished. She kept it. I visited her in the hospital. The father didn't want anything to do with it. She's still living with her mother, I think.' She handed him his card and walked swiftly away.

CHAPTER 4

He held his face against the cool windowpane. A current of salty air slid across the glass. He inhaled, feeling its cleansing effect. When he remembered it was ozone attacking the mucous layer in his nose, he headed downstairs.

Warren scanned the breakfast room. The tables and chairs were packed closely together. He'd have to almost walk sideways if he wanted to go as far as the bay window without knocking into something. An athletic, older couple in slick raincoats were the only others in the room.

'Good morning,' he said, filling a bowl with cereal.

'Morning,' they replied with the faintest of Scandinavian accents.

He poured in the milk while searching for somewhere to put the cardboard packet, then sat at the nearest table. 'It's not been the best summer so far, has it?'

'We're from Denmark,' chuckled the man. 'As long as it's not snowing, we're happy.'

'Retired?'

'No, but she thinks I should be.' The woman remained focussed on her bowl of fruit. 'I build boats made of wood.

It's the family business. Our sons have taken over but I go in most days.'

The owner entered the room and descended on the buffet table, checking all the items. She picked up Warren's discarded cereal box.

The Danish woman said something to her partner. 'Would you have me sit in an armchair all day?' he replied.

The owner stood by Warren's shoulder with the packet. 'Would you like a full English breakfast?' He nodded, staring at the offending item. 'Poached or scrambled?'

'Scrambled.' Warren swallowed. 'Is there a hospital nearby?'

She paused. 'Are you unwell?'

'No, no. I'm writing a story on infant mortality and need to check something.'

'The nearest is in Westhaven or there's the old one in Portland.' She left the room.

The Danish man handed his partner an ordnance survey map. He turned to Warren. 'What are you researching?'

'In general, I focus on unexpected or unexplained events. Usually, it's people who say they've seen fairies at the bottom of the garden. Weird stuff like that. Crop circles and the like.' The man stared at him blankly. 'It's for a magazine called The Skeptic's Handbook.'

The woman titled the map to the horizontal and spoke to her husband. He grunted something back.

'We call them trolls,' said Warren.

The couple turned sharply towards him. 'I think I heard you say the word "Neisser." Small troll-like creatures. We ran an article on them just after I started. I believe the myth began in the sixties near Silkeborg. I hope I've pronounced that correctly.' The woman made a small nod. 'Cows were found with their throats cut and locals said they'd seen a small figure, dressed in brown with a pointed hat. It remains unsolved. Perhaps they're waiting for their next victim.'

The woman folded the map and handed it back. She mumbled something and they both got up. He bumped the edge of the table with his thighs, making the cutlery rattle. 'We must begin our hike,' he said, and they left the room.

Warren dropped off the camera for repair before taking a taxi to Portland Hospital. If the Prof complained at the cost, he'd just cover it himself. When he'd first lost his leg, he'd spent a lot of time in hospital having dressings done prior to trialing different prosthetics. It had taken a lot of time before he got used to his altered weight distribution. Crutches had been painful to use, and he knocked many things over with them. Each time, his mother told him not to worry about it, but he did. His father internalised his pain. Mother thought it was what eventually killed him. The guilt had formed a knot inside and triggered a stroke.

Portland Hospital was a red-brick, pizza box built in the seventies sitting so low to the ground it appeared to be cowering from the sea surrounding it. Warren waited at the main reception desk after asking to meet with someone senior. He began to doubt why he was even there. It was a long shot that they'd know anything and even if they did, with patient confidentiality, would they tell him anything. Maybe he should just go. The receptionist tapped him on the arm – he hadn't heard her calling him. She said the Chief Administrator would see him.

Warren followed her directions to an ante-office. Inside, a woman with blue-grey curls told him to sit. She sat behind two monitors. Plant pots were scattered around the room. He realised that each one was at a different height.

Warren suddenly realised she'd said something to him. 'What? Sorry?'

A curt voice resonated over the screens. 'You can go in.'

A woman in a cream suit stood in the open doorway.

Warren leapt up, wobbling as he stuck out his hand. 'Thanks for meeting me at short notice.' He followed her into the office. The gold lettering on the doorway was repeated on the certificates hanging on the wall.

She sat down, adjusting her skirt beneath the table. 'What can we do for you? Mr...?'

'Warren. Call me Warren. This is going to sound really odd, but the magazine I work for was recently sent a photograph of a dead baby with a missing finger. Bizarre, I know. We don't even know if it's genuine. Other information leads us to believe the picture was taken somewhere on Portland. I've only just got started on the investigation. Arrived yesterday. Thought the hospital would be a good first port of call. Have you had any babies born or brought to you like that recently?'

The Chief Administrator regained her composure. 'That sounds awful. And, to answer your question, no, I can't think of anything like that in the last few months. We get the odd toddler who's caught a finger in a door but not so much to lose it. And never a baby.'

'Could it be genetic?'

'Possibly, but extremely rare. Which finger?'

'The ring finger on the right hand.'

'Unlikely then. Birth defects of that type affect the smallest digits. Could be caused by something toxic to the embryo during pregnancy. Most likely, though, it was lost during an accident.'

'So if the child had been brought into A&E and it was suspicious...'

'The police and child services would have been informed immediately. If it had died in suspicious circumstances, we'd perform an autopsy. If there *was* an active investigation ongoing, I wouldn't be able to say any more. But I've not seen anything like that as long as I've worked here.'

'How long would that be?'

'Two years in this role and before that, another five as a surgeon. We do have a records archive downstairs but that's staff only.' She glanced at her computer. 'Is there anything else?'

'No, you've been very helpful. Thank you.' As he held the door handle, he turned back. 'What was the name of your predecessor?'

Dr Halstead pulled the keyboard towards her. 'Dr Rhodes,' she said 'He's retired now but still lives in nearby.'

He pulled the door shut and found the assistant on her hands and knees, brushing pieces of a broken pot and soil into a dustpan.

'Be careful,' she said, without looking up.

Warren launched his right foot up and over to clear her legs. 'Do you need any help?'

'I'm fine. It should be fine.' Her face remained focused on the floor. 'Did you find out what you needed to know?'

'Perhaps. Is there any way you could let me into the archive?'

She stopped brushing and turned her head. 'I've got the door code but unless Dr Halstead's given me a nod, I can't give it to you.'

'Do you have children?'

'No, why do you ask?'

'Oh, I'm trying to figure out if someone might be able to have a baby in secret. No kids myself, so I've no experience to fall back on.'

She laughed. 'Not sure why you're asking me. Some women choose to have home births but they're still recorded.'

'Aren't they risky?'

'Not if you know what you're doing.' She clambered to her

feet and stared at Warren. 'I'm going to need to run a hoover round this.'

'I'll get out of your way. Thanks for your help, Mrs…'

'Plowright.'

He made his way to the exit and loitered. When he heard her door shut, he turned around and headed back inside. One of her monitors had several square notes stuck to it. He took a photo of the couple containing a string of digits.

After several wrong turns, Warren found the archive in the basement, next to the mortuary. He tried the first code on the keypad. The door didn't open so he scrolled to the next. A squeak made him turn his head. An orderly was pushing a trolley of records at the far end of the corridor. He looked for an exit, trying several doors until the mortuary door opened. Listening, he heard the trolley push the door open. How long would he have to wait?

Two male voices rose in volume and one commented on the lock still being broken. Warren the darted across the room but there was only a wall of metal coffins. Most were shut but one or two were slightly ajar. He pulled one open and climbed in. He wriggled inside, using his palms against the walls to pull it almost shut. A sliver of light passed across his face through the remaining gap.

'This the one,' enquired a male voice.

'Cremation for you, fella,' confirmed another.

They moved closer. Cold air seeped through the gaps between his clothes. preceded the grating of metal as a body was slide into a container. A clunk nearby shook him.

'Time for a tea,' said the second voice.

'Is this one meant to be open?' Asked the first.

Warren hadn't had the time to determine if he'd be able to get out if the door was shut. He ran his fingers over the back of it. It was completely smooth surface. He'd have to shout out.

'Leave it. There'd been some leakage, so I cleaned it this morning. Let it dry.'

Warren heard the door shut and exhaled. He waited for several minutes before pushing himself forwards. He tumbled off, taking the weight on his good leg. It cramped up and he rolled onto his back. He rubbed at his calf.

Warren listened outside the records room but could hear nothing. The next key code let him inside. A metallic chill enveloped him as the door clunked shut. The lights flickered on. On the left was a large bank of metal drawers; on the right, chest-high filing cabinets. In-between, a single desk with several folders. One of these contained records of the refrigerated coffins. None contained children.

The filing cabinets were arranged by year then alphabetical by the name of each patient. There was no other indexing system. A dead end.

CHAPTER 5

After lunch in the hotel, he took a taxi to Chessil beach. He took of his coat and sat on the sea wall. The sun had baked the sand as white as paper. The distant sea tumbled in then slid out. He unfolded the printout and rescanned the image. The picture wasn't a high resolution. The surface could be sand but equally it might be concrete or carpet. It wasn't wood and it was too dark to have been taken in the quarry.

Warren let the document close along its deep folds. He read his texts and emails. The Prof had told Harris to drive to Norfolk and get pictures of the crop patterns. Harris was livid and tried explaining they'd look like all the others. He wanted Warren to come with him. Faith wanted to know if he'd tried any of the beech sap products. He hadn't. The image of the baby swirled around his mind like a tornado of barbed wire. It's just one baby. One that might have died of natural causes. But how common was that? He'd have to find out.

He rang the office. Glade answered. She was an American student working part-time as an intern at the magazine. 'Do you want to speak to Miriam?'

Professor Miriam Stanzen had become Editor just before Warren arrived. She'd taken a chance on him. Her role at the Skeptics Handbook was an honorary position. Her 'real job' was research into European mythology. Glade was one of her postgraduate students and had started at the same time as Warren.

'I'd prefer not to speak to her. She'll ask how I'm getting on with the weeping statues article. If she asks, tell her I'm working on it.'

'Are you?'

'I can't, not now.' He switched the phone to his other hand. 'This baby thing is more important. There's something I need your help with.'

'Related to the article?'

'Not really, but-'

'I'm only meant to carry out research for the next issue she said, 'Don't let Warren send you on any wild goose chases. I don't know what that means but I don't know if I can help.'

'This isn't one of those things and it shouldn't take long. It's big data stuff so could be a good training opportunity. But let's just keep it between us for now.'

'What do you need?'

'I'll email you the details later.' Warren stood up and began to walk back towards the hotel. 'One other thing. Can you get me the address of a Mr Rhodes. He lives in Portland and was the previous Chief Administrator of the hospital. If he's ex-directory, ask Harris to help you. He knows a few workarounds.'

The Danish couple were sat at the same table in an empty breakfast room. They returned his "Good Morning" with a nod. Warren wanted to sit somewhere further away but felt forced to sit at the same table. He wasn't normally one for sticking to social norms. He ate with the fork in his right hand. But to sit somewhere further away would've felt rude.

He stretched over to grab a newspaper from the next table. It was the local paper and mostly adverts. But he'd learnt to sift information quickly and had finished it by the time he'd eaten his cereal. The only story of mild interest featured a woman who'd found two dead porpoises on the beach. A photograph of the three of them was rather unnecessarily included. The two corpses were so close, their noses nearly touched.

As he finished his tea and checked his emails, the camera shop rang. The body of the camera was still functioning, but the lens was unrepairable. They'd be able to sell him a similar one. He'd collect both on the way to the train station. He had one visit to make first.

Warren walked along a short row of narrow Georgian houses. They stood defiantly between several set of much larger modern houses. They faced the bay; an absence of buildings opposite gave them an uninterrupted vista. Each garden was neatly manicured. Number thirty-eight was near the middle. Ivy spread from it in both directions.

Warren stood beneath an arch over the door. Roses twisted up and climbed up the pillars. He felt the sunshine on his back as it broke through the sea mist. He swung the knocker.

A man with grey hair and a red V-necked jumper opened the door. His blue-grey eyes blazed behind his round, metal glasses. He held the door half-open. 'Can I help you?'

'Are your Henry Rhodes?' He nodded. 'My name's Warren Stance. I'm a journalist. Could I ask you some questions about you time working at Portland Hospital?'

'That was quite a while ago, I don't think I'd be able to help you. What precisely is it about?'

Warren stepped forward. 'It'd be easier if I came inside.'

'For whom?' The knuckles on the hand holding the door

turned white. Warren stood still. A few seconds later, Rhodes opened the door and led Warren inside.

The house's low ceilings made his head sink into his shoulders. Warred caught a glimpse of the lounge, a bookcase opposite the entrance. They went though the galley kitchen into the garden. It was full of plants, many tropical, their large leaves hanging over others. The largest lined the perimeter, making it hard to judge its size. It was cool and dark. A sandstone water feature reflected what little sunlight had crept over the house.

Warren felt edge of the pitted bowl perched on a worn pedestal. 'What's this?'

'It's a font, rescued from a church destroyed during the reformation.'

Rhodes directed him back to a corner next to the house to sit in a semi-circular, wooden gazebo.

Warren shuffled around the table. Ash tray and secateurs sat in the middle. Roses snake up the pillars into the trellis roof.

Rhodes sat down on one of two metal chairs on the outside. 'What would you like to know?'

'I work for The Skeptic's Handbook. It's a magazine that examines strange occurrences and debunks urban myths.'

Rhodes spun the secateurs on the table. 'To what end?'

'Sorry?'

'What are trying to achieve?'

Warren had never been asked to defend the magazine's purpose. Of course, it was meant to entertain. He had no doubt there were many that read it but still believed in fairies at the end of the garden regardless of what they disproved. But that wasn't why he'd left a better paying job to work on it. He'd seen the harm that came from conmen or the loan sharks preying on the poor. But there was something purer too.

'To debunk charlatans mostly, and promote rational thought.'

The secateurs slowed to a stop. 'But people aren't rational. I spent my working life watching families grabbing comfort from wherever they could. What gives you the right to try to take that away?'

'I'm not. We're not. But blind hope is open to abuse, so we highlight it when we find it.'

Rhodes picked up the secateurs and began to snip away at the rose stems. 'What do you want from me?'

'I'm investigating the death and probable mutilation of a baby.'

'I've seen nothing on the news. Where was it found?'

'It hasn't but we think there's a link to here.' Rhodes turned to Warren. 'Portland.'

'Why do you think there's a link to here?'

Warren crossed his legs. 'I'd prefer not to say.'

'You said it was…mutilated.'

'Mutilated, yes. It had lost most of one finger. I spoke to your successor, Dr Halstead. She said it's unlikely to be genetic.'

'What do you think caused it?'

Warren rubbed his left knee. 'We covered something along the same lines in a recent issue, although that was related to adults. This type of injury is sometimes associated with rituals, such as the Japanese Yakuza punishing a gang member for a mistake.'

Rhodes dropped the collection of inch-long stems into the ashtray. He sat back down, examining the secateur's blades. 'I still don't see how I can help you. What Dr Halstead said is true and unless there's a body, I don't see there's anything really to write about.'

Warren uncrossed his legs. 'Perhaps you're right.' He leant his arms on the table, feeling the damp wood under his fingertips. 'But perhaps you could tell me if there were any similar cases of infant mortality when you ran the hospital?'

'No.'

'Are you sure?'

'I'm certain.' Rhodes pushed his chair back, scraping it across the paving stones. He stood. 'I don't think there's much more I can tell you. I've got things to do, so if you don't mind.' Rhodes indicated to the garden. Puzzled, Warren stood. 'There's a side gate at the back.'

Warren paused by the font. 'Was Mrs Plowright also your assistant?'

'We worked together for a few years. She was a clumsy woman but charming enough to get on with.'

Warren walked towards the back of the garden, plants sliding across his body until he reached the exit.

CHAPTER 6

Warren sat in the hotel lounge starring at the landscape painting above the unlit fake fireplace. It hung at an angle. He lifted his leg onto the beetroot shaded footrest.

He called the office hoping to speak to Glade. 'Glade, how are you getting on with that-'

'This is Margaret.'

'Apologies, I thought you lectured on a Monday.'

'Summer term's finished. Can I remind you that Glade is not your private secretary. She's a shared resource for the magazine when she's not carrying out research. Have you finished the article?'

'I'm still working on it.'

'Get it to me by the end of the week. Harris needs your help with a new crop circle. You'll need to go to Norfolk with him.'

Warren tried to argue that he needed to stay in Portland. He didn't fancy trekking all the way to the north of England. Glade had given up the information on his progress and the Prof had deduced the story had gone cold. Even if he was sure it hadn't.

Warren packed without using his system and checked out. He'd stay overnight in Bristol. Harris agreed to delay his journey and pick him up in the hybrid.

———

Warren watched Harris slide silently to a stop. He swung his suitcase through the heavy door. Keplar watched him struggle. 'Faith'll be in to top up your food.' The cat wandered into the lounge. Warren shook his head and left.

Warren opened the boot. 'I dreamt you'd seen sense and exchanged it.' He pushed Harris's bag and a metal case to the side and slotted in his suitcase.

Harris patted the roof. 'We got sixty miles to the gallon last week.'

'With zero to the gallon of enjoyment?' Warren let a car pass then got in.

Harris told him, from what he'd seen walking the crop patterns was that they weren't circles but did show symmetry. But without an aerial view, he couldn't be sure. Experience had shown him it was usually either agricultural students or older guys with too much time on their hands. This didn't appear to be either.

After checking in, they met in the bar. Harris lowered his half-finished pint as Warren entered. 'You still doing that unpacking thing?'

'You should try it.' Harris downed his pint and got up. 'The owner says there's a a good curry round house the corner, you can have a pint there.'

Warren and Harris sat with a plate of poppadoms between them. Harris added a large spoonful of lime pickle to his side plate.

'I don't know how you can eat that stuff,' said Warren, breaking a poppadom into pieces. 'You've ruled out the usual suspects.'

Harris crunched into a triangular piece laden with relish and swallowed. 'Jonesy says he's retired.'

'Do you believe him?'

'I paid him a visit. He's just had a hip transplant.'

'What about that couple from Cambridge?'

'This isn't anything like their style. Or anyone's we've seen. That's why I told the Prof I needed a hand.

Harris reached for the final poppadom, paused, and looked up at Warren, who nodded as he reached for his pint.

———

The breakfast room had a conservatory-style section on the far side. He saw Harris sat there and had to hold his hand up as the glare from the metal case shone into his eyes. Warren settled for cereal. Harris chewed on a sausage as Warren sat down. 'Skipped cereal, did we?'

'I had some already. Were you working on your article like a good boy?'

'Not you as well.' He shovelled in a mouthful of corn-flakes. 'I did a bit more before coming down. What's the new one like?'

'Better camera, greater stability.'

'Let's try not to break this one.' Harris nodded as ran his toast around the inside curve of his plate.

'How's your sister?'

'She's still off work. You'd not know she had PTSD from meeting her. But we were in a shop last week when a police car went by. She broke down in tears.'

'Blimey.'

'She's looking at other careers, but I can't see her not going back.'

. . .

Outside, Harris opened the boot and put in the case. 'Do you want to put your camera in?'

'I'll hold onto it.' Harris shrugged and closed the boot.

They arrived at a small farmhouse with two large, metal barns. A man in Wellington boots and khaki shirt rolled up to his elbows, came out to meet them.

'This is Nathan Wilkes,' said Harris. 'Two of the crop patterns are on his land.' Warren shook his large, outstretched hand.

'So, do you think you'll catch the bugger? The police were round, they're not hopeful.'

'If it's someone new, it will be bloody difficult unless they've left something behind.' Harris lifted the case. 'But if they have, a piece of rope or a plank, we might track them down.'

'Are you still okay for us to take some pictures?' said Warren.

The landowner looked over their heads. 'Aye, but I'd make a start soon, the weather's turning.'

———

Harris and Warren stood at the field's edge, unpacking the box. A breeze blew through the wheat field ruffling the spikes. 'Will it be okay?' asked Warren.

'As long as it doesn't get any stronger.'

Harris handing Warren the remote. It resembled a games controller with two sets of joysticks but was square. Warren uncoiled the strap wrapped around it and looped it over his head.

Harris lifted the drone from its foam insert and placed it on a flattish patch of ground. He pulled out a tablet that was underneath. Warren started the drone's propellers, looking at Harris who stepped back. He pulled one the joysticks forward and it rose quickly into the air. 'Where now?'

Harris pointed into the field. 'Take it towards the middle.' He watched the camera image displayed on the screen as Warren guided it. 'Move it left.' Warred adjusted the position of the drone, allowing it to hover autonomously each time. 'Stop! That's it; leave it there.' Harris bent closer. 'It's degraded somewhat but the overall shape is visible. Have a look.' Harris tilted the screen.

Warren stood shoulder to shoulder with Harris. 'Zoom out.' His eyes zig-zagged over the image. 'I've never seen anything like it, have you?'

'No. I'll take some pictures.' Rain droplets landed on the surface. Harris wiped it with his sleeve.

The crop pattern was about six metres in height and ten metres in width. The flattened wheat formed an undulating curve that rose and fell four times.

'Let's check the others,' said Warren, bringing the drone back.

The remaining three crop patterns were within a two-mile radius. The area was mostly wheat fields split by a few roads and farmhouses. Rain fell in thick apostrophes.

Harris held the controller. 'Got it?'

'Yes, let's go.'

'I'll bring it in. I hope it's okay.'

'Hold on.' Warren wiped the screen. 'Could you send it left.' He looked up, checked his bearings, and pointed. 'Towards the stile.'

Harris guided the drone towards it. 'What can you see?'

'I'm not sure.' He tilted the tablet, letting the water run off. 'Bring it in and we'll go take a look on foot.'

Warren stood up to the stile located under the cover of a several small trees. Water dripped off the leaves in heavy droplets.

Harris caught up, shaking the rain from his raincoat. 'What was it?'

Warren nodded upwards. Above the stile, caught on the end of a branch, was a red bobble hat. 'Do you think you could reach it?'

Harris stepped onto the first step. 'Give me a hand.' He leant on Warren's shoulder and gripped the top of the stile. He couldn't reach it.

'Hold on,' said Warren, picking up a small branch. 'Try this, short arse.'

Harris tried to push the hat off, but it stuck resolutely. 'Pull it,' said Warren. On the next attempt, it fell off. The branch sprung up, shaking water into Harris's face. Warren picked it up.

Harris stepped down. 'What do you think? Perhaps a toddler on their dad's shoulders?'

'Wouldn't they have spotted it coming off?'

Harris wiped his face. 'Maybe they'd couldn't reach it or didn't realise 'til they'd gone too far.'

Warren stared over the stile. A two-story farm house sat on the edge of the next field. Smoke drifted out of the chimney. 'Why don't we ask?'

Warren and Harris sat in the car; warm air blew hard from the fan. Rainwater rushed under the car. Harris uploaded the images from the tablet to the Skeptics Handbook server while Warren drew the position of the crop patterns on the map.

'Done,' said Harris. He leant across. 'What've you got?'

Warren looked through the windscreen. 'That house is in the middle of them.'

'So, it is? Could be a coincidence.'

'Let's find out.' Warren pulled the laptop off Harris's lap. 'Drive.'

They parked on the verge opposite a small wooden gate, labelled Roper's Farm, set in a waist-high stone wall. The rain had petered out. Water splashed over their shoes as they squelched towards the house. Warren glanced at the upstairs windows. One the two facing him had its curtains drawn.

A woman answered after several knocks. She was tall with tightly cropped blonde hair. She was drying her hands on a tea towel. A warm, yeasty smell followed.

'Sorry to bother you while you're in the middle of something,' said Harris 'but could we ask you a few questions.'

She stared at the hat in Warren's hand. 'Are you from social?'

Warren lifted the hat. 'No, we're not.' Her eyes followed it. 'We found this nearby and thought it might belong to you.'

She stepped forward and examined it. 'Might be. Where did you find it?'

'About a mile away, at the edge of the next field to yours. Close to one of the crop patterns,' said Harris. 'Quite a job getting it down.'

'We ain't got nothing to do with that. I've spoken to the police already.' She folded the tea towel. 'It'll be those agricultural college students. Happens every few years.'

Warren held the hat higher. 'Would you like a closer look?' She nodded, tucking the tea towel over a nearby radiator. She took the hat in both hands, rubbing it softly with her thumbs.

'I thought it looked like a young child's hat. Do you have any?' said Harris. The woman didn't answer.

'Everything all right, Norma?' They turned to face a man approaching. He wore a long green raincoat, a shotgun broken over his forearm.

Norma looked up. 'They're asking about the damage to them fields. I told them its probably them students again. They found this hat over by the edge of Mulligan's.' She lifted the hat up. 'It looks like yours.'

He paused then continued. Warren and Harris parted to let him through, his waxy jacket brushing against them. He cocked the gun and rested it on the floor beneath the radiator. He took the hat. 'I often go for a walk at night. I must have dropped it' He handed it back to his wife. 'Is there anything else?'

'Have you had a look at the crop -', began Harris. Warren pulled him away.

'Thanks for all your help.' Harris reached inside his jacket for a business card, but Warren pulled him again, making him drop it into a muddy pool. 'What's going on?'

'I'll tell you over dinner. It's your turn to pay.'

CHAPTER 7

Over dinner, Warren told Harris he didn't think the hat belong to Mr Roper. All his clothes were working ones – marked or torn. The hat was pristine. 'iIt's your story but I think we should try the nearest school,' he'd said.

In the morning, they worked on other articles in the hotel. Warren waited for Harris in the lounge. The armchair was newer than his own but didn't feel worn in. He squirmed to get conformable as Harris entered the room, 'Sorry about that. Helen and I had some things to discuss.'

Warren held up an arm and Harris pulled him up.

Children blew out from the school like confetti. Most ran to their parents. Others chatted in small groups, phones in hands.

Harris and Warren walked through the playground. A woman stood under the entrance's awning, wrapped her grey shawl tighter around her neck, and strode out.

A football bounced off Harris's shin. Her head snapped to the side. 'Michael, keep that football under control.' She stopped in front of them. 'I'm the headteacher, can I help you?'

Harris took out his notebook. 'Have you heard about the crop patterns?'

'Our PSCO mentioned it last week. I made a request at assembly for information, but no one's come forward.'

'We're writing an article about them for a magazine, said Warren, 'Does every child in the local area attend this school?'

'All of them that can. And since you're going to ask, I don't think one of our students is responsible.'

The football hit Warren's left foot, twisting his leg. 'Michael!' shouted the Headteacher. The ball spun on its axis. Warren leant onto Harris's shoulder to reset his prosthetic. A boy arrived and picked up the ball. 'Michael, what did I tell you? Look at what you did?'

'Sorry, Miss.' He ran off, ball close to his chest.

She looked at his leg. 'Are you okay?'

'I'm fine,' said Warren, standing straight and letting go of Harris. 'We should go.'

Harris opened his notebook. 'Have any kids been excluded from school?'

'Not this year.'

He pulled the pen top off with his mouth. 'What about last year?'

'Two. A brother and sister. The Metcalfe twins. The incident was outside the school, but it was decided they should be home-schooled.'

Harris wrote. 'Where do they live?'

'I don't think I can tell you that.'

Harris waved his pen in the air. 'Data protection, I know, but we'll find it anyway.

She shrugged her shoulders. 'Then you don't need me to tell you.'

• • •

Most of the parents had left as they approached the hybrid. Harris paused with his hand on the door handle watching a child being secured into a car seat. Warren called the office.

'Hello,' said a voice.

'Glade, we need an address.'

'It's Miriam. Glade's on BlueCrystal, she'll be back later.' BlueCrystal was the University's supercomputer.' I've seen the photos of the crop circles. Have either of you seen anything like them before?'

Harris got in the car. 'No, we haven't.' Warren got in the car. 'But they look mathematical to me. Maybe sine waves.'

Harris mouthed, 'Who is it?'

Warren held his hand over the mouthpiece. 'The Prof.'

'What?' said Miriam.

'Nothing.'

'Do you have any idea who made them?'

'Perhaps. That's why we need an address. We can look for it ourselves if Glade's busy.'

'Send what you have through, and I'll ask her to look at it when she's back. What about the baby photo story'

'I've not thought much more about it.'

'Harris you said it could be a sign of ritualistic behaviour.'

'If it was an adult,'

'Well, regardless. The nature of a ritualist behaviour is that its repeated. Get back down there as soon as you've finished with the crop circle story.'

A quick search on the computer gave them a single entry for Metcalfe in the area. Warren gave Harris directions from his phone while looking ahead.

Harris bit into a chocolate bar. 'Where did you get that from?'

'Box under the seat. Emergency rations.'

Harris parked in a cul-de-sac on the eastern side of the

island. The sound of a piano became audible as they approached the Metcalfe's two-up two-down. Harris rung the doorbell. He squeezed the laptop under his armpit. Warren stretched over, looking for a gap in the front room's curtains. A fair-haired man answered the door, holding a schoolbook.

'Mr Metcalfe?' asked Harris.

'Yes, who are you?'

Harris switched the laptop to his other arm. 'We're investigating the crop patterns in the area. We wondered if you knew anything about them?'

'No, I don't,' said Mr Metcalfe, closing the door.

'What about your children?' said Warren. The door stopped moving. 'Perhaps we could speak to them?'

'Only Josie is here. Josh lives with my mother most of the time.'

'Can we see her?' said Harris.

'Josie's not very comfortable with strangers.'

'Is that her playing now?' said Warren, leaning away. 'It's lovely.'

'No. She doesn't play anymore.'

'Well, perhaps we could speak to you, instead. It won't take very long,' said Harris. 'It's just a few pictures on a laptop.'

Mr Metcalfe nodded and led them inside the narrow hallway. Warren closed the front door. A row of dark coats and umbrellas enveloped the wall behind it at the foot of the stairs. A red bobble hat hung bright above them.

The kitchen was compact with white panelled cabinets. Children's paintings were stuck to several of them. Family photographs were stuck to the fridge with magnetic neon letters. The rest spelt out, 'Josh & Rosie.' They huddled around a table, littered with textbooks and pens covered.

Warren leant towards the fridge. 'Is that Disneyland?'

'Yes, it is. Three years ago. I think my wife enjoyed it as much as the kids.'

'That's right. I think it was as much for my wife as the kids.'

Harris swivelled a textbook so he could read the title. 'How long have they been home-schooled?'

'Nearly six years. I do most of it, but we have a tutor for maths and science. Music's still her favourite.'

The music was still audible. Warren realised it was purely the piano. He'd originally thought he might have only heard a solo within an orchestra. 'Does she play the piano?'

Mr Metcalfe shook his head. 'Not any more. Now, what did you want to show me.'

Warren nudged Harris, who'd been flicking through the pages of the textbook. He stopped and opened the laptop. Mr Metcalfe studied the crop patterns. 'You don't think Josie did these, do you?'

He looked up, pushing his seat back. 'She couldn't. She's doesn't leave our sight. Anyway, she'd never be able to get there on her own.'

Harris closed the lid. 'Perhaps her brother helped her?'

'He doesn't live nearby. Is there anything else. I need to get back to marking?'

'Not from me,' said Warren, slapping Harris's leg. 'But my colleague's been thinking about home schooling, haven't you?'

'Have I?' Harris gripped the laptop. 'I have.'

Warren got up. 'So perhaps you could give him some pointers while I use your bathroom. Then we'll be gone.'

Mr Metcalfe pointed back through the kitchen door. 'It's just outside, under the stairs.'

Warren closed the kitchen door behind him, opened the toilet door and ran the tap, leaving the door ajar. He entered the sitting room. The music was louder than he'd expected. He shut the door quickly.

A pink boombox sat on the mantlepiece. It was covered in

stickers. Further along, in the corner by the windows, stood a baby piano.

Opposite both, Josie was sat on her hands on a pale green sofa in jeans and a loose jumper. In front of her, on a long coffee table, were several schoolbooks and an open notepad.

Warren pointed at the piano stool. 'Can I sit down for a minute?' She nodded, making her chest tilt forward. He pulled the seat towards her, near the edge of the table. He sat down, placing both hands on his thighs.

Warren tapped one of the textbooks. 'Homework?'

'Geography. I hate it.'

'I did too.' He glanced at the piano. 'Do you miss playing?' She frowned and shook her head, making her hair pile onto her shoulders. Her eyes became wet.

Warren pinched the bottom of his left trouser leg and raised it. She tilted forward to examine the black, carbon fibre rod. She stared into his eyes then fell back against the sofa. Harris's voice became audible. 'Can I see?' She turned her head to the window, biting her lower lip. She pulled out her right, then her left hand, resting them on her thighs. Each of her fingers was misshapen. Several were crooked and most of them had enlarged knuckles.

'What the hell are you doing?' Shouted Mr Metcalfe, entering the room. Josie shoved her hands back under her thighs. Harris followed and shrugged.

Warren pushed himself up as Josie's father sat next to her. 'I'm sorry, I had to see for myself. In every recent photograph, she was either wearing gloves or had her hands in her pockets. Even when it was sunny.'

Mr Metcalfe put his arm around his daughter who had begun to cry. 'Don't worry, Josie, it's not your fault.' He looked up at them. 'They're going now.'

Warren joined Harris by the doorway. 'We'd like to know what happened? After that, we'll never bother you again.'

Mr Metcalfe got up and forced them from the room. He

leant around the door frame, 'I'll be back in a minute. Put your headphones on.'

'Don't be angry with him.'

Warren bumped Harris's upper arm and pointed a finger towards the coat rack. Harris was still staring at it when Mr Metcalfe started speaking. 'It was Josh. They'd spend all their time together. In or out of school. He used to enjoy listening to her play. He'd make her play for hours. But his behaviour at school became difficult and he was diagnosed as bipolar. The medication worked for a while.'

Harris put his hands in his pockets. 'What changed?'

'He didn't like her playing anymore. It riled him and she knew it too. She was at my mothers, and they were getting on fine. But something happened with one of the livestock and she had to go and help. The two were left inside. My mother had her own piano, but Josie hadn't been allowed to use it. She must have started playing.' He leant against the bannister.' Josh slammed the lid onto her hands so hard she passed out.'

'My god,' said Harris.

'So, Josh moved to my mother's. Josie's had several operations. The doctors say she could play but she won't. I think she blames herself and she doesn't want to see Josh because she thinks she hates her. We keeps them apart.'

'And Josh?' said Warren.

'He's still living with my mother. Near the damaged crops.' The music from the sitting room stopped. 'Now, please go.'

Warren's phone rang as they got in the car. It was Glade. Harris started the car.

'Hold on,' said Warren, covering the phone with his hand. Harris waited. 'Back to Roper's farm.' Harris shrugged his shoulders and started the car.

Warren listened. 'That's what I thought. Hold on, Harris

will want to hear this part.' Warren set the phone to speaker mode. 'Tell us again about the patterns.'

'The crop patterns *are* sine waves.' I measured their frequency and amplitude's. The amplitudes vary but the frequency remains the same: two-forty hertz. I'll send you the marked-up images.'

'What about the other thing? The Prof said you'd got a slot on BlueCrystal.'

'Don't worry, I fitted in your runs between mine. The data from The Crown Estate was easy to get but it's going to take some time to make sense of the results.'

'Send it through when you get something,' said Warren before hanging up.

On the way to the farm Warren explained what had happened with Josie. 'No wonder she doesn't want to go to school.'

They parked on the verge a few metres past the gate. Harris opened the laptop and paired it with his phone. Warren looked at the sign on the gate. 'A few of the oldest pictures showed a different father,' said Warren. 'It was Mr Metcalfe senior. His mother must have reverted to her maiden name. Roper.'

'They've downloaded,' said Harris, clicking on the attachments. Warren leaned over. Glade had overlaid measurement lines to the peaks and troughs.

Warren sat back in his seat. 'Two hundred and forty hertz.'

Harris stared at the pictures. 'Do you think it's significant?'

'I think we should go.'

'We just got here.'

'Drive!' said Warren, slumping low into his seat while pointing over his left shoulder.

Harris turned. Metcalfe was approaching them, holding a

shotgun. 'His son must have have told them we'd been over.' Harris started the car. Warren peaked over the windowsill, spotting movement in the upstairs bedroom. The car's wheels spun on the slick, long grass before it dropped off the verge with a bump. The side window behind Warren shattered propelling tiny pieces of glass around the car. Harris bucked forward making the car spurt forward. 'Shit!' Harris sat back, glancing in the rear-view window, trying to regain control. A second shot shattered the rear window. They turned a corner and didn't stop until they reached where the hedges became walls.

Harris and Warren sat in the corner of a pub in silence. Two pints grew stale on the table. Warren stretched out to his and stopped to pick a cube of glass from the folds of his coat. His arm shook and he withdrew it.

Harris felt his left ear, examining the semi-dried blood on his fingers. 'What do we do?'

'If we report it to the police, we'll never get back there.' Warren sighed. 'But it's your story, what do you want to do?' As long as he'd known Harris, he'd always been determined. A finisher. He'd told Warren he's always the last to leave the cinema, even as a child. It drove his wife mad.

Harris grimaced, drank the rest of his flat pint, and stood up. 'Want anything?' Warren shook his head.

Harris returned from the bar sipping a fruit juice. 'I got you something anyway,' he said dropping two packets of crisps.

'Are *your* ears still ringing?'

Harris nodded and turned to the window. 'I hope it doesn't rain. The missus needs the car for next week.' He put down the drink and pulled out his phone. 'I'd better go outside and give her a call.'

Warren opened the second packet, turning it to face Harris as he sat down. He stared at the crips, picked up his drink then

put it back down. 'She wants me to go back. It's too dangerous. She says it should be a police matter.'

Warren leant back making the chair creak. 'What do you
want to do?'

'I want to see it through to the end.'

'You know you should go home. I'll keep you involved
with progress; it will be as good as being here.'

'How will you get around without a car?'

'I'll think of something.'

'If I can find a garage, maybe they can do a quick repair of
the glass and I can get the other damage fixed back in Bristol.
What will you do?'

'Take me to the station.'

Harris, drinking a small amount of fruit juice. 'Are you
heading home?'

'Sort of.'

CHAPTER 8

Warren yawned as he sat at King's Lynn station. The ringing in his ears had made it difficult to fall asleep. He phoned Faith and his mother as he waited for the train to London. Families and students filled the platform.

Warren worked on the train. The internet connection was patchy, but he managed to do some research on the crop pattern's rate of repetition.

It was dark as he exited Bagshot station. The streetlights lit the mature canopies of the trees like lampshades as he walked. As a small child, they'd felt like sentries, watching as he and Faith recreated what they watched on screen. Now they stood as a complex organic structure, photosynthesising and respiring, in a chemical silence.

His mother answered the door and they hugged. She looked around him. 'No suitcase?'

'I'm going back tomorrow. Any food going?'

His mother warmed some food while he told her about the shooting. She'd not been as shocked as he'd been expecting.

In the morning, they drank coffee in the garden, watching

collar doves flutter around the dovecot like impatient ballerinas. His mother pointed at one: 'He's the bully, always pushing in.' She reached for the cafetière. 'Do you want some more coffee?'

'No thanks.'

'Are you sure you need to go back. Couldn't you switch to a different story.'

'Not with Harris off it already. There's no one else. It was only rock salt. He only meant to scare us.'

In his previous job at the Oxford gazette he'd been one of a much larger team. Leads on stories were exchanged freely. Since you really knew which would lead to something significant, it was low risk to your career. The collegiate atmosphere remained too until the growth of online news forced reductions in permanent staff. He'd been one of the first to leave.

His mother turned the slim mug in a circle by its handle. 'Do you think it will even start?'

'I hope so.'

'He'd be pleased you're using it after he made the modifications, but couldn't you wait to Harris's car is repaired?'

'I don't want to put him in any more danger. I'm only using it out of necessity.'

'But it's okay to put yourself in danger?'

'I've got less to lose.'

He breathed out and turned the key. Nothing. He tried again and it started. His mother moved backwards, letting the Lancia Fulvia Sport roll out of the garage. It crunched on the gravel. Warren stopped next to her, flicking stones towards her.

'Sorry!' He wound down the window. 'Are you sure don't want a lift to rehearsals?'

'No, that's all right. I'll see you in a couple of weeks, won't I?' Warren frowned. 'For Peter's birthday.'

'Of course,' he bluffed.
'Be careful.'

It would take Warren just over an hour to get to Oxford. His father had bought it after he'd retired. It had need significant repairs. He'd converted it himself, knowing it would reduce its value. When it was finished, he'd driven all of them for lunch in the country. His father had asked him if he'd wanted to drive back. He'd refused. His father fell ill shortly afterwards.

Faith lived in a small, terraced house in Yate. She and Peter's father, James, had both sold their flats before they'd married. This was the house they'd bought. Faith should be on her own if Peter had been picked up. It was short notice but he'd reminded her that James had done it to her several times.

He swung her bags into the boot. 'Did you remember the printouts?'

'They're in the sports bag.' She walked around to the passenger side and stepped back. 'So, you decided to drive it?'

'I had no choice,' Warren said, opening the driver's side door. 'That's why I needed you.'

'Thanks,' she said, getting in.

Warren pulled across his seat belt and scanned her. 'I thought you'd be wearing it.'

Peter's being teased at school, so I didn't want to upset him. I'll change when we stop somewhere.'

Faith examined the car. 'The last time I sat here was when Dad took me to the Sixth Form ball. Do you remember, he dressed up like a chauffeur? It was so embarrassing. Jules and Geeta were in the back. He'd started to lose weight by then, but he still looked distinguished. I don't know where he got the hat from.' She leant her elbow on the window and rested her head on her fist. 'I never told him how much that meant.' She wiped away a tear with a knuckle.

They stopped at a service station near Yeovil. Even those that had been upgraded infuriated Warren. They channelled you through a succession of shops selling over-priced emergency supplies or artery-clogging outlets when all you wanted to do was use a restroom This one was typical. At the end of the wide entrance walkway was a circular seating section surrounded by food counters. The toilets weren't even visible.

Warren sat with some bought lunch while Faith got changed. He'd attended her *passing out* ceremony - her graduation - with his mother. She'd marched in her dark blue uniform with the other officers in her class around a parade ground. It drizzled non-stop but their white gloves flashed like a magician's doves peaking out of their sleeves. Her eyes had beamed with pride and hope, matched by Warren and their mother.

Warren took a first bite from his sandwich as she sat down. 'Still fits, then?'

'What did you get me?' She said as she turned the packet.

'They'd run out of cheese, so I got you egg and cress.'

Faith pursed her lips. 'What did you get?'

'Coronation chicken.'

'Sounds nice.' She tilted her sandwich to look at the filling.

He grinned. 'Do you want to swap?'

'No, thank you. Enjoy your antibiotic-pumped, caged slate of protein.'

Getting up to leave, she'd left half of it. Warren looked over her uniform. 'How does it feel?'

'It feels fine,' she said. 'You realise if anyone reports me, I might be fired.' She said, feeling the lapel between thumb and forefinger. 'So this better be worth it?'

'Are you still getting flashbacks?'

'They're *not* flashbacks. Not in the sense of seeing what happened again. It's more that the sensations of how I felt come rushing back so fast I can't stop them. I'm paralysed. The counsellor said it's perfectly normal. I want to go back but how can I when something might trigger another one.'

'You should take as long as you need.'

'But I can't. At some point I need to make a decision. They'll only keep paying me for so long.' They sat in silence. On the way up, Warren had explained what had happened with the farmer. 'So how long do you think this will take?'

'We got close to an answer. It would be good to finish the story for Harris.'

'Do you think everything's okay with the baby?'

'I think his wife's nervous. It's their first one but I think there's something else.'

'I still think you should have reported the shooting. It might be real bullets next time?'

Yelling echoed echoed around the forecourt. They turned as a bald man in a waxy green jacket shuffled towards them. 'Officer,' he said, 'Officer. They've caught a shoplifter.'

'Do you remember what to do?' said Warren. Faith punched him on the shoulder and strode towards the man.

'Why don't you show me the way.'

She was led to a woman in dark trousers and a checked blue jacket holding a young boy by his arm. He wore shorts and tights, torn t-shirt. In her other hand, she gripped a few magazines. He tried to shake her off and she squeezed. 'Ow!' The boy shouted. 'Let go of me.'

'Little rascal,' said the man.

Faith turned to him. 'Thanks for your help.' He scanned her face as she waited.

'Oh, I see,' he said and wandered off.

Faith turned to the couple. 'What's happened?'

'I'm the manager in the newsagent. He tried to steal these magazines,' she said, swinging them forwards.

The boy continued to wriggle. 'She's lying.'

'It's on CCTV if you need it. There's a bunch of them group of travellers out the back.'

Faith stepped towards them. 'Why don't you let go of him so I can have a word with him alone.'

The manager let him go and the boy ran behind Faith. 'I want him charged.'

Faith looked at the manager. 'I don't think that's really necessary, is it? He's too young for formal charges.' She bent her knees and faced the boy. She turned to look at the manager and the boy's head followed. 'Now do you promise not to come back and bother this woman?' The boy looked once at Faith and back at the manager who frowned. He looked back at Faith and shook his head.

She stood up. 'Come with me,' she said to him, walking towards the exit. He followed close by, sticking his tongue out at the manager.

When they got outside, the boy overtook Faith and walked around the side of the building. They'd startled two chefs smoking.

The boy stood at the edge of a field, a clear path through the wispy grass visible. He tugged on the bottom of his t-shirt. 'You arresting me or what?'

'What's your name?'

'Kieran.'

'Well, Kieran, if you promise not to do this again, I won't arrest you.'

The boy folded his arms. 'Okay.'

'Go on, then.' He turned, dropped his arms, and ran through the gap.

When Faith turned the corner of the shopping centre, Warren was standing by the entrance. 'We should get going.'

. . .

Warren parked close to the Roper's farmhouse, resting the car on the grass verge. They walked down the centre of the narrow lane. A stone wall ran along the property's perimeter. When the reached the gate, Warren sat on the wall. 'This is close enough for me.'

Warren watched Faith rang the doorbell. In full regalia, she looked invincible. She took off her cap as she waited. It was hard to fathom what she had been through and if she'd ever recover enough to go back. Someone opened the door and a conversation started. A few minutes passed. She waved him over.

Warren slid off the wall and walked up the path. He glimpsed movement above him and when he looked up, he saw a pair of curtains close. Ms Roper was stood at the door. They exchanged an awkward smile. Mr Metcalfe Snr was stood behind his wife, watching each step of Warren's approach. Warren stood behind his sister with a view into the house. At the end of the hallway, a door was open into a kitchen. A shotgun sat on the table.

Faith turned to Warren. 'I've spoken to Mr Metcalfe and Ms Roper. They're willing to cooperate if you follow certain rules.'

'Can *I* have a rule that he doesn't shoot at me?'

'Your luck it was only birdshot,' said Mr Metcalfe Snr.

Faith held up her hand. 'I've given him a warning and explained that we'll overlook it this time. They've agreed to let you speak to their son on the condition you don't upset him. His name's Josh.'

'I'm sure he didn't do it,' said Ms Roper. 'He's not like that.'

Mr Metcalfe Snr pointed at Faith. 'She promised that anything he says remains private.'

Warren moved closer. 'What if I don't write anything that could allow anyone to identify your family? Our readers will want to know who made them.'

Ms Roper looked at her husband who nodded. 'All right, then,' she said, stepping to the side. Faith and Warren entered the house.

Mr Metcalfe Snr waited with Faith downstairs as Warren followed Ms Roper upstairs.

She knocked softly on the door. 'Josh, that man is here. Can we come in?'

'Yes. I'm on the computer.'

The room was dark. Josh was lit by his computer screen which he stared at intensely. His mother brushed past him. 'Let's open the curtains. What have I told you. It's not good for your eyes, is it?' The sunlight filled the room, washing over the computer screen. It was small with bare walls, except for a football-shaped clock above the bed. Josh clasped his hands between his legs, making the veins stick out on his skinny arms.

She rested her hands lightly on his shoulders, causing him to sit straighter. 'Now, I've told Mr Stance that you had nothing to do with that damage in the fields. But he wants to ask you some questions, anyway. I'll be in our bedroom across the hall if you need me.' She kissed him on the head and left the room, leaving the door open.

Josh watched his mother leave without turning his head. He began to interact with his computer.

'Can I sit on the bed?' said Warren, moving closer. Josh nodded slightly.

Warren sat down on the end stretching out his legs. 'What are you playing?'

'Championship Manager.'

'How far have you got?'

'Champions League Semi-Final. Lost 2-1 against Bayern Munich.' He reached out and manipulated the mouse.

'That's good. Do you play any other games?'

Josh stuck out an arm to pull a curtain closed, darkening the screen. 'Minecraft.'

'What are you building?'

'Cambridge.'

'Really? Sounds complicated. Do you visit there a lot.'

He shook his head. 'We went to listen to Shostakovich's Cello Concerto No 1.' Josh let go of the mouse and moved his fingers in small patterns.

'Do you like music, Josh?'

He nodded several times. 'I'm not allowed to listen to it.'

'Do you what a frequency is?' Josh stared over the monitor at the wall. Warren took out two pictures of the crop patterns and placed them on the keyboard. Josh glanced at them. 'Did you make these?'

Josh rocked back and forth. He began to mumble. Warren leant across the room and gave the door a door a push, sending it till it rested against the frame.

'No one will be angry with you.' Warren stood and leant over Josh's shoulder, making him flinch. Warren traced the s-shaped curves with a finger. 'These are sine waves aren't they?' Josh nodded. 'Used to make sure the orchestra is in tune.' Josh said something inaudible. 'Say it again.'

'They're for Josie.'

'Do you miss her?'

Josh began to rock back and forth.

'I think she misses you too.'

Josh began to chant Josie's name. His rocking became more vigorous, and he hit the desk with his stomach, making the monitor wobble. He got louder. A torch rolled off the desk. Warren heard voices downstairs. He stuffed the printouts into his jacket as someone came up the stairs. He put his hand on Josh's arm to steady him, but it was thrown off.

The door swung open, and Ms Roper came in, followed by her husband. 'What's going on!' He shouted.

She brushed past Warren, crouching next to Josh. 'What did you do, did you touch him?' Josh stopped chanting and began to hit his clenched hands against his head.

'I'm sorry,' said Warren as Mr Metcalfe Snr grabbed him by the arm, pulling him out of the room. Warren pulled out the red bobble hat and stretched out to give it to Josh. 'This is Josie's.'

His mother snatched it. 'It's okay, Josh, he's going now.'

Mr Metcalfe Snr pushed Warren down the stairs. Faith stood at the bottom. 'What did you do?' she rasped.

'I want the two of you to leave, now.'

'Let go of Mr Stance, Mr Metcalfe.'

Mr Metcalfe released Warren. At the bottom of the stairs, Warren turned around. 'I'm not leaving until I speak to you both first. You'll want to hear what I say.'

Warren and Faith sat in the lounge facing two similar prints of a Mediterranean countryside. Mr Metcalfe Snr leant against the wall by the door, watching them. Ms Roper entered the room and closed the door. 'He's okay,' she said to her husband.

Mr Metcalfe Snr pushed himself off the wall and leant forward onto the back of the armchair, making the material around his shoulders taught. 'We had a deal.'

'We're really sorry?' said Faith, nudging Warren.

'I am,' said Warren, 'truly.'

Ms Roper rubbed her husband's arm with her hands. 'He wasn't to know Josh didn't like physical contact.'

'How is he?' asked Warren.

'He's lying down. That hat still must still smell of her, he won't let go of it.'

'Has his behaviour got worse since Josie and Josh were kept apart?' said Faith.

'He's not been in any trouble since I've been here,' said Mr Metcalfe Snr.

Ms Roper walked around her husband to sit in the armchair. 'We thought it would get better, but it's been getting worse. When they were younger, I'd often find them asleep like two pups in one of the barns. They'd be gone for hours exploring.'

'When I saw the same hat here as on Josie, I figured that they'd been bought for both of them,' said Warren. 'Josh admitted to causing the damage.'

Ms Roper looked up at her husband. He let go of the armchair and stood beside her. 'We'll pay for any damage.'

'Will he be charged?' said Ms Roper, wringing her hands.

Warren turned to Faith. 'I'm sure something can be worked out,' she said. 'When did you buy the hats?'

Ms Roper sat down into an armchair. 'We bought them last year. It was one of the last times they were together. They'd see each other most weekends. We were in a shopping centre, and they were getting on fine. Josie wasn't wary of him anymore. She was old enough to understood that he hadn't meant to hurt her. They'd walk around hand in hand with their matching bobble hats.'

Mr Metcalfe Snr put his hand on her shoulder. Ms Roper breathed out. 'An orchestra started playing Christmas music on the ground floor. Josh got excited. He started swinging Josie around by her hands. Initially, it was fun, but he went faster and faster. We'd just gone into a shop. I thought they were with us.'

'When he gets overexcited,' said Mr Metcalfe Snr. 'He can be difficult to stop.'

'Well, he slipped and let her go. You know these floors are so polished now. She slides into the glass barrier overlooking the band. If it had shattered, she'd-.'

'But it didn't,' said Mr Metcalfe Snr, gripping her shoulder.

'And they've not seen each other since?' said Faith.

'We thought it was for the best,' said Ms Roper. 'I didn't know he'd react in this way, damaging those fields. They're our neighbours, I don't know how we're going to explain it to them.'

'We'll manage,' said Mr Metcalfe Snr.

Warren stood up. 'The patterns in the fields. He's sending a message telling her he misses her.'

Ms Roper looked at her husband. 'I don't understand.' He shook his head.

Warren took out the photographs, smoothing several of them out on his thighs. He handed them to Ms Roper. Mr Metcalfe Snr leaned over her as she shuffled through them, her eyebrows furrowed.

Warren pushed himself up from the sofa. 'They're sine waves, repeating at a frequency of four hundred and forty Hertz. It's the frequency most musical instruments are tuned to. Including pianos. He's telling us he misses her.'

'What should we do?' said Ms Roper.

Warren turned to Faith. 'It's up to you of course, in agreement with the school. There's still a risk to having them together of course, but I think there's a bond between twins which is being stretched too thin.'

'Will you arrest him?' said Mr Metcalfe Snr.

'I don't think that's necessary,' said Faith. 'If you'll speak to your neighbours and compensate them, it can be kept a private matter. I don't see the public benefit of bring charges against him.'

'Thank you,' said Mr Metcalfe Snr.

'Yes, thank you,' said Ms Roper, handing back the printouts to Faith as she followed Warren out of the house.

'You might want to fit a lock to his window. Or confiscate the torch, just in case.'

Halfway down the path, Warren looked back up at Josh's window. Josh was standing there. Warren waved. Josh stepped back and the curtains shut.

Faith sat in the passenger seat, holding the printouts. 'This one look different,' tilting it towards him as started the engine.

'Those were closer to four hundred and thirty-two Hertz so higher than the others. There's a theory that the lower frequency resonates with the Heart Chakra, repairing DNA and restoring both spiritual and mental health.'

'That sounds interesting. Do you think it's deliberate.'

'I doubt it. It can't be easy to maintain the right distance between intervals as you wander up and down in the dark.' Warren pressed hard on the accelerator, making them lift out of their seats as they bumped dropped of the verge. 'And all that stuff about healing properties.' Faith turned in eager anticaption. 'It's all bollocks.'

CHAPTER 9

Faith had slept most of the way. As kids, they'd sit in the back and play games, inevitably it would end in a fight. One game guaranteed to end in punches was 'reg plate duelling.' Each in turn would pick a number plate from a car and make an amusing phrase from the first three letters. What started as "Rabbits Chew Pastries" soon became "Slugs Dance on Warren" or "Farts Like Faith".

They hit rush hour traffic outside Northampton and Faith woke up as the car came to a stop. 'Where are we?' She yawned.

'About halfway,' chuckled Warren.

'What's so funny?'

His phone buzzed in his pocket, and he handed it across. 'Check that, would you?'

'It's from Harris. He wants to know how we got on. Shall I tell him?'

'Don't forget to mention the bit about the frequency.?'

'That *was* pretty clever of you,' said Faith, typing away. 'Especially as you couldn't get a decent tune out of the recorder.'

Warren waited in the car as Faith collected her clothes

from the boot. She stood by the driver's side as he wound down the window. She was still in uniform.

'You're good at it, you know?'

She half-smiled. 'It was good to feel useful again.'

———

Warren stood with his arms crossed in Bristol's Queen Square by their bench. It had become their usual bench after careful analysis. It faced the flow of commuters that came and went between Temple Quarter and the Harbourside. It was neither under a tree nor in full sun. It was the second closest to the coffee stand.

Warren unfolded his arms, took the cup, and refolded his arms. 'How's the family?'

'Both fine. Helen's settled down now I'm home again.'

Warren told Harris what had happened. Harris had sat on the bench, avoiding eye contact, sipping at his coffee.

'It's still your story,' concluded Warren. 'You should write it.'

'Not anymore. You solved it. To the victor, the spoils.'

'We'll co-author, then?'

Harris rotated the cup between his hands. 'There's no need to do that.'

'Is everything okay?'

'I've handed in my notice.'

'What?' Warren began to pace. 'You said everything was okay.'

'I need something with less travelling and frankly, more money. I'm going back to work as an IFA.'

Harris had spent several years as an independent financial advisor. 'I thought you hated that.'

'I did, but I've or will have -.'

'Don't say it.' Warren ground a foot in the gravel. 'Responsibilities. What about responsibility to find the truth? To dispel lies or debunk the belief in the occult? Educating the ignorant? Holding back wave after wave of those for whom rational thinking is an afterthought. Who else is going to do it?'

Harris shook his head and got up. He began to walk back to the office but paused, 'It's just a job, Warren,' before continuing.

The The Hare On The Hill was almost empty. Warren would rarely come without Harris, but this seemed an appropriate evening to do so. He sat at the bar, watching the foam of his beer dissipate on the inside of the pint glass. The process is two-fold. First, the bubbles expand as gas moves from one bubble to another. This is called coarsening. Secondly, the liquid drains away, bursting the bubbles.

The dog's tail wagged against his prosthesis as it followed his movements with its eyes. The vibrations travelled up his body, dissipating in his abdomen.

Kelly leant over the bar. 'Jessie, stop that.' The dog looked from Kelly to Warren. 'She thinks you're Harris. He gives her some of his pork scratchings Harris, I'm sure of it.'

Warren showed the dog his palms. The dog turned and left, tracing a familiar route to the back of the bar, its nails making a tick-tacking noise along the wooden floor. He picked up Warren's glass. 'Another?' Warren held up his hand up. 'If she bothers you again, just push her away.'

'It's people that bother me.'

'They can be trouble, all right. Where's Harris?'

'I didn't ask him.'

'I see. You two had a falling out?'

'He's quitting. Probably for good.'

'I opened this pub with my partner. He designed it and was in charge of the renovation work.' Kelly scanned the room. 'Did a fine job. But the day-to-day stuff wasn't for him.

"Not exciting enough," he said. I was doing more and more of it. I asked him to leave. He went the same day.'

'I'm sorry, I didn't realise.'

'I've still got the pub; she'll not be leaving me.'

'Maybe I will have another.'

CHAPTER 10

Warren twisted the bag of used cat litter and dropped it in the bin. Kepler waited by his food bowl, oblivious to the house keeping. When Warren stopped, the cat looked up. 'Give me a minute.'

Warren filled a clean bowl with cat foot from a pouch on the kitchen counter. He placed it on the floor and left the flat to the sound of the cat's low contented growls as it chewed.

The Prof was reading a set of papers at her desk. She tended to use the screen for emails but always printed off their articles for editing. If she had academic work to do, she'd always return to her other office.

Warren stared at Harris's empty desk.

'Just us?'

Miriam peered over the top of the papers. 'Harris's working from home and Glade will be in later.' She placed the bundle onto the desk. 'Harris sent in the first draft of the crop pattern story. But he's left you to finish it while he wraps up.'

Warren peered around his monitor screen. 'So, he told you?'

'That he's leaving. Yes. End of the month.'

Warren sighed. The Prof came and sat on the edge of Harris's desk, facing him. It creaked slightly as she adjusted her position, taking off her reading glasses and letting them rest on her chest. 'He'll be missed.'

'Will you replace him?'

'I've got a meeting with the owners next week. I'll be proposing it but there's no guarantee. We'll have to manage as best we can.'

Warren slid his chair sideways so that he was sat in 'Didn't you have a meeting last week?'

'That was a board meeting and Harris hadn't handed in his notice.' She leant forward. 'As long as subscriptions remain stable and advertising doesn't fall any further, I think we can afford to replace him.'

'The trends have all been downwards.'

'One major story could turn things around.' Miriam returned to her desk. 'Did you find out anything further regarding the photograph of the baby?'

Warren spun slowly in his chair. 'There's been nothing reported in the press and there's no similar historical examples locally of that type of disfigurement. It's unlikely to be congenital but it's impossible to confirm from the photograph alone. The angle of the hand doesn't allow a good enough view to determine if its a recent cut or not.

Warren stood up. 'I feel it's good enough to go back to Portland for a few days. Perhaps, Glade could do some field work?'

Miriam chuckled as she moved forward. 'The University would never allow it and nor would I for that matter. Perhaps your sister could help out again?'

Miriam left to meet academic colleagues for lunch. Warren was alone. He tore a piece from the middle of a ham and cheese baguette he'd picked up on the way in. He scanned the white office walls, feeling the blood seep from his head to his stomach.

When his mother had entered his hospital room in tears, he'd realised something was seriously wrong with his leg. She'd taken the comic book out of his hands and held his hand.

'What's wrong, Mummy?' She dropped her head and started to cry. 'Where's Dad?' He looked towards the door. He caught parts of an angry conversation. His mother wiped her eyes then cleared her nose. 'They're going to have to operate on your leg, Warren.'

'Will it mean I can play football again?'

'In time, perhaps. They're going to take you in to surgery later today. You'll be given an anaesthetic which will make you fall asleep. You won't feel anything.'

'Will I remember it?'

'No.' She gripped his hand tighter. 'The surgeon is going to explain it to you. But to stop the cancer spreading to the rest of your body, the surgeon is going to have to remove -.'

His Dad burst into the room...

'Warren...Warren,' said Glade. He broke his gaze and found her next to his desk. She held a cup of coffee towards him.

'I saw Miriam heading up Park Street.' Warren took it. 'She told me you were in and with Harris not being in, I thought I'd pick one up for you.'

Glade placed her drink on the desk and slid a rucksack off her shoulders.

'Going somewhere?'

'I'm visiting Birmingham.'

Warren swivelled to face her, holding the coffee in both hands. 'On you own?'

'No.' She sipped her coffee. 'With my partner.'

'Thanks for doing that work on the crop patterns. Did you hear that we found the person responsible?'

'Harris told me. It's a shame he's leaving, isn't it?'

'I never liked the bugger really.'

Glade's mouth opened. 'You're joking?' Warren smiled and nodded. 'We'll need to plan some leaving drinks for him.'

'And a gift?'

'He'll be happy with anything alcoholic.' Warren stretched out his legs and slid his hands into the pockets. 'We'll be including your marked up photographs of the crop patterns for the article. Did you manage to locate the metrics for Portland Hospital?'

'It took a freedom of information request, but I got them.' She swivelled the screen towards him. He pulled in his legs and walked over to examine the spreadsheet. 'I couldn't find anything unusual. The hospital's rates are similar to others with a similar catchment.'

'Including infant mortality rates?'

Glade switched to a new tab. 'They're close to the national average.'

'What about emergency visits to the hospital or emergency calls?'

'Normal too.'

'What about GP visits?'

Glade furrowed her brow.

'Emergency callouts by doctors.'

'They weren't available.'

Warren stepped backwards and fell into his chair. 'So, we've got nothing? A picture of a mutilated baby that may or may not be recent and a postcode centred on a hole in the ground.' He put his hands behind, leaning back.

'There was something else,' she said, opening another tab. 'Portland has a higher rate for home births than anywhere else in the country.'

. . .

When home, Warren moved the box of supplements into the hall cupboard. After dinner, he sat with the laptop on his legs, looking at the picture of the baby boy. It looked so pure and unblemished as if nothing could harm it. The porcelain skin and its plump chest. Then you saw the finger.

Warren jumped up, dropping the laptop on the seat of the armchair. He pulled out a large plastic box from the bottom of the hall cupboard. It was full of cables, plugs, chargers, and pieces of electronic gadgetry. He couldn't remember what most of them did. He pulled out a projector from the black spaghetti. It took another few minutes to find the relevant cables to operate it.

Once powered, it emitted a burning smell as a square of light lit the wall. He shut the curtains and watched the ghostly image solidify. He stood close to the wall before moving back. There *was* something else there. It could be bruising or something under the skin made visible after death, but he didn't think so. There were two intersecting lines across, black across her chest, forming a cross.

CHAPTER 11

Warren had to park at the end of Faith's street. As he wandered towards it, he took off his jacket. He never checked the weather. Not through any lack of faith in its scientific accuracy, just that he didn't think it was worth putting in the effort. He wore the same cloths most days and if it rained, he'd go inside. He could normally guess how the weather would be each morning on his way to work. Today was going to be hot.

Warren and Harris had discussed the cross, or *mark* as Harris preferred to call it, for over an hour. Harris had dealt with all sorts of religious motifs. Although the Christian cross was the most familiar, there were many other variations, including the type commandeered by the Nazis. Symbols had power. Most often they signified a common belief system, quickly identifying people and places to them. They could be graphical forms but bled into forms of dress. Warren found it all a turn-off He found that many of those using them, reckoning it gave them a misplaced power. And that status often led to abuse.

James was outside, putting Peter's bags in the boot of his four by four. Peter saw Warren and ran towards him. 'Hi,

Uncle Warren,' he shouted before colliding with him, knocking him off balance.

'Hello, Pete. What've you got planned for your birthday?'

'McDonalds and Air Hop.'

'Sounds dangerous.'

James shut the boot and stood behind Peter. 'I guess I should thank you.' Warren tilted his head. 'For making it possible for me to have Peter for half-term.'

Faith approached carrying two bags. 'I hope to have her back before the end of the week.'

'That's not what your sister thinks. She's packed for a month.' Faith dropped the bags at her gate and headed back to the house.

'I'd better go in and stop her from bringing anything else.' Warren turned to Peter, 'Goodbye, mate. We'll be back in time for your birthday.'

Gerry ruffled Peter's hair as he was about to speak. 'Have you said goodbye to your mother?'

'Yes,' said Peter, shrugging him off.

'Get in the car, then. Let's get going.'

Warren entered the house unobstructed. Before the break-up, someone was always in motion, coming in or going out. Or the whole family were packing for a family outing that he'd been invited to. The house was quiet. Boxes of Beech Miracle lined the hallway. He swung the door shut.

'I'll be down in a minute,' came Faith's voice from upstairs. 'Will I need my uniform?'

'Bring it just in case.' She scowled at him before ducking back inside.

Warren made a pot of tea. Faith dropped a bag in the hallway and hovered in the kitchen doorway.

'Where's Peter?'

'They've gone.'

'He didn't say good-bye.' Warren moved the pot to the

table and sat down. Faith shrugged before pointing back down the hallway. 'Do you need any refills?'

Warren shook his head. 'I'm pacing myself. I don't want to get too healthy too quickly. It might be dangerous.'

She took out two mugs from the cupboard. 'You do want my help, don't you?'

'I'll get the milk.' He began to get up.

'Stay there.' She went to the fridge.

'Have you come to an agreement on childcare?'

'Not completely. He'll spend the week with me unless Gerry finds somewhere to live closer to the school. Weekends will be split and the same with holidays.'

'That sounds workable.'

'I hope so. When you're in a couple, you start off making joint decisions but when life gets hectic, it's whoever's able to make the decision first that gets their way.'

'Which used to be you, I bet.'

Faith smiled as she picked up her mug with both hands. 'Usually.'

'I'll try to let you get your way as much as possible.' Warren scanned the cupboards. 'Any biscuits?'

'They're not part of our diet at the moment.'

'Let's hope the hotel has some.'

———

It was overcast as they arrived at the hotel. Faith bounced up the steps, a bag in each hand, and waited for him under the awning at the top.

'You promised me sunshine.'

The owner was on duty. He wore a different sleeveless jumper, but it was equally tight across his chest. Warren took a breath as approached the counter. The owner turned from the computer screen.

'Welcome back, Mr Stance.' He waited for Faith to draw parallel. 'This must be your sister.'

'Hello,' said Faith, shaking water droplets from her jacket. The owner tilted forwards, glancing at the marks they made. 'Sorry about that.'

The owner turned to Warren. 'Will you be dining with us tonight?' He pushed two sets of keys across the surface.

Warren checked with Faith. 'What do you think?'

'You promised me fish and chips on the seafront.'

'Did I?' Warren picked up the keys, handing one set to Faith. 'I did, didn't I?' Faith nodded vigorously. 'Maybe, tomorrow.'

Warren and Faith walked along the sea front. It had stopped raining, but the paving stones remained a dark grey. They picked a restaurant and ordered. 'How does fish and chips fit within the Faith diet?'

'Fish is full of omega oils; I just won't eat all of the chips.'

'More for me, then.'

After they ordered, Faith asked, 'So, what do we know?'

'We know that someone sent us the picture of a male baby, almost certainly dead. She's missing the third digit on his right hand which is not likely to be genetic. There's been nothing reported or recorded publicly of anything similar in the last ten years. The phone number was hidden and the location they sent led nowhere other than a quarry and some empty houses.'

'I think you should report it anyway.'

'I'd like to get a bit further with it. The police aren't equipped for this type of thing.'

'Of course they are,' she said, shaking a piece of tartare sauce coated fish at him before eating it. 'What's going on in that head of yours?'

Warren put down his knife and fork. 'You really want to know?' Faith nodded as she chewed. 'The number of child abuse cases in the UK involving witchcraft has risen by over fifty per cent in the last three years. During an exorcism, they might tie the child to a chair in a locked room for over a day without food. They'd take turns to whip, beat, or rub chilli in its eyes.' He put down his knife. 'In America, there are over eight thousand Satanist covens. The penalty for leaving one is death by being knifed, with one stab wound for every year of the person's life.'

Warren picked up his cutlery and glanced at Faith. 'No need to stop eating.'

CHAPTER 12

There were five churches in Portland. Two were not in use and one was shut for repair. St George's was the largest and in the centre of the island and seemed an appropriate one to start with.

A tower sat over the entrance to a long, dark grey building with a ribbed roof. White pockmarks pitted the walls. It was surrounded by gravestones. Those facing the sea, leant backwards like drunks against a bar.

Inside, box pews ran from the back to the altar. Walking between them, they passed under two duck egg blue pulpits. Galleries ran along each wall.

Faith stopped to read an information panel. 'It says the church was built by a local mason whose grandfather supplied the Portland stone used to build St Paul's Cathedral.'

'I can show you where it comes from if you don't mind getting dirty.'

Somewhere ahead, a heavy door swung shut. The altar was a standard gold cross below an egg-shaped candelabra.

Hidden from view until they stood below it, was a woman on her knees, cleaning the shelves within a display case in the corner. Besides her was a dark alcove lit by a sliver of light from the base of a side wall. Warren moved towards the alcove, avoiding the woman's feet. He bumped into a pew causing it to scrape across the floor.

The woman turned and began to get up. 'Excuse me, could we ask you… Mrs Plowright. This is a surprise.'

She got up, using the heavy wooden cabinet to bring her to standing. 'Hello,' she said, holding a yellow cloth close to her chest.

Warren beckoned to Faith as she caught up. 'Mrs Plowright works at Portland Hospital. Most of the time.'

'I'm a volunteer. Weekends mostly. Tidying up, putting things back in the right place.'

'If you remember, I came into the hospital to discuss something with your boss. We're investigation a photograph that was sent to us of a baby. Something in the image suggests a religious connection, hence our visit today.'

Faith pulled the pew back into alignment. 'We were wondering if you'd ever heard about any cults or covens on the island?'

'I don't think I'd even know what one was,' said Mrs Plowright. Warren side stepped towards the alcove.

'Perhaps a group of people meeting secretly?' said Faith. Mrs Plowright shook her head.

Warren saw the light on the floor. 'We might as well go then.' Warren strode into the alcove, feeling for a handle above the line of sunlight.

'You can't go out that way,' said Mrs Plowright. Warren found a metal handed and pushed down on it. The door opened outwards, and he stepped through as Mrs Plowright and his sister followed.

'Warren, you need to come out of there,' said Faith.

A black dog outside began to bark. Warren scanned the graveyard and stepped forward. The dog growled. Warren saw a man shuffling through the graveyard a hundred metres away. He stepped forward and the dog grabbed his right leg. He grabbed the door frame to maintain his balance and shook his trapped leg. 'Faith!' he cried as she arrived at his shoulder. 'I'm okay,' said Warren, waving his free hand in the direction of the graveyard. 'Over there!' Faith flew.

Mrs Plowright shuffled through the doorway. 'Let go of him,' she said to the dog, kicking it in its rib cage. It skulked away as Warren set off after his sister.

Faith slid between gravestones as she pursued the man. Warren stumbled over the uneven ground. Wispy grass sprung from tight blocks of earth. He put a hand on a head-stone to gain some leverage. As he pushed off, it shifted, and he nearly fell. The dog ran past him. 'Faith,' he called breathlessly.

Warren found her holding the man by the shoulder of his jacket. It gave the impression that he was hanging in mid air. She let go of him and the jacket settled back over his slight figure. He wore brown corduroys and a green hunting jacket, stuffing was visible one side. The dog was sat at his feet, panting. It growled as Warren approached.

'Easy, girl,' said the man, stooping down to rub its belly.

Warren felt a trickle of blood running down his leg. 'Your dog's got quite a grip.'

'Under the Dangerous Dogs Act, it could be destroyed,' said Faith.

'Please don't,' said the man in a reedy voice. He crouched down to stroke its head. 'She's all I've got.'

Warren rubbed his injured leg. 'So why did you run off, Mr Plowright?'

'How did you... 'Mr Plowright stretched his neck to looked around Warren.

Faith followed the man's gaze. 'Your wife's on her way.'

Warren stepped towards him, blocking his view. 'It was you at the quarry, wasn't it?'

'My wife will be able to explain when she gets here.'

'I think I deserve an explanation - I fell a long way. You might have called an ambulance.'

Mr Plowright held onto the dog. 'I'm sorry about that, I really am. Jenny gets quite excited when she's outside. I did wait to see if you were all right. I saw the truck come in— '

'Which nearly ran me over.'

'Yes, I saw that which was when I knew you'd be okay. The man got out to help you.'

'Why did you run?' said Faith. He didn't answer but stood up and looked for his wife. Warren turned around as she arrived at the scene.

'Is everything okay, Harold?' He nodded. 'Maybe we should go back inside.'

They walked back in silence, the dog tracking Harold.

'Do you volunteer here too, Mr Plowright?' said Faith.

He glanced at his wife. 'It's Harry. Yes, I do. I look after the graves, most of time, giving tours. Many of them belong to people killed at sea.' He stopped by one. 'This is captain Thomas Page. In 1869, he spotted a ship adrift in the channel. Just over there,' pointing out to sea. 'He swam out to it, but no one was on board.'

'A ghost ship,' said Warren.

'It was the brig Lavonia, fully laden with coals on route to Amsterdam. He piloted it back to shore and a month later he hired a crew to complete its journey. It sank. No one survived. Most of them are buried here. They never found any of the first crew. Before each disappearance, the locals reported seeing a fireball land in the sea.'

'Let's keep going,' said Faith, striding ahead.

Warren sat in one of the pews and stretched out his legs. Blood had stained the fabric of his trousers. Mrs Plowright whispered something to her husband. Faith crouched down and rubbed the dog's belly as it stretched out on the cool flagstones.

'Why did you run off, Mr Plowright?' asked Warren.

'You don't have to say anything to him, Harold,' said Mrs Plowright, a hand on his arm. 'He's not a policeman.'

'I am,' said Faith.

'Where's your uniform then?' Snapped Mrs Plowright.

Faith stood. 'Uniform or not. I still carry all the same legal powers.'

Mr Plowright gripped his knees. 'I'd seen you walking towards the church, and I recognised you. From that quarry. I didn't want Jenny to get in trouble. I waited to see you weren't hurt, didn't I? I'm meant to keep Jenny's out of trouble.'

'I've told him to keep that stupid dog on its lead, but he doesn't listen,' said Mrs Plowright.

'I've always wanted to have one, but my husband never wanted one. Peter, my son, is always begging me to have another one. Do you have children?'

'Just one,' said Mrs Plowright. 'But she died at birth. A long time ago, now.'

'I'm so sorry,' said Faith.

'Was she born at Portland hospital?'

'Yes,' said Mr Plowright.

'Did you ever consider a home birth?' said Warren.

Mrs Plowright looked at her husband. 'That sort of thing wasn't an option back then. We should be getting home. Is there anything else?'

Warren crossed his legs, making the fabric rub across the teeth marks. 'Do you know what making the mark of the cross on a baby might mean?'

Mrs Plowright locked her arm in her husband's. 'You'd need to ask a priest or a vicar about that. Try St. Andrew's, it's nearby.'

CHAPTER 13

Warren and Faith drove through Easton into Portland's town centre. They'd decided to get a drink before trying the next church. Small, terraced houses lined the straight roads. They parked on one side of the central green square. The trees formed a boundary within the iron fence, leaning over as if reaching for something.

Warren winced as he got out of the car. Faith stood with the door open. 'We should go back to the hotel so I can have a look at it,'

'I'll be fine,' said Warren, limping towards the nearest row of shops. 'Get us a table, I'll only be a minute.' He handed her a book. 'Take this.' He walked past the café, throwing his voice over his shoulder. 'And a coffee.'

Warren passed the counter looking for Faith. The café had low ceilings with several alcoves. Framed photographs hung on the powder-white walls.

'There you are,' he said, ducking under an arch.

Faith was sat, flicking through the book. A cup of reddish liquid sat in front of her. She put down the phone and picked up the cup from the low table. Warren scrunched up his nose as he sat down next to her. 'It's full of anti-oxidants,' she said, taking a sip.

'So is normal tea but *it* doesn't smell like potpourri.' Warren looked at his watch. 'We might as well have lunch.' He sat down and picked up the menu. 'Have you had a look, yet?'

'The chickpea salad, please.'

'On its own?' She nodded.

He studied the menu. Chickpea salad was one of the main dishes on a small list. He was going to struggle. She lifted her head. 'Is that TCP?'

'It was all they had, and I didn't want to lose the other. Although, if I continue to have this amount of bad luck with dogs, I might just go fully bionic.'

Warren ordered despite Faith's offer to do it for them. On his return, he looked closer at the photographs. They were pictures of landmarks and the cliffs around the island.

'What do you think about those two?' said Faith when he returned.

'I didn't think there was a lot of love there?'

'I've seen worse.' She leant back. 'I'd have expected them to have provided a bit more gossip.'

'Because it's a small community?'

Faith nodded and paused for a few seconds. 'Do you think that baby's body will be found?'

'I doubt it. Whoever took the photograph either left it where it was or disposed of it. If they'd left it, someone would have found it by now.' Warren followed a waitress passing by with food. 'But if the death was linked to some form of cult behaviour,' pointing at the book. 'That means several people know about it. We just need one of them to break the silence.'

Faith wafted a small, tatty paperback with a lurid cover of a woman shrieking as a vampiric figure loomed over her. '*The Horrific History of Dorset* by Derreck Foster. Published in ninety-eighty-one. Hardly a bestseller.'

'Doesn't' mean it's not true.'

A waitress with long red hair brought them their food. 'Do you need anything else?' She asked after moving back to standing.

'Have you got any low-calorie salad dressing?' said Faith.

'I'll get you some.' She looked at Warren.

'I'm fine,' he said. 'Do you know much about the photographs on the walls?'

'Not really,' she said, running her hands through her hair. 'The owner picks what goes up.' She looked at the nearest. 'I know they're taken locally. This one's inside the underground tunnels.'

Warren hadn't noticed that one. It was taken inside somewhere but he'd not reapplied it had been a tunnel.'

'Where are they?' said Faith.

'We've tunnels all over. There's the RAF ones at the top. Then the Victorian cliff tunnels. My mother even said they're some secret ones hidden under the hospital. No one believes her, though.'

The waitress waited briefly, then left.

Faith had offered to drive but Warren insisted. He swallowed two painkillers as they set off to St George's. It led to nothing. The vicar had been polite although Warren found him condescending. He'd remarked several times on Warren's torn trouser leg which annoyed him further and stated that a child had never been marked in service he'd been a part of. They asked him about cults and birthing pools and at that point he'd ask them to leave.

It was dusk as they arrived at the ruin of St. Andrews Church. It was on the east side of the island, perched above a cove. Most of it had fallen into the sea but it was still accessible.

Faith received a text as they exited the car. 'Mum wants to know if you're still coming through for Peter's birthday.'

'When is it, again?'

'The seventh. We'll be at Mum's on the Sunday.'

'I'll take another look, I'm sure I'm free. What shall I get him?'

'Anything to do with mountain bikes. Or a voucher for clothes,' said Faith, crossing over the road. Warren followed.

They stood at the top of the hillside, looking down onto the remains. None of the roof was in place and most of the walls had gone. The rectangular floor was lush grass. The sea stretched out behind it.

'What do we hope to find in this wreck?' said Faith. 'There's not even any one to speak to.'

'Then we'll be no worse off than when we started.'

They walked down a stone pathway that terminated at a stone archway. At the level of the church, the sea was hidden.

'There seems even less now that we're closer,' said Faith.

Warren walked the perimeter. The walls were about a metre high at their tallest. Each had greyed and been dusted with moss. A gap on the seaward side displayed a sign, "Danger of Falling". He leant over it: the sea quietly buffeted the base of the cliff.

Faith overtook Warren moving in the other direction. She stopped. 'I guess that's it.' Warren was stood on the northern most side, pulling at vegetation covering the wall. He reached over the edge to pull more away, making a gap. He took off his coat. 'Come here and grab the other arm.'

She ignored him and looked over the wall, about half a metre in height. 'You're not, are you?' She looked over the edge. 'Let me do it.'

Warren knelt and edged backwards to the edge. 'I've only got one leg to break. Take it.' She took the other arm of his coat just as he swung his legs over, beginning to drop. She braced herself as the coat became taught. He slid down the face, branches bending and snapping. He let go making her stumble backwards.

'Are you okay?' she shouted.

Warren spat limestone from his mouth. He swivelled his body on a narrow outcrop so that he felt stable. He pulled ivy from around him in long chains.

'What is it?' said Faith, her head peering over the top, her chest balanced on the wall.

Warren looked up at her. 'A font, I think.'

'Is that all?'

Warren examined the stonework. It was a lighter colour than the rest of the remaining building. He felt around the base to see if he could get his hand underneath to move it. It was stuck firm in the thin layer of earth. He grabbed at something nearby.

'Pull me up.'

Warren brushed leaves and twigs from his body. Faith handed him back his coat. 'I hope it was worth it. It's probably been there for decades.'

He reached into his trouser pocket and held open his hand. Inside his palm were half a dozen cigarette butts. Someone had been here recently, several times by the varied state of them. There wasn't much left to determine the brand without being sent for some form of testing. It wasn't much help on its own but with less and less people smoking, it at least narrowed the field.

Warren set the television to play BBC Five Live and ran a bath. Faith had gone for a run. Water slushed over the side as he climbed in. Pre-match banter seeped under the door. He looked at his legs. He was used to it by now but when everything was in pairs: legs, arms, eyes, people, it still looked wrong.

He moved his thighs up and down, creating small waves.

Water slid over the edge. He slid underneath with his eyes shut. The image of the baby filled his head, its eyes open but lifeless.

———

The waves lapped over it as if tasting it. It sat on the wet, strip of fresh sand connecting Portland to its parent. An earth bank separated Chessil Beach from the only road in or out of the island. Cars drove along it, their passengers oblivious to what was on the other side.

But a curious dog smelled its odour borne on the ozonic breeze. It sniffed and poked at it with its nose. It realised it wasn't food, that it couldn't be eaten, but it was familiar.

'What is it, Oscar?' said his owner, catching up with him. 'What have you found?' The dog moved away. 'It's just a doll, you silly animal.'

She turned it over with her walking stick. The dead eyes were like marbles but the bloated flesh was real.

———

Warren dried himself on the edge of the bed. It throbbed. The bite marks on his calf were red but it didn't appear infected.

His phone rang. It was Faith.

'There's another,' said a breathless, female voice.

'Faith, what's happened?' He stretched for the remote. 'Another what?'

'Baby,' said Faith. 'On the beach.' Warren regained his balance and silenced the tv. 'Warren. Are you still there?'

'Where are you?'

The police had erected a square cordon using metal poles and yellow tape. The untwisted sections glowed in the fading light. A few onlookers hovered at the edges. In the centre, a small marque sheltered the body and a couple of forensic officers. Faith stood outside the cordon, talking to a police officer. She had a blanket draped over her shoulders. A 4x4 stood between them and the distant sea.

Warren held up his camera as he approached. 'Too late for this then?'

'Warren!' said Faith, pulling the blanket closer as she nodded to the man next to her. Beneath the regulation uniform, his tall, wiry figure held firm against the ragged gusts. Specks of dried salt ringed one side of his glasses. 'This is PC Matthews. I've given him my statement so we're free to leave.' Faith slid the blanket off her shoulder.

'Who found it?' said Warren.

'A woman walking her dog,' said PC Matthews, looking over Warren's shoulder. Warren twisted to observer a tearful woman, comforted by a police officer, a dog at her feet.

'I'd just run past her when she screamed.' Faith held the blanket towards the officer. 'Can we go?'

'Since your brother's here, perhaps I can just confirm some things.' Faith's lips pursed as he opened his notebook, his long fingers flicking through it to her notes. 'Your sister say's you've evidence of a similar victim but that it's not been reported?'

Warren flashed his eyes at Faith. 'Our magazine was sent a photograph but there was nothing to confirm it was recent. Or even real.'

The PC tapped the page with his pen. 'But it's why you're in Portland?'

'About the same time as the email, I was sent a location in Portland, centred around the quarry,' said Warren. 'But it didn't lead to anything.'

'Like I said.' Faith glanced at the notebook. 'If we'd found anything substantial, we'd have come forward.'

'I think my boss will want to speak to the both of you. Can you come into the station to give us a full statement? You can bring copies of the material you received.'

'Now?' said Warren.

'If you- '

'Could it be tomorrow?' said Faith. 'I'm cold and I'd like to get back to the hotel and get changed.' PC Matthews flicked the pages of his notebook. 'You know where we're staying.'

'Okay. I know she's in tomorrow,' said PC Matthews. 'Staff appraisals in the afternoon.'

'Thank you,' said Faith. 'Let's go, Warren.'

Faith grabbed Warren's arm, leading him away, as PC Matthews rolled up the blanket.

'I'd like to talk to the woman,' whispered Warren, indicating to a route around the cordon.

'That's not your job.' Faith tugged Warren towards the car park. 'I'm cold.'

'So was the baby.'

Faith let go of him and turned her hand face up. 'Give me the keys.' Warren turned turned towards the cordon. His head dropped and he let out a sigh. He moved to her side, and she gripped his arm, pulling herself into his warmth.

Warren opened the pizza boxes on Faith's bed as she dried her hair. He pulled out a slice, catching the end as it flopped downwards. Faith turned off the hair dryer and sat down on the remaining end corner, sending a wave towards him. As the ripple subsided, he bit into into his slice.

She opened the lid of the second box. 'This one must be mine.'

They ate in silence. As children they'd only ever done that when they'd been told too. Usually after they'd been fighting at the dinner table. Both knew that that what they'd witnessed today was not something trivial, or to be ignored. Both had experience of counselling. Talking it out was something they both knew to be of value. But now that both had seen it, would talking still work. Neither seemed to think so.

Faith closed the box, a couple of slices remaining. 'I'm done.' Warren picked it up and place it on top of his. He bent forwards to drop both by the door. 'What did the woman say when you spoke to her.'

Faith waited till he faced her. 'She was too upset to say much. It had been on its front when the dog had found it.'

'Was there anyone else nearby?'

'No one suspicious but I passed plenty of people.'

'Did it look similar to the boy?'

'A similar age but the body was more bloated.' She looked at the boxes on the floor. 'What did you get?'

'Hawaiian.'

'They still do that?'

'It's a classic.' Warren stretched out a hand. 'I think there's a slice left if you want to take off the meat.'

'No, thanks. Ham shouldn't be that shape.'

'Did you get a chance to check its hands or see if there were any markings on its chest?'

Faith shook her head as she picked up a piece of pepper off her thigh.

'Did it have all its fingers?'

'Let's talk about it tomorrow.'

Warren began to respond but stopped. He picked up the boxes and left the room. He'd had more time to process the discovery and he'd only seen a picture. He entered the room and briefly considered how he might fit the boxes into the small tin bin that seemed to be every guest house and hotel room he'd ever stayed in. He balanced them on top and switched on the television.

Knocking on his door woke Warren up. He turned towards it, keeping his eyes shut. The knocking continued. 'Who is it?'

'Faith. Are you coming for breakfast?'

'I'll meet you downstairs.' He rolled back on his back and looked at his watch. It was eight.

Faith was talking to the Danish couple. They were the only diners. The conversation stopped when Warren entered.

He filled a bowl with cereal and milk. It sloshed over the edge as he sat opposite her.

She twisted back to face him. 'Clumsy.'

'I'm guessing no one slept well?' He smiled at the couple. The looked down at their map, spread across the table.

Faith dabbed at the puddle of milk. 'Did you?'

'If I say "Yes", does that make me a bad person?'

'Maybe,' she said getting up. 'I'm getting some more fruit juice; do you want some?'

'Apple.'

Faith returned with two small glasses. As Warren ate, Faith stared at her glass, her fingers gripping its side.

Warren dropped his spoon into the bowl, jolting her to attention. 'I've not been doing this very long, but you should know this better than me. You need to detach your emotions. This is work. Letting your feelings take over will cloud your judgement.'

Faith picked up the half-eaten slice of toast and held it between them. 'When Peter was born, you know the first thing I did. It'll seem illogical to you.'

'Go on.'

'Most mothers do it.' She put down the toast. 'I counted his fingers and toes. Each one, from one to ten. Twice.'

———

Portland Police Station was a single level, peach brick building on the east side of the island. Silver windows ran around it like a thick belt holding everything in. A few cars were parked outside it.

An officer stood up from her desk as they entered the small waiting room. Its pale blue walls escaped upwards from the similarly coloured floor. A notice board with a variety of campaign leaflets and some chairs littered the space. Faith and Warren waited in front of the glass divide as she approached. They'd not discussed the second body or the interview since breakfast.

The police officer smiled as she approached, preventing Warren for surveying the room behind her. A wisp of highlighted, brown hair skirted the edge of her right eye. She tried to return it to its clip.

'We've got an appointment,' said Faith. 'It was arranged by PC Matthews. I'm Faith.' The officer looked down at the appointment book, nodded and left. Warren shrugged and turned to face the row of plastic chairs. Their backs had created a grey scar across the wall.

As Warren headed for the nearest seat, the internal door opened. It was the same PC. 'I'll show you to the interview room.' At the end of a dim corridor, she ushered them into an interview room. 'I'll let them know you're here.'

'Thank you,' said Warren, searching for a name tag.

The interview room had a small table with chairs either side of it. The colour scheme had been continued. 'Are they all like this?' said Warren.

'Usually,' said Faith, sitting on the far side of the table. Warren sat beside her and tried to get comfortable. The plastic chair creaked. 'Stop that.'

Someone had entered and they snapped towards her in unison. She wore a tight grey suit gliding into the chair. Her hair was short giving her porcelain skinned face a wide circumference. She slid an A4-sized folder onto the desk and chased it into the seat. PC Matthews edged into the room. He pulled the remaining empty chair to the back wall.

The file was open. 'I'm Detective Inspector Pale,' she said, flicking through the pages. 'You've already met PC Matthews. He'll be taking notes.'

PC Matthews bolted upright, tugging a notebook from his back pocket. He searched for a pen. 'Now, Mrs Walters, you've already given an account of how you found the body, so we'd like to cover the information your brother has.' She turned a page, releasing a pen. PC Matthews followed it towards the table's edge.

Faith scanned Warren. 'We're happy to do that.'

'For your brother's benefit, I'll make this clear…' PC Matthews stretched forwards to pick up the pen. DI Pale flicked her eyes towards him and sighed. 'This is an informal interview. You're not under arrest.'

'That's a relief, I've got plans later,' said Warren.

Faith knocked Warren's knee with own. DI Pale examined Warren before turning to Faith. 'You're not currently working, are you?'

'No, I'm on extended leave due to- '

DI Pale raised her hand. 'I know. I spoke to DI Foster this morning. We trained together at Hendon.' She studied Faith. Warren watched the exchange. A small provincial police force wouldn't have experienced the type of serious crimes Faith had been exposed to. It seemed unlikely they'd be able to cope with what might be happening here. 'He's hoping to have you back soon,' she continued, escaping back into the folder. 'Anyway, that's not what we're here to discuss.' She turned back several pages. 'I understand that you were first on the scene?'

'Second,' said Faith. 'There was a woman walking her dog.'

'Oh yes, here it is.' DI Pale looked up. 'What did you think?' PC Matthews pen pressed into paper.

'I think there's some sick bastard killing babies,' said Warren.

'There's no need for that,' said Faith.

DI Pale angled herself at Warren as he folded his arms. 'You're a journalist,' tracing a finger down the page, 'for a magazine…The Skeptics Handbook. I can't say I've ever seen it in any newsagent.'

'It's written for a select audience.'

'You were sent a photograph of another baby a couple of weeks ago, but you didn't report it. Why?'

Warren remained silent. Faith knocked his knee. He scowled at her, unfolding his arms. 'People send us pictures all the time: two-headed animals, weeping statues, lights in the sky. Most are natural phenomena or hoaxes.'

'But you thought this one plausible enough to travel here.'

'There were other factors. Plus, anyone willing to go to the extent of faking a picture of a dead child needs to be dealt with.'

'It was a boy.' Faith nodded. 'What were its injuries?'

Warren pulled out the cube of paper and unfolded it. He spread his palm across the the surface before pushing it over.

DI Pale pulled it closer, leaning over it. 'It has a missing finger.'

'If you look closely, you'll also see a faint cross on its chest.'

'There wasn't any evidence of mutilation to the body found last night,' said DI Pale. 'But I don't think we've checked closely for any markings.' She turned to PC Matthews, waiting for him to finish writing. Catching her gaze, he shook his head.

'I didn't see anything,' said Faith.

DI Pale pushed back the paper. 'Well, the body found yesterday is definitely real. Can you send us the image?' Warren nodded. 'Preliminary autopsy results are due tomorrow. The Tox screen will take another few days - the samples have to be sent to the mainland.'

'We'll hand over what else we have and stay out of your way as much as possible,' said Faith.

'*You* might,' said Warren, turning to her. 'I've got a story to write.'

'Warren, we can't interfere with an active investigation.' Warren decided it was best to not respond. His policy of asking forgiveness rather than permission had served him well. Faith would have to go along with it. 'Is there anything else you need?'

'Not at the moment.' She closed the folder. 'Will you remain on the island?'

'As long as necessary,' said Warren.

'I don't think it will be very long,' said Faith. 'I need to get back home before the end of the week.'

DI Pale stood up and shook their hands. 'Well, I'm sure if Mr Stance performs his investigation under your supervision, we won't have a problem.' She pushed the chair under the table and turned, pausing by PC Matthews. 'Can you see them both out after confirming the first contact details from Mr Stance's phone?'

PC Matthews closed his notebook and jumped up as DI Pale opened the door. She held it open and swivelled to face them. 'We're a small community here. Everyone's connected to each other in some way. We've not had something like this happen before. At least not as long as I can remember. But thank you both for coming in.'

Warren and Faith sat in Easton Square on the single metal bench. Two mothers with prams rolled past chattering away. Faith flicked through pages on her phone. Warren stretched out his legs and looked up at the weak tea sky. 'I need a cigarette?'

'What?' She didn't look up.

'Or perhaps a cigar.' Warren drummed his hands in his trouser pockets. 'A Cuban cigar. They always look so-'

'Stupid?' She turned to him. 'You wouldn't smoke, would you?'

'No, but I like the idea of it.'

'You've never tried, have you?'

'Not really.'

Faith shook her phone at him. 'I remember.' He crossed his legs. 'When you came running into the house. Your Japanese friend, whose dad was a diplomat…what was he called?'

'I can't remember.'

'Morio. That's right. When Morio told you that lighting a piece of straw and inhaling the smoke was just like smoking a cigarette.' Faith giggled. 'That was it wasn't it?' Warren pulled in his legs and rose to his feet. Faith gripped her throat. 'Water! Water!' followed him as he strolled away.

At the corner of the park, Faith stopped in front of the car. 'Where now?' Warren checked his watch. 'Let's get a coffee before going anywhere else.' He stepped into the road. 'I need to write Glade an email and work on an article. We could have an early lunch?'

Faith remained on the pavement. 'After that massive breakfast?'

'We could speak to the woman who found the baby.'

'Why?' Faith scanned the road for traffic.

'She might have seen some markings.'

'Don't you think I didn't look?' Faith wondered if she did see a car coming whether she'd bother to tell Warren.

'I'm sure you did. But you might have missed something.'

'You're joking, aren't you. Well, I don't know how you're going to contact her, you don't know anything about her.'

'But I bet you do.'

Faith moved to put her hands on her hips then relented. 'That doesn't mean I'm going to tell you, does it?'

'You wouldn't be mean to your little brother, would you?'

'I might. I seem to remember I enjoyed it, but you'll need to not be run over first. Come back on the pavement.'

Warren moved to the back of the car and opened the boot. He tucked his laptop under his arm. 'Let's go across the road to the cafe. Perhaps you'll reconsider over an herbal tea.'

Faith strode past him across the road. 'You're buying.'

CHAPTER 14

They sat in a different alcove of the White Stones Cafe. The tunnel pictures were still up. Faith made some calls as Warren looked at emails. He asked Glade to find the woman's address from the details Faith could remember. Warren had seen the woman's surname on the files in the police station. Faith spoke to Peter. He'd had an argument with Gerry over going to some party with his mates. Someone from Human Resources called her about her return date to work. She'd be able to go back in stages, a day or two a week initially.

They'd ordered lunch not long after they'd caught up with their lives at home. Sitting together, they were forming a new partnership. Warren would hesitate to call it one and Faith would never consider what she was doing other than a favour for her brother. But despite their differences and frequent successful attempts at winding each other up, both would admit that they were making progress together.

Warren shut his laptop as a waitress brought their lunch. 'Glade should text us the details. She should be in the office today.'

Warren bit into his burger, reviewing the nearest photographs. 'Did you know that Switzerland has twenty-thousand bunkers?' Faith shook her head as she swallowed a mouthful of falafel. 'With sufficient warning, the whole population could fit inside them. In the event of a nuclear armageddon, Switzerland would become the world's only superpower.'

'Mrs Marcham, 22 Clovens Road,' said Warren, reading from the screen. 'Let me check where it is…It's about fifteen minutes from here. But then so is everything.' He pushed back his chair. 'I'll go and pay.'

Warren was still queuing when Faith reached him. 'Is Peter going to be, okay?'

'He'll be fine. Gerry may be an asshole, but they'll patch it up. I just think Peter's missing me.'

'Did you say when you'll be back?'

'I told Peter I'd not be much longer. I had a brief chat with Gerry and said pretty much the same thing. I think he's enjoying having Peter around. It's just been a while since he's had him this long. They're probably getting on each other's nerves. Peter can be a bit tricky, especially with his exams approaching. But I can't expect Gerry to have him too much longer.'

'Peter's his son too for god's sake.' Warren swiped his card and asked for a receipt.

'I know, I know, but it's a joint responsibility. He did more than his fair share when I was signed off.'

He folded the slip of paper and tucked it into his wallet. 'He can always stay with me.'

'You know he's allergic to cats.' Warren held the door open. 'Actually, I'll just go to the toilet.'

'I'll be outside.'

Warren read the postcards in the newsagent's window next door: chiropractic medicine, acupuncture, naturopathy, aromatherapy, reflexology. He wiped his mouth with the serviette he'd been clutching in his hand and threw it in the nearby bin.

'Everything okay?' said Faith.

'Let's go.'

Ms Marcham lived in Chiswell, high on the southern edge of the island. Her road ran above a local school. Houses were spattered all the way to the bottom, marking the start of Chessil Beach.

Her blood red house sat in the middle of a row of grey contemporaries. Faith rang the bell and they waited together. Warren took a step back as a shadow appeared behind the glass facade, wary of another dog encounter. The woman opened the door unaccompanied. 'Can I help you?'

'Ms Marcham,' said Faith. The woman nodded but showed no recognition. 'It's Faith,' pointing at herself. And this is- '

'Oh, so it is. I'm sorry. It was so awful wasn't it, I can't get it out of my mind. Oh, I'm so sorry, you were saying something.'

'This is my brother, Warren.' He stepped closer. 'Can we ask you a few questions?'

'Are you part of the investigation now?'

'Not exactly,' said Warren. 'If we come in, I'll explain.'

Mrs Marcham led them into the lounge. 'I'll make some tea.'

The dog appeared to be asleep by the fireplace. The upper eye opened for a few seconds then snapped shut like a heavy steel shutter. 'This is the type of dog I like,' said Warren, moving past it to the window.

Faith sat on the pink rose-emboldened sofa. 'You're close to the beach from here?'

'What's that, dear?' said Ms Marcham from the kitchen.

Faith stood up. 'I'll give her a hand.'

Warren rubbed his left thigh as he looked around the room. Multiple photographs of Ms Marcham with dogs and dogs on their own, littered the flat surfaces. Rosettes were stuck to several of them.

Faith entered followed by Ms Marcham, a tray held tight to her stomach. 'Mrs Marcham was telling me she's lived her forty years. Her son's on the mainland and her daughter is working in France. Her son works for the navy in Portsmouth.' Warren smiled. It made it appear he was interested. His sister was genuinely interested in the minutiae of other people's lives. He wasn't.

Ms Marcham put the tray across a footrest, creating a seesaw of blue and white crockery. 'We'll give it a few minutes to brew.' She lifted off a side plate. 'Would you like a biscuit?'

Warren took one and sat by Faith. 'Thanks.' The dog woke to a sitting position and followed the biscuit's path into Warren's mouth.

'Not for me,' said Faith. 'Why don't you sit down.'

Ms Marcham sat in an armchair in front of the the tea set, clasping her hands between her thighs.

'How often do you walk the dog?' said Warren.

'Every day, morning and night,' said Ms Marcham. 'Unless the weather's really awful. Then we'd wait in and go out later.'

'The same route each time?' said Faith

'Yes.'

'Could you have missed the body during one of your previous walks?' said Warren.

'No, I don't think so. It's a narrow beach. We wouldn't have missed it, would we, Oscar?' The dog remained fixed on the remaining half of Warren's biscuit. 'How do you think it got there?' Her voice trailed off.

'I think,' - began Warren.

'We don't know,' said Faith. 'They're carrying out some tests which will tell us more.'

'Did you get a close look at the body?' said Warren as he consumed the rest of the biscuit.

Ms Marcham's fingers formed interlocking patterns. 'No, not really. Once I realised it was real... I just couldn't look it at anymore.' Ms Marcham put her hands to her face. Faith stood, looking at Warren as she did so, moving to the side of Ms Marcham to lay a hand on her shoulder. 'I know, it was awful.'

'Do you still compete with Oscar?' said Warren.

Ms Marcham let her hands slip down her face, leaving red wet streaks. 'Not anymore. He's too old, aren't you boy?' She clapped her hands and the dog waddled into her hands.

'How do you take your tea, Ms Marcham?' said Faith, pouring.

'White, no sugar,' said Ms Marcham, rubbing Oscar's ears.

'It was on its back when you found it?' said Warren.

Ms Marcham nodded. 'Until I turned it over with my walking stick.' She took the cup from Faith. The dog settled at her feet. 'I don't really need it, but you get all sorts of things washed up on the beach. One doesn't want to touch something with your bare hands when you don't know what it is.'

Faith held out a cup for Warren which he ignored. 'Did you see any markings on it?'

'Markings?'

'Like a cross,' continued Warren. Faith pushed the cup out again, making it rattle on the saucer.

'I can't remember. It was a grey-white colour, that's why I didn't think it was real. If I'd know it was real, I wouldn't have touched it.' The words sputtered out like a newly filled hose pipe. She raised the cup to her mouth in jagged stages.

'You didn't do anything wrong,' said Faith, pressing softly. 'I think we should go, Warren.'

Warren sat still in his seat. Faith drank her tea and

returned it to the tray. Warren stood up. 'If you think of anything else, we're staying in the Fairview,' he said. 'No need to see us out.' He paused at the door. 'Where were your children born?'

'Portland hospital.'

'Do you know anyone who's had a home birth?'

'No, I can't say I do. Why would someone take the risk.'

CHAPTER 15

arren spent the morning composing an email to Glade. From Faith's description the baby's body had spent time in the sea. But how had it got there? Dropped in from the beach, from a boat or some other way. What if it had been thrown in from a clifftop. There was something both poetic and macabre about that. But where could it have come from? Could they work backwards, modelling tides and currents to find a possible entry location. It was likely too much for Glade to do on her own, but she had the whole of the University's research expertise to pull from.

Faith jogged past the window. She came straight into the breakfast room. He passed her the local newspaper as she sat down, her cheeks flushed. It showed her the front page - the dead child was the main story.

'You're mentioned,' he said.

'Let me see.'

'I've not finished it yet.' She held at one hand as she drank with the other. 'They spelt your name wrong.' Warren turned the page.

'You're reading the next article.'

'So?'

'You're impossible sometimes.' Faith stood up. 'I'm going up for a shower.' Warren's phone chimed, holding her in her spot. Warren continued to read. 'It might be important.'

'It can wait,' said Warren, chasing her from the room.

Warren put down the paper and checked his phone. There were two messages. The recent one was from Harris. He'd had a meeting with a firm of Independent Financial Advisors in Reading. The commute would be long, but he'd be able to work from home a few days a week.

The second had been sent in the middle of the night. It was another GPS coordinate -about ten minutes' drive away. This time accompanied by a time: ten am.

'Shit,' he said, dumping the paper on his plate and looking at his watch. They had forty-five minutes. 'Faith' he said, repeating it until he reached her room.

She either couldn't hear or was ignoring him. He breathed in and knocked again but there was no response. He pressed his ear against the door: the hair dryer was running. He banged the door with the base of his palm. The dryer stopped. 'Faith, we've got a text. We've got to leave in twenty minutes.'

'Okay!'

'I'll bring the car round.'

He was looking at his watch as Faith opened the passenger side door. He turned off the radio.

'You should take up running,' she said, pulling the seatbelt across. He gripped the steering wheel. She glanced at his leg. 'You know I keep forgetting. Well, some other form of sport.'

'Maybe hopping will make it into a future Olympics too.'

'Just drive.'

He caught the map as it slid off his legs on the first corner. 'Hold the map.' She took it. 'I've marked it.'

They drove along Portland Beach Road, past Chessil

Beach. Traffic was light after rush hour. Warren pushed the car through the speed limits and amber lights.

Faith examined the markings within the circle.'What are those?'

'Without looking, I think you're looking at the former gun battery or the old prison. As the prison's sealed up, my guess is that we're at the battery.'

'I thought you said it was something to do with guns.'

'The ammunition was kept in underground tunnels.'

'Tunnels?'

'Don't worry, I'm going to drop you off nearby. The text message said to come alone. Dad's binoculars are in the glove box.'

Faith took them out. 'What if someone sees me?'

'Pretend your bird watching.'

Their father had tried several hobbies when he retired. Bird watching was one of the few that lasted more than a few months. For each, the books were bought, internet searches completed, and equipment purchased. Occasionally, Faith and Warren were enticed to participate.

'We're here, I think,' said Warren stopping the car. Faith nodded, folding the map. They were in a car park overlooking Portland Port on the top of island. Two other cars were parked close, but they saw no one nearby. It was just after ten. Faith tussled with the wind for control of her coat.

'Be careful,' she said as Warren struggled up the bank in front of the cars. There was a large square expanse of short grass. At the far end, the gaping mouths of the battery beckoned him. About halfway across, he scanned the wisps of marsh grass skirting the edges. Faith should be in there, but he couldn't see her. Hopefully, no one else would either. If the deaths were connected as he expected, they'd not be welcoming to someone in their midsts talking.

Reaching the edge, he stood where a gun would have, looking down into the concrete trench. Steps led down at each end. Ammunition from the tunnels would have been delivered up to the weapons. Their blackness was impenetrable. He wondered if he'd been tricked again. He'd need to get closer.

As Warren stood at the steps nearest the car park, something swung out from the furthest tunnel before returning inside. He skipped down the steps and peered into the first tunnel. There was an odour of wet coal. Light dissipated within less than a meter of entering. He moved slowly towards the second, hoping Faith could make out his movements.

At the second, he could see a doll hanging against someone's leg. Their top half was invisible. When he stepped inside, they withdrew. He couldn't see anything, and fine gravel shifted underfoot as he followed her.

'Stop,' she said.

As he waited for his eyes to adjust, Warren listened to her breathing: quick and rasping. Her shape formed around it. It was a skinny, young woman, shorter than him, wearing a cotton dress covered by a dark puffer jacket. It was pulled tight around her face.

'What's this about?' His voice slid down the walls.

'Shush.'

Warren hated waiting for anything. Whether it be someone else to arrive or a parcel to be be delivered. Her concentrated on her: the breathing was still fast, and she smelt faintly of talcum powder. 'Did you send me the picture of the baby girl?'

'Someone helped me.' Her voice was childlike.

'Who?'

She shook her whole body. 'I can't say.'

'Was it your baby?'

'Her name was Susie. She liked cuddles and milk and sleeping. They took her away from me. I want her back.' She turned her head sharply towards the entrance. 'What was that?'

Warren grimaced as he examined the white square for movement. 'I can't see anyone.' He turned back. The darkness had slid down her body. The doll's legs swung against her. 'Who took your baby?'

Kaylin lifted the doll, hugging it to her chest. 'I can't tell you.'

The woman's breathing quickened. The cool air trickled around his ankle, and he shook his leg, making him lose his balance. He stuck one hand out to the wall.

'Why did you contact us?'

'Someone read me the fairy tales in the magazine.'

'The Skeptics Handbook?'

'It had pictures of statues and goblins.'

'They're not fairy tales-'

'Shush! I can hear someone.'

A shadow flashed past the entrance. She grabbed his arm, her sharp nails digging through his clothing. 'Can you find my baby?'

'I don't think he's alive.' She let go of his arm. 'I'm sorry.'

She sighed. 'Oh well,' she said swinging her doll, 'I'll get-'

Something large crunched towards them. They were hit by light, she screamed, and Warren threw his hand in front of his face. A large hand yanked him forwards, the light flashed upwards and then nothing.

Someone was shaking him hard by shoulder and calling his name. He'd fallen off his skateboard and then what? He wished they'd stop shaking him. He'd hit his head on a lamp-post. Faith had told him to stop halfway but he'd kept going. It was her voice now. He'd made it to the bottom of the hill but as the slope flattened, he lost his balance.

'Warren. Warren! What happened?' He opened one eye, squinting at the light being shone over him. It was Faith.

He was on the ground, looking up but he wasn't eight

years old. But Faith looked just as angry. He covered his eyes as he opened the other. He tried to lift his head but fell back. His felt the back of his head. It was dry but sore and sharing its discomfort to his forehead in sharp pulses.

'Someone went into the other entrance. I went back to get the torch. They must be connected.'

'Who was it?' He lifted himself onto his elbows. Everything spun, forcing him back to the ground.

'Are you okay?' She said, putting a hand on his chest.

'Were they male or female? Old or young?'

'I couldn't tell, they were too well covered. But not small.'

'Did you see where they - '

'Enough of the questions. You're probably concussed. Let me see.' She moved her hand to his chin, pushing it sideways. He rotated his head, and she circled the beam over the back. She lifted his hair to reveal his scalp. 'There's no blood, but you've got a hefty bruise forming.'

'Help me up.' She placed the torch on the ground and pulled him up. He took a step then stumbled.

'Maybe we should wait a bit?'

'Let's just get outside,' he said, reaching for the wall. Faith looped his other arm over her shoulders, and he gripped her lightly. He trailed his other hand against the smooth wool as they shuffled out.

The attacker must have known this area well enough to realise they could outflank him. As well as strong, they'd been light enough on their feet to surprise him. Kaylin had been right, there had been someone stalking them.

Outside, the sun burnt holes through his eyelids. 'Any sign of them?'

She scanned the immediate area but holding Warren up, didn't allow her to see far. 'I don't see anything. I could use the binoculars.'

Warren didn't think he'd stay upright if she let him go.

'Don't bother, they'll be long gone. If it had been a struggle, we'd be hearing screaming. Let's go.'

About halfway across the field, Warren was able to walk unaided. He felt woozy, almost drunk but his vision was clear. He'd never ridden a skateboard again after his mishap.

Ten minutes later they reached the car. Warren rested his back against the car's boot. He wiped sweat from his fore-head. Faith dropped the torch and binoculars onto the back seat. She stood beside him.

'We need to get you checked- '

'There were two cars here when we arrived.' He looked at the remaining red mini. 'This was here, I think. But what was the other one. It wasn't new, a classic I think, but...' Faith shrugged. 'Did you see anyone get in or out of the cars?'

'I was focussed on you.'

'If you'd come straight in rather than going back for the torch, we might have caught them.'

'Don't blame me for this. It was your plan for me to wait so far away.' She pushed herself from the car.' This is just like you. You always blamed me for whatever went wrong.'

'I'd hoped you'd show a bit more common sense. You're meant to be the expert.'

'You'd know why I did that.' She kicked at the ground. 'If you just stopped for a moment and thought about something other than this vain attempt to make headlines.'

Warren took out his phone. Faith got into the driving seat, leaving the door open.

When Warren flopped into the passenger seat, it began raining. He rested his hands on his thighs. 'I hadn't realised you still had an issue with the dark.'

'It's not just the dark.'

Warren directed her towards Easton. He tried to focus on the horizon, but each turn made him feel sick. His brain felt like a wet sponge pushing against the inside of his skull. The young woman clearly had learning difficulties. It had been quite upsetting but at least they were closer or were they. Was it worth the risks they were taking, these were clearly dangerous people.

He'd taken the job at the magazine for a bit more excitement. But getting smashed on the back of the head wasn't what he'd expected. Perhaps he'd made the wrong choice. The Oxford Gazette still hadn't filled his position. But they were here, and they'd met a key figure in solving the whole thing. But who was she and how could they find her? If she was unable to look after herself, she'd need some sort of custodial care.

Faith's brow furrowed. 'Hold on, where are we going? This isn't the way to the hospital.'

'I want you to meet someone first.'

Warren stepped out of the car and collapsed to his knees. Faith rushed around to kneel beside him. 'Are you okay?' She examined his head. 'We should really get you looked at. You don't have to keep doing this, let the police take it from here.'

'They're not here now are they.' He used her to drag himself upwards. 'We need to do this now.' He braced himself against the car and tried to focus on the spiralling house. 'Who lives here?'

Warren glanced at the cars parked nearby. 'Mr Rhodes. Former hospital administrator.' He reached for the gate like a novice swimmer reaching for the side. 'Keen gardener.' He knew this was likely a waste of time but, what did he have to lose. He felt like he might pass out at any minute, and he was gasping for a final gulp of air before going under.

Warren slapped the bell with his palm. He pressed again. 'Let's try the back door.'

A radio was playing Russian Easter by Rachmaninov. He banged on the door, regretting it immediately, as each thud echoed in his head.

Warren stretched his neck upwards to angle his voice at the gap between gate and the top of the fence. 'Mr Rhodes. Are you in?' The radio continued. 'I want to ask about a woman. A young, disturbed woman.'

'Maybe he's out and just left it on.'

Warren climbed the steps and pressed his body against the door, angling his face into the gap between it and the frame.

Faith stepped towards him, placing a hand on his exposed shoulder. 'Warren, what are you doing?'

There was no one visible. The foliage hid everything below head height as far as the house. The curtains were drawn but he saw no one inside.

Smoke drifted from the far-left hand corner. 'Mr Rhodes. Mr Rhodes. Are you in the gazebo? This won't take long.'

Warren stepped back down as Mr Rhodes opened the gate. His cheeks glowed around a grimace.

'How can I help you?' He smiled briefly at Faith.

'Looks like you've been exerting yourself.' Mr Rhodes ran his hand through his thin grey hair.

'Just doing a bit of tidying up.' He probed Warren's bloodless face. 'Are you okay?'

'He's had a bit of a fall,' said Faith, 'I'm his sister. Warren thought we should have a chat.'

'I'd like to help but it's been a long time since I examined anyone.'

'No, no, we're going to the hospital straight after this.'

'I'm fine,' said Warren. 'I want to ask you something.'

Rhodes looked over his shoulder. 'It's not really a good time as it happens.'

'Do you have company?' said Faith, trying to look past him.

'Yes, but that's not- '

Warren fell towards the steps. Rhodes and Faith, both caught him, trying to keep him upright. 'You'd better come in.'

'Thank you,' said Faith, helping her brother into the garden.

'Put him back there.' Rhodes pointed through the garden to the far corner. Faith shepherded Warren through the fonds, flicking the blades and bending the stipes.

'Craig, give us a hand,' shouted Rhodes over their heads.

A tall, bald man stood was stood in the gazebo, grinding a cigarette into an ashtray. He strode towards them, his white t-shirt flexing beneath a set of turquoise overalls. He lifted Warren out of Faith's grip, carrying him to the gazebo and depositing him on the nearest side of the curved bench.

'Thank you,' said Faith, putting her hand on Warren's shoulder as she stared into his eyes.

'I'll get him a glass of water,' said Rhodes, passing by them.

Craig tipped out a cigarette from a carton.'He should go to hospital,'

'That's what I told him. My brother can be quite stubborn.'

'I'm okay,' said Warren, throwing out a hand to grip the table's edge. 'Who are you?'

The man lit his cigarette and drew from it. 'Craig and I were roommates,' said Rhodes, emerging from the house. 'He helps out in the garden sometimes. I'm not as fit as I used to be.'

Warren jabbed towards Craig's arms. 'Hence the scratches.'

Craig ran his right hand along his left forearm, smearing blood. 'That's right.'

Rhodes put the glass down. He turned his hand to Faith. 'Would you like something.' 'No, I'm all right.' Warren considered which hand would offer the least risk of fainting.

She nudged Warren's outstretched arm. He released the table to reach forwards, his hand shaking.

'Actually, a glass of water would be good.' She watched the glass reach Warren's mouth, clinking against his teeth.

Craig smiled. 'Craig, would you get Faith a glass of water?' Craig hesitated, twisting his cigarette between his fingers. 'Please.' He got up, ducking under the trellis.

Rhodes sat down in his place and picked up a pair of shiny, mint-green gardening gloves. The cigarette burnt.

'You haven't asked us what happened?' said Warren, returning the glass.

'It's none of my business,' said Rhodes, his shadow-edged eyes piercing the fog. 'I can see that we're both risk takers. Risks can be managed but they can never be completely mitigated against. I've never been scratched because I wear gloves and I cover my arms.' He held out his arms. Two strips of thick, pink tubular bandage ran bicep to wrist. 'The trouble comes when you rely on others and they're not so careful.' He stubbed out the cigarette.

Craig returned with a glass of water and handed it Faith. He sat down on the outer seat and reached for his cigarette.

'Some people complain that roses have thorns.' He twisted the gloves in his hands. 'I see it as a test.'

Warren leant back. 'A test of what?'

'Resolve. To maintain a focus on something for long enough to achieve salvation. Methodists say that salvation is for God alone. I disagree.' He swept his right arm in an arc over his head. Multiple rose branches were threaded through the cross-hatched frame. Pink and white heads reached through the gaps. 'These roses are not meant to be climbers. They had to be persuaded to do so.'

Faith placed a hand on Warren's shoulder. 'I think we should be going if you're feeling better.' Warren didn't respond, so she shook his shoulder. 'Warren.'

'Yes, let's go,' he said, turning towards her. He leant on the table and pushed himself up. Faith grabbed his arm and they headed for the back gate. Rhodes followed.

Warren stopped. 'My question.'

'What?' said Faith.

Warren forced himself in front of her. 'What cars do you drive? And the colour.'

'A Volvo Estate,' said Rhodes. 'Blue.'

'Have you driven it today?'

'I've been here all day.' Warren turned to Craig.

'My car's in the garage,' said Craig, remaining seated. 'A red Ford Focus.'

Faith held the door shut as Rhodes locked it. When she stepped onto the pavement, Warren was shuffling down the middle of the road. 'What the hell are you doing? 'The car's this way.' She waved. 'Get out of the road! '

Warren continued. Faith ran along the pavement till she was parallel. His head lolled from side to to side. 'Warren, come back on the pavement.' She looked back and forth. 'There's a car coming.' His pace quickened. The car behind him continued, sounding its horn. When it reached him, he disappeared. 'Warren!'

She ran into the road as it drove away. Warren was stood with one hand on a car bonnet. It was a blue Volvo estate.

'Warm.'

'Do you think it's the missing car?'

'I'm pretty sure it was white, so neither of theirs, but we do know he's willing to lie to us.'

CHAPTER 16

They sat side by side on green plastic chairs facing two snack machines. The hospital felt busy but in control. Nurses, orderlies, and doctors skipped past carrying documents or pushing patients. A father and son sat behind them. Warren heard stories of storks and train sets as he filled in the admissions form. Faith chatted with Peter. Things had improved with his father.

Faith ended her call with a jump to her feet. She stretched her back, yawning. They'd been waiting for over half an hour. This wasn't what she'd signed up for when Warren had asked for some help with a story. She'd lied about the torch. It had been in her pocket all time she watched through the binoculars. She hadn't lied about what she'd seen. Or hadn't seen. She'd stood outside the tunnel for about a minute. The torch was in her hand, on, and pointing at the ground. Her arm refused to lift it and her legs refused to budge. But she'd signed up to the police force to stop people hurting other people. Getting hurt doing that, was part of the deal, wasn't it.

'Are you going to get something or just stare at it?' said Warren.

She fed the machine and entered the code for a cereal bar. Nothing happened. She repeated the sequence. Another code followed by another yielded no prize.

A bald, bandy-legged man scuttled towards her brandishing a set of keys like a duster. 'Hold on.' He flicked through them. 'It's a bit temperamental.' He selected a tubular key. 'What did you want?'

'One of those,' she said pointing, 'D4'.

The man squinted inside before opening the door. He picked out two of the items. He bundled them into her hands and locked the cabinet.

'Thanks,' she said. 'That's kind of you.'

'No problem. I think it should be free, myself, amount of time they make you wait.' He flicked his head at Warren. 'Is your man, okay?'

'Warren.' Warren held the pen above the admissions form but was staring into the distance. 'Not really but then he wouldn't be Warren. But thanks for asking...'

'Seymour.'

She tapped her breastbone. 'Faith.'

Seymour smiled then nodded. 'Right, better get back to it.' He dropped the keys into the baggy pocket of his grey overalls and ambled down a corridor.

Faith handed him a bar. 'Here you go. My turn to buy *you* lunch.'

He turned it over and read the label. 'I didn't request this for my last meal. '

'Just eat it.' She sat down, examining the empty form. 'You might be in shock; this will keep your sugar levels up.'

'If I don't choke to death first.'

She waved her open packet at the document. 'You haven't even started it yet.'

'Anything stuck to a clipboard is either bureaucratic or extremely dull. It's usually both.'

He signed and dated the bottom. 'Happy?'

'Give it to me.' Faith took it from him. 'I'll try to find out what's taking so long.' She stood up, nearly colliding with a woman who'd turned on her heels.

'Mr Stance?' said Dr Halstead. 'You're back.'

'You can't keep me away from here,' he said, tearing a piece off the bar. 'I think it must be the food.'

'There's a canteen down the corridor,' she said, turning her head in its direction. 'It should still be open.'

'Maybe later,' said Faith, creating some space between them. 'He's had a bump on the head.' She held out her hand. 'I'm Faith, his sister.'

'Are you a journalist too?'

'No. I'm a police constable.'

'We don't tend to shake hands here. Hygiene.' Faith dropped her hand. 'I read the newspaper article about the other baby.' She lowered her voice. 'Was it mutilated too; it didn't say?'

Warren leaned forward. 'If it was, not in any way that was easily visible.'

'Well, let's hope they're not connected.' She glanced at the clipboard. 'You shouldn't have to wait long once you've handed that back. Nice to meet you. I'd better be getting back to my office.'

'Say hello to Mrs Plowright,' said Warren. Dr Halstead hesitated then joined the white and blue traffic lanes.

Faith scowled at Warren before striding to the reception, the clipboard swinging at her side. Warren pinched the bridge of his nose and leant back, squeezing his eyes shut.

Someone tapped his upper arm. The smell of stale cigarette smoke ran across his face, trying to hide the alcohol underneath. He opened the nearest eye to its source. Seymour. Sitting in the next chair, he rocked sideways. 'So, you two are investigating this baby thing?'

'The death. Yes.'

'Got any suspects?'

'Not yet, would you like to be one?' The man guffawed, exposing a mouth of missing teeth. Warren turned his head. 'How much did you hear?'

'Most of it.' He tapped the nearest ear. 'Ain't nothing wrong with my ears. It's the eyes that are going.' The laugh returned. 'Lucky I'm not a surgeon.'

'Indeed.' He didn't know the rules about hospital staff drinking on duty. Smoking would be allowed outside although he doubted many of the staff did. Janitor's always had store rooms, didn't they. A perfect place for a dash of something alcoholic. If he ignored him, he'd hopefully return to his cubby hole. Warren closed his eyes.

'There's been things happened with babies here before.'

'What?' Warren bolted upright. His head throbbed in retaliation. They were the only two on the row. Faith was chatting to the woman at reception. 'What do you mean?'

'It was before Dr H,' flicking his head towards the hospital's innards.

Warren turned towards him. 'What happened?'

'I can do better than that.' Seymour lifted his chin. 'I can show you.'

'When?' *Mr Stance to Exam Room 2* bounced across the waiting area's walls.

Faith strode over, beckoning him. 'Warren, that's you.'

'When?' repeated Warren, pushing himself to his feet.

'I finish at eight.'

'Come on,' said Faith, beckoning faster.

'I'll meet you outside,' mumbled Warren, standing between them.

Faith seized Warren's arm, drawing him towards her. 'What were you talking to him about?'

'Nothing important.'

'Warren, you can't keep hiding things from me. You asked me to help. Do you not think I could do that better if you told me what's going on in your head?'

They had an early dinner at the hotel. Neither of them spoke much. The food was bland but it made a change from fish and chips. Warren paused outside his room as Faith put her hand on his arm.

'Promise me you'll rest.'

'I might watch some tv in bed.' Faith nodded and let go of his arm.

Warren was older than Faith but following the loss of his leg, Faith had turned protector. He'd never argued. She seemed to enjoy it. She'd taken on bullies twice her size. Although she'd rarely win, she never lost. Her ferocity so completely surprised her opponents that by the time they'd decided whether it would be fair to hit someone smaller, they'd already lost.

An hour later, he left his room with television still on. If Faith found out he wasn't resting, she'd be furious. His head pounded despite the handful of paracetamols he'd swallowed.

Seymour crushed a half smoken cigarette under foot in a disabled parking spot in the hospital car park as Warren got out of the taxi. Seeing Warren, Seymour took a deep drag from his cigarette before stubbing it out using the metal plate on the wall. He tucked remaining finger of tobacco into his chest pocket.

'Evening,' said Warren.

Seymour headed to the building's front corner. Warren followed, Seymour's speed surprising him. It grew darker as they turned. Seymour unlocked a gate at the edge of the car park. It clanged shut.

At the end of the narrow path, they arrived at a loading bay. Two battered, blue dumpsters squatted in front of a graffitied, corrugated metal door. To its left was a single door, a light above emitting a urine-coloured glow.

A rattle of keys preceded the door, scraping open.

Seymour bent over to pick up a torch from the floor, burrowed between empty bottles.

Warren followed Seymour through a dimly lit, dank corridor. The torch disclosed black puddles allowing Warren time to adjust his footing. They went through another door and down a flight of steps.

'Be careful,' said Seymour, descending, 'they can be slippy.' Warren clenched the handrail, letting its cool surface slide under his palm.

At the bottom, a flickering light lit another series of pools. Seymour shined his torch over them and above to the mouldy walls. 'They were due to knock down this side of the hospital. It got approved ages go but when Dr H started, she put the kibosh on it. Didn't have the money or something.'

'What was this all used for?'

'You'll see.' Seymour pushed open a wide door. The beam flicked across the room's large square floor and windowless walls. It settled on the far wall: there were two round heavy metal doors side-by-side. 'This was the incinerator and autoclave room.' They approached, Seymour focussing the beam on the ocular pair.

Seymour flicked the beam across the room, pitching Warren into darkness. 'Over here was the cold room. All the freezers were sold off.'

Warren wriggled his toes, feeling the dampness beneath. Pulling out his phone, he used the torch to illuminate the ovens. 'What went in these?'

'The left one's the autoclave. It was used to sterilise glass stuff. But it didn't get used much once everything became plastic. That's when this one became useful. All the used medical stuff went in there along with quite a few other things.'

Warren peered through the letterbox window. 'What sort of things?' He angled the light to peer inside. It was empty.

'Anything plastic that's been used in surgery or the like, bits of tissue, old blood samples. And foetuses.'

Warren spun round. 'Are they meant to do that?'

Seymour's gaze fell to his feet. The light followed. 'They should really be cremated or buried. The parents should be asked.'

'Why hasn't anything been done about this?' Warren moved to the centre of the room. 'It's unbelievable.'

Seymour sighed. 'I came down here once. The previous administrator was in here with someone else. They looked surprised by my coming in. I came fairly often but I guess he didn't know that. He came straight over to me, blocking my view. I couldn't see what they were doing.' Seymour lifted the beam and lit up the incinerator. 'I'd never seen him so angry.'

Why would an administrator be somewhere like this and why so angry. He was effectively the boss of the hospital, so nowhere was off limits or not part of his responsibility. But still, this was like the boss of Microsoft touring their server room. A perfectly legitimate thing to do, however unusual 'Who was with Mr Rhodes?'

'You know, him?' Seymour stiffened. 'I don't want no trouble.'

Warren rocked on his heels, crossing his arms. 'I'll keep this private. Do you remember what the other man looked like?'

'No, they didn't have all the lights on. Looked pretty sturdy, though.'

'Did you ever see them down here again?'

Seymour shook his head. 'The place was closed shortly after that. Contracted it all out for collection. Bags and bags of the stuff all pied up outside.'

Images of bloody tissue and unformed babies swirled around Warren's head. He started to waver and felt a chill run through his body. He lunged towards a chair he'd seen pushed against the far wall. His phone flashed light across the floor. He fell into it, dropping his head between his legs.

Seymour illuminated Warren's hunched body. 'You all right?'

'I'll be okay. Just give me a minute.' Warren tried to purge the thoughts from his mind. But it was like being told not to think of something, you couldn't help but focus on it. He concentrated on his breathing.

'We should be getting back. We're not meant to be in here.'

Warren inhaled deeply as he pulled himself upright. The chair remained rigid. He was sure it had wheels. He crouched down beside it, directing his phone underneath. There was a piece of dark material stuck under both front wheels. He lifted the seat and pulled at it. Its wet form dragged across the floor, uncoiling as he raised it.

He stood, holding it at arms length as he walked towards Seymour. 'Shine your light on it.' Warren craned his neck around it. It spun slowly between his finger and thumb, liquid beginning to drip from the thin material. It was smothered in black mould. A single section became visible. It must have been protected by being on the inside. The item had been white. In the middle of the patch was a smiling teddy bear.

'Looks like something for a baby,' said Seymour. 'My grandson's got one like it.'

'Can I take it?'

'Be my guest,' said Seymour, chuckling as he turned towards the door, waving the torch. 'Just keep me out of it.'

Warren held the clothing in front of him as he followed. An occasional drip caught the torch light, as it landed by his feet. It could be nothing, but wouldn't standard issue hospital clothing be plain.

CHAPTER 17

Warren woke to knocking on the door. He freed his ears from the soft pillow. Faith was calling him. He slid to the edge of the bed and swung his legs out from under the covers. She continued.

'Hold on.' He hopped towards the door, grabbing the handle. He pulled it open.

Faith stood outside, holding a side plate. 'You missed breakfast, but I've saved you something.'

'Please come in,' he said, jumping back onto the bed. It bounced in acknowledgement. She slid the plate on the table below the tv.

'How are you feeling?'

'Better. I think.' He moved to the end of the bend and considered the food.

'I tried your door when I went down.' She bent her head towards his, blocking his view of the plate.

He leant back. 'What are you doing?'

She scanned his eyes. 'I read that if your pupils are dilated, it could mean you're still concussed.'

He leant forwards, pushing her thigh sideways, and grabbed a wrinkled sausage. 'Did I pass?'

She smiled. 'I think you'll live.' He swallowed the remains of the cold sausage and switched his attention to the bacon. She opened the coarse yellow drapes, reviewing the exterior. 'Why don't we take the day off?'

Warren chewed on the drying sliver. 'And do what? Whenever we had the day together during the holidays, we'd usually finish at each other's throats.'

She turned around, framed by the light. 'We're adults now.' She held up her hands as if deciding between two melons based on weight. 'It looks like another sunny day.'

'Maybe we could compromise.'

'What do you mean?' She shoved her hands into the small pockets of her trousers.

He pulled the dish off the table and held it on his thighs. 'No brown sauce?' She shook her head. 'Let me finish this first and I'll explain.'

She poked a tongue into her cheek. 'I need to use your toilet?'

'What's wrong with yours?' She closed the bathroom door.

'Yours is nearer.'

He shrugged and picked up a button mushroom. It squirmed into his mouth. 'No butter either,' he muttered, rotating a slice of brown toast.

The door found open. The top two buttons of her trousers were undone. 'What the hell's soaking in the sink? It looks like a bodysuit.' He considered what to say, suddenly feeling full. They couldn't send it for DNA analysis, it was too contaminated for that, and he couldn't just hand it to the police and ask them. They'd think he was crazy. 'Did you go out last night?'

He never enjoyed being told off by his sister. Or anyone for that matter. However, he'd worked out that as long you gave the impression of listening and didn't interrupt or object, you could pretty much zone out of everything they were saying. He told her what he'd been up to.

By the time she'd finished, his food had gone cold. He slid the plate back onto the table. 'What would you like to do as a day off?'

'You're unbelievable.' She put a hand on her hip. 'Let's stay nearby. We could go shopping for Peter's birthday presents.' Clearly, the punishment wasn't over.

'Shopping.' He flopped backwards. 'Community service would be less painful.'

'A day of gentle walking in the sunshine is what you need.' Warren stared at the ceiling. Perhaps it would fall in if he concentrated.

Getting no reply, she returned to the bathroom and began to rinse the clothing as

Warren got dressed.

Weymouth's city centre was full of brightly coloured families laden with plastic bags. They moved like giant amoeba, sections expanding and retracting as children pushed out or fell back from their parental nucleus. Pensioners shuffled in pairs or gossiped on benches.

After a couple of hours, Faith had found several small gifts. Warren had bought an item and refused to tell Faith who it was for.

'Why won't you tell me?' They climbed the hotel's steps. Faith had bags in both hands. Warren gripped his prizes under his arm.

'Wait and see.' They approached the reception desk.

The receptionist's gaze flicked from Faith to Warren's package. Her mouth fell open. She tracked the see-through box as he approached the stairs. Warren generated a smile. It wasn't returned.

'I used to have a doll like that,' she said, her voice quivering.

Warren checked the package. He'd gripped the figure around its neck. Warren flipped the box up, holding it in his hands to face her. A corner of the young woman's mouth flickered.

'Birthday shopping,' said Faith, brushing past her brother.

Warren nearly dropped the box. He squeezed it against his chest making the plastic crackle. He followed her upstairs.

'Oh, Mr Stance,' said the receptionist. 'I've a package for you.'

Warren exhaled as he reversed back down. He twisted towards her. 'Just put it on top.' She laid a small white box on top and turned her head sideways. 'Who's it for?'

'I keep asking,' hollered Faith from the landing, 'but he won't tell me.'

'It's not really for any one *specific* person.'

'Mine was called Jemima,' said the receptionist. 'I'd take her everywhere with me. She was like a sister.'

'I don't suppose you have a weighing machine?' said Warren.

An hour later, Faith knocked on Warren's door. 'I've got some for you, can I come in?'

'Yeah,' he said. 'It's open.'

Faith pushed at the door, allowing the dissonance of chatter to flood inside.

'What is that?'

'French school kids,' she said entering, one hand outstretched. 'I brought the weighing-.' Faith let the electronic weighing balance drop against her thigh. 'What the hell are you doing?'

Warren was stood at the end of the bed, one knee pressed into the dolls legs as he sawed into its stomach with a penknife. He grinned. 'What does it look like?'

The doll's packaging lay across the bed and over the floor. The other lay unopened on the bed. She kicked the door shut with her heel. 'That was expensive. It shed real tears.'

He held out his empty hand. 'Pass me the tracker.' Faith scanned the room. She had no idea what she was looking for.

Warren was never the most technical, but he'd picked up quite a bit working with Harris. He'd got hold of the GPS tracker and express posted it to the hotel. When Warren had told him what he'd intended to use it for, he'd expected several questions, but Harris had just focused on the technical requirements. That suited Warren. He didn't' like explaining things. Harris had been a communication specialist in the army.

Faith had met Harris a few times and never knew why they called him – it wasn't his Christian name, not even his surname, but she didn't dare ask.

Warren threw his right arm back, pointing the blade towards the table under the television. The white package lay open under the tv. Inside, sitting half on top of its grey protective foam insert, was a black block the size of a chocolate bar.

She handed it to him. 'What is it?'

'GPS tracker.' He handed her his phone. 'It's on. You should be able to see it on the software's map.'

She examined the flashing dot on the map, zooming in. 'It's pretty accurate.'

He squeezed the tracker through the slit in the doll's skin. 'To a couple of metres.'

'So, are you finally going to tell me what's this for?'

Warren closed the knife, standing up straight holding the doll. 'Can you place the balance on the table.' Faith obliged. He zeroed it and put on the doll. 'A couple of pounds light.' He moved the doll back to the bed. 'What was Peter's birthweight?'

'Seven pounds two ounces.'

'Did you ever want another?' said Warren, escaping to the bathroom.

'Who says I might not?' She snapped. She perched on the

bed, inspecting the doll. Its eyes sparkled. She stood up, craning her neck. 'So, are you going to tell me?'

Warren reappeared, cupping several small toiletry bottles. 'Can you get yours?'

'Not until you tell me what's going on,' she said, hand on hip.

Warren lobbed the bottles towards the doll. 'Sit down.' He leant back against the windowsill. She sat on the edge of the bed, her back to the doll.

'If the autopsy confirms that the body was not left on the beach, then it's likely that it was thrown into the sea. But where from? Glade's already checked ship movements but nothing has come close enough. If it was thrown into the sea, finding out where it started from might give us an idea of who did it and stop the next one. To do that, we'll need to test different entry points using our knowledge of prevailing currents. Glade's narrowed down the possible locations to a couple. The doll will allow us to confirm which one.'

'What do you mean, *the next one*? If it was a distressed mother, why would it happen again?'

Warren shrugged his shoulders. 'I hope you're right.'

Warren came out of the bathroom to find Faith lying against the headboard, staring at her phone. There were an additional dozen toiletry bottles pooled around her feet.

'Make yourself, comfy.'

They were going into town for dinner. Faith would be glad return home. She missed her son. Faith didn't think Warren missed anything, even his cat. 'What?' said Faith without looking up.

Warren stopped drying his hair. 'Where did you get those from?'

'Mmm,' said Faith, wiggling her toes. 'They were in a cupboard at the end of the corridor.'

Warren winced as he rubbed the bump. 'See how many

you can get in.' He examined the white towel for blood before throwing it on the bed.

Faith sighed and started stuffing the bottles into the doll. Warren put on a shirt as slid the towel over its face. Faith filled the rest of the cavity, using another four bottles. 'I think that's the most I can get in.'

'Check the weight.' Warren picked at a roll of black tape.

Faith rested the doll on the balance. 'Six pounds, 12 ounces.'

'It will have to do.' Warren stretched out the duct tape. 'Hold it horizontally with your hands at each end.'

Faith held it as instructed at arms length. Warren wrapped several layers of the tape over the doll's chest. He cut through it with the penknife. 'That should do.'

He took it from her and examined it. 'Jesus,' said Faith. 'It's monstrous. I wouldn't want to find this without knowing what it was.'

'We'd better make sure we get there first, then. You can do the other one. I'm going down to the bar for snacks.'

A morning shower surprised the town like an annoying second cousin. It sought out imperfections in the concrete. Faith arrived at the hotel wet. She'd run through town to avoid the beach and got lost.

Warren was sitting in the foyer, holding the doll in its box on his lap. The Danish couple swung past him. Faith stood inside the door, water running down her legs. Seeing her, they moved into single file formation. Faith smiled at them, standing aside to let them out. They blanked her.

Faith and Warren examined each other. 'I don't think there's any way back, is there?'

'And there I was hoping for a Danish penpal.'

'Sorry, I'm late.' She put a foot on the stairs. 'Do I have time for breakfast?'

Warren pressed his fingers into the box's plastic window,

leaning over it to peer into the breakfast room. 'If you're quick.' Faith shot upwards.

A group of schoolgirls descended. Warren slid the doll under the chair as they passed. One of the groups saw it and was briefly distracted before the conversation sucked her back. They congregated in the hallway. More joined them. Warren pulled out his laptop and connected his headphones.

Warren started the engine. Faith held the doll between her knees, facing the dashboard. 'Are you sure you're well enough?' He nodded as she studied him. 'Where's the first location?'

'Glade and I spoke while you were getting ready. She said the boss is getting impatient but not to worry. Anyway, the first one's near the quarry. It's close to Chessil Beach so it won't have far to travel. If there're any problems with the design it should still get to us.'

'I was thinking about your *idiotic* late-night trip to the hospital. You said the collection of the clinical waste had been contracted out.'

'That's right,' drawled Warren.

'Did Seymour say who the firm was? Maybe someone from it might remember what was going on.'

Rain fell heavily. Warren visualised the two blue bins outside the hospital. He stopped the car at the lights. They were still green. They had been a name on he outside of them. It was white, smeared in dirt. The driver of the car behind sounded his horn.

'It was Draper, I think. Draper…Engineering Services.' The car overtook them as the lights turned red. 'But isn't it likely that they'd have stopped it by then.'

'Unless the contractor was in on it too.'

Warren parked parallel to a metal barrier fifty metres from the bus stop he'd used to visit the quarry. Inside was a large patch of gravel with two parked trucks. They'd not seen another vehicle for the last mile.

'Shall we wait it out?' said Warren, looking up through the windscreen.

Faith zipped her raincoat up to her chin. 'I'm set.'

He frowned. 'One last check.' He fished out his phone and checked the GPS signal. The dot hovered on their current location. 'Let's go, then.'

Warren pushed the barrier open from its pointed end and held it for Faith. She stood at the hinge, reading the metal plate fixed within its apex.

'Might it have been *Draber* Engineering Services?'

'Could have been.'

She followed him in. 'It also says *Private Property*.'

'We'll only be a minute,' he said, turning up his collar. The barrier swung shut. They crossed the gravel, passing behind the trucks, until they reached the edge and into wispy grass and small trees.

A wet branch bent by Warren's shoulder whipped across Faith's face. 'Careful,' she said, wiping the water off her cheek. 'I think this is a waste of time. One photo of a dead baby and one washed up along with an odd couple, doesn't make for a conspiracy.'

'Do you remember that Magic Eye craze when we were kids?' She mumbled in agreement. 'Everyone found them so easy. 'Just stare at it, Warren. it's easy.' I could never do it; you had no problem. They say it's a gift entrepreneurs have, to assimilate disparate events: economic, social, technological, and spot an opportunity. For me, I get a sense that there's a gap too, but it's not to be filled by some new business or widget. More like a wound that has never healed. Or a crack, ready to burst.'

The vegetation thinned as the ground fell away. The rumble of the sea rose through the *ratatattat* of the rain. Trees gave way to bushes and grass to rocks. The edge arrived as an absence.

Warren ducked his head over. 'This is close enough. Give

me the doll.' Faith offered the box. He grabbed it and pulled out the doll. He let it dangle by an arm, feeling its weight. He turned around. 'Hold my belt.' She grabbed it and he leant over the side. He estimated the distance from the cliff face to the sea. It would need to travel a few metres. He felt sick and retracted back to standing. He pressed his feet into the slick blades of grass. He faced the sea, the wide expanse left nothing to focus on. He began to swing the doll. Faith tightened her grip. His legs felt hollow.

Warren tried to centre himself, providing a solid foundation. But however much he believed he was stable; he knew deep down that he wasn't. Most of the time, he didn't think about his missing limb. And nor did anyone else, particularly if he was wearing trousers. Sure, if you looked closely, you might see a slight rocking motion to his gait, but most weren't that observant. Or just didn't comment. But he'd lost count of the number of times, particularly as a teenager, he'd toppled over through overconfidence or being drunk. As an adult, he was a bit more circumspect. And standing on the edge of a cliff, was no time to be reckless . 'Actually, you'd better do this,' he said, handing her the doll. 'Nice and high.'

Faith dropped the box. Warren grabbed the back of her raincoat. Faith bent her knees, swung twice, then hurled the doll up and over the side. At the top of its arc, it hung facing them, then fell, cartwheeling below their line of sight.

A large truck stood in the far lane, indicating its intention to turn in. A man in a blue, short-sleeved shirt stretched against his midriff, leant on the barrier, watching them approach.

'You've blocked the entrance.' He glanced over his shoulder. 'You're creating a tailback.' Warren searched for a car behind the truck but saw none. 'This is private property; you can't be in there.'

'We're just going,' said Faith, walking faster.

'What was that thing I saw you throw?' Warren and Faith changed glances. 'It looked like an animal.

'It was'- began Faith

'You're right,' said Warren, stepping forward. 'It was my...cat.' He felt Faith's hot gaze on his neck. 'He passed away, the poor bugger. He loved fish so it seemed only fitting to give him a sea burial.'

The man's lips puckered, dragging his eyebrows to his nose. He let go of the gate allowing Faith to push it open. The man returned to the truck. On the cab door it read *Draber Engineering Services* in small white letters.

Faith saw it, nudging Warren. 'I don't suppose you ever made collections from the hospital?' said Faith.

He looked over his shoulder, hanging from a handle. 'Not me. I only do Portland stone. You'd need to speak to the boss to find out about the other stuff.'

'Who would that be?' said Warren.

The man hauled himself into the cabin, knocking his cap as he slammed the door shut. He wound down the window and pulled his cap into place. 'Corinne Draber's in charge since her father died.'

Faith pulled back her hood, 'Where does she work?'

'The Head Office's in Portsmouth but she's as often in Queen's Spa over in Weston.' He chuckled. The window slid shut and the truck rattled to readiness.

Faith got into the car and Warren reversed, then pulled away. 'Check the GPS,' he said, handing her his phone.

'Seems to be working,' she said, twisting the screen towards him. 'What are you thinking?'

Draber connected both the hospital and the quarry. They had trucks going back and forth across the island all the time. Often the best way to hide anything nefarious was in plain sight. After a while, you ignore the parked cars on your street. They become background noise. And long gone were the days when people were friendly with their postman, let alone milkman. Nowadays, it was anonymous delivery drivers dropping of parcels on your doorstop and rushing off. If there was someone trying to find ingenious, if somewhat dramatic ways, of disposing of a child's body, an anonymous transportation system could fit their warped modus operandi.

Warren faced her with a grin. 'How would like a bit of pampering? I'll tell you on the way.'

'Why do I think I'm going to be disappointed,' she said, turning away.

As they drove into Weston, Faith scanned for somewhere to park near Queen's Spa. Faith had checked its website's list of treatments and created a shortlist in her head. Some of them she didn't recognise. If Warren was going to ask her to go inside to spy on Corinne she'd at least get something from it.

The last time she'd had a fancy treatment was a two-for-one voucher offer her friend, Jules, had got online. It was in a fancy gym, and they'd gotten so drunk afterwards, Jules's husband had to come to pick them up.

Warren slowed the car, signalling when Faith pointed to a gap. It was right outside the shopfront, bookended between two premium cars. A white four-by-four whined as it overtook them.

'Couldn't get much closer,' she said. Warren cancelled the signal and accelerated, throwing Faith backwards. 'What the hell are you doing?' He leant forward, pointing his left forefinger at the diminishing car. The numberplate read "Draber".

After twenty-five miles, they reached Winterbourne Monkton, a village between Avebury and Maden Castle. Expansive houses hid behind grass and gravel.

The Mercedes turned into a gravel driveway. Warren crawled past, completed a U-turn, and parked on the opposite side.

A woman in black gym kit pulled a sports bag from the

boot one-handed. Her ponytail swished as she went inside, gripping a dog with her other arm.

'At least it's small,' mumbled Warren, opening his door.

Faith grabbed his arm, holding him inside. 'Give it a few minutes. It'll be less suspicious.'

Warren tried to remember when he'd developed a dislike of dogs. Faith said he was frightened of them because he'd been pinned to the floor by one as a child. That wasn't true, exactly, although he didn't like to think about it. He thought some of them looked perfectly acceptable. Cute even. But they weren't man's best friend. Best friends don't bite chunks of flesh from you like a hyena.

The doorbell's deep timbre reverberated inwards. The door opened and Warren was eye to eye with the dog. It growled, exposing a set of gleaming sharp teeth between wisps of shiny hair. The woman tilted her head at Warren.

'Don't mind my brother. He's scared of dogs,' said Faith. 'Are you Corinne Draber?'

'I am.'

'Could we talk to you about your business?' She looked puzzled.

'Draber Engineering Services,' added Warren.

'If you're anything to do with my brother, I've told him to stop bothering me.'

'I know how you feel,' said Faith, making Corinne laugh. 'We're nothing to do with him. I'm a police officer and my brother's a a journalist. We've got some questions regarding some of the contracts your company had. It shouldn't take long.'

Corinne led them to the gleaming white kitchen with black appliances. The monochromatic palette was interrupted by a single fruit bowl on the empty worktop. 'I know I'm listed as the business owner, but it really runs itself. I turn up to the odd management or board meeting, but I find it so boring. But if I don't turn up to those things, I might not get to live like this,' she said, swishing one arm through the air. Rather unenthusiastically, Warren thought.

Warren and Faith sat on two high stools at the breakfast bar. Corinne placed the dog on the floor. It danced around her ankles as she filled its bowl with biscuits.

'This is what my kitchen would look like without Peter,' said Faith to Warren.

'What?' said Corrine, reappearing on the other side.

'Pete's her son,' said Warren. 'Bit messy.'

'You said this wouldn't take long,' said Corinne, holding the edge.

'Yes…yes,' said Faith. 'When did you take over the business?'

'After my father died. At the start of the year. It was a heart attack.' She pushed off and leant back against the cooker. 'He lived life to the full. Even before my mother left him, he was either at the office or the golf club. He never stopped.'

'Do you work from home a lot,' said Warren, looking around.

Corinne smiled. 'I own the business, but my brother *runs* it. It was all set out in the will. My father's idea of a joke, I think.' She folded her arms. 'My brother's not happy about it.'

'So do you know anything about the contract with Portland hospital?'

'My brother would know more about that, you'd need to ask him.'

'Do you have a number or somewhere could we find him?' said Faith.'

'You can ring the main office. But first thing tomorrow morning you can catch him at the golf club. It's called Came Down, just off the A354''

'Enough?' Faith said to Warren, hopping of the stool. He nodded and slid

to the floor. 'We'll be going. Thanks for your time.'

Warren stood at the doorway, leaning against the frame. 'I don't suppose you know a Mr Rhodes. He was Portland hospital's Administrator. He's retired now, lives in Weston?'

Corinne picked up the dog, holding it close to her chest as it squirmed. 'No.'

'We'll see ourselves out,' said Faith, tugging Warren's sleeve.

They ate late. The sea sat black outside, weak moonlight dusting the tops of silent waves. Faith talked about Peter's upcoming birthday. Warren feigned listening. He couldn't see any solid connections between the people they'd met, and the bodies discovered. Or if the incinerator had been used for anything it shouldn't have been. And what about the girl with the doll in the cave – if they could find her, that could reveal everything. Had she been telling the truth and would someone with learning difficulties even know if they were.

An experienced detective can tell if someone's lying. Warren didn't have that skill, neither did Faith, he thought. But even knowing the target doesn't mean you can pin anything on them. It just gives you a focus of where to apply the pressure. Faith knew better than him that cases are solved when someone admits to something criminal. After that, the evidence tends to fill the gaps of knowledge. They needed someone in the know, to tell them if there was anything even in what they found to be a story let alone demonstrate any criminality.

'Where is it now?' Said Faith.

Warren woke his phone, spinning it to face her. 'About a mile off the coast.'

'I'd have expected it to have been further north by now.' Faith took a sip from her fruit tea, scrunching up her nose.

'No good?'

'It's okay.'

'Never as good as your own, is it?'

'I don't imagine they filter the water.' She tapped the side of her cup. 'I do need to get back at some point, Warren. When do you think you'll have enough for an article?'

Warren harrumphed. 'We're a long way off. What's the hurry?'

'Gerry has to go away for work next week. Someone needs to pick up Peter from school.'

'Can't Mum do it?'

'I've asked her. She's not keen on doing it on her own. You know what she's like. If one around, she'd do it. I think I'll need to go back tomorrow, I'm sorry.'

Warren twisted his cup in its saucer. 'I really appreciate you being here. With Harris gone its-.'

'Couldn't you ask Harris to come back? He never liked working in finance, anyway.'

'His pride won't let him. Maybe when he's got bored of it.' He let go of the cup. 'If you have to go, I'll manage. Hopefully, there won't be another one.'

Faith's cup clattered onto its saucer. 'That's not fair.'

'I know.'

CHAPTER 18

You've got five minutes,' said Warren, taking Faith's bags out of the boot. She yawned as he handed them to her. He shut the boot and scanned the tracks for incoming trains.

'You could come home too,' she said, putting the strap of one bag over her shoulder. 'I'm sure the local police will find the woman.'

'You know I don't think it's that simple.'

''There was no mark or mutilation on the boy. Why do you still believe there's something going on?'

'Just a feeling.' Evidence's objective but when there isn't any, subjective is all there is. 'Say "Hi" to Mum.' Warren caught a train arriving in the distance. 'You'd better go.'

Warren never liked golf but he didn't hate it, either. At school, he played all the obligatory sports. Golf wasn't one of them. But he had played with his father before the cancer. He watched it on television occasionally along with many other sports. If he had to rank golf as a spectator sport, it would be near the bottom.

Came Down's clubhouse was a single story, brown and

stone building perched above the course. A golfer crunched past him, pulling a trolley, as he got out of the car.

In the bar, small groups of players circled dark tables, littered with side plates of bacon sandwiches. A solitary man, wearing a pale blue jacket stood at the bar. Warren approached him. The man was leaning against the bar, pushing the jacket's decorative gold buttons against himself. He drank slowly from a dark pint of flat beer, exchanging short sentences with the barman.

'I wonder if you could help me?'

The man pushed himself from the bar. 'Depends on what help you need, son.'

'I'm looking for Mr Draber.'

'I will get the Pro,' said the barman.

'Don't worry, Pedro,' said the man, holding up a hand. 'I'll deal with it. I'm the club President here, Gerry Murphy. Maybe I can help?'

He led Warren to a window overlooking the final green. A woman slotted the flag back into the hole and shook hands with her opponent. 'Have you played here?'

'I don't play. My balance's not so good.'

'That's a shame. It's a great course. Not long in yardage but it's traditional. Not like the target golf you see nowadays. Yet, all hazards are visible. Good for a newcomer.'

'Well, if I change my mind, it'll be top of my list. Corinne Draber said he'd probably be here.'

Murphy steered them to another window. They watched several golfers practising their putting. They lined up half a dozen balls, hitting each one in turn at a one of the flagged holes.

'Do you know Mr Draber?'

'I was good friends with his father. Harry was a long-standing member of the club. His handicap never rose above ten. He was a good committee man. Never missed a meeting.'

He leant towards Warren. 'Felix's more of a hacker but don't tell him I told you. Got a bit of a temper.'

'Is he here?'

'Yes, that's him. Over there,' said Murphy, nodding towards the green. 'In the pink jumper.'

Warren watched Felix take a put. His chestnut hair bulged out of the sides of his black baseball cap. The hit ball ran half a metre past the hole. He prodded the club's head firmly into the turf. Jim tapped the window and shook his head as Felix looked over. He sneered as leant over to address the next ball in line.

'Can I speak to him?' said Warren.

Murphy glanced at Warren's shoes before directing him. 'Go round that corner and into the changing room. From there you can head out to the practice area.'

Warren hesitated. 'What was Harry like as father?'

'He was good with the kids. He brought them here from when they were nippers. Corinne was good, really good but she just stopped. Felix, he's always been keen as mustard, always trying to grab Harry's attention. But he's not got the mentality for golf. You need to be in control of your emotions. Felix, well, he seems to be battling himself as much as the course.'

'Do you know if a Mr Rhodes was ever a member here? He used to run the hospital.'

'Rhodes. He still is. But as a non-playing member. He served on the committee at the same time as Harry. They pretty much ran the show. He still comes in to check on the roses. When you leave, you'll see them climbing up the side of the greenskeeper's hut.'

'Thanks,' said Warren, turning away. 'I'll look out for them.'

Warren sat on a wooden bench to read a text. It was from the cat sitter: Keplar had thrown up in the hallway. She'd cleaned it up. He typed out a reply. *He'd need to leave her a gift next time.*

As he stood, a half-naked man, blood dried on his forehead, sitting opposite, pointed at a small white and red sign fixed to the wall: *No Mobile Phones.*

'Sorry,' said Warren, dropping his phone in a pocket. 'Bank manager.'

Warren stood on the paving at the edge of the putting green. Felix Draber missed a putt. 'Come on,' bemoaned Felix. He examined the club's head, wiping his thumb across the face.

Warren stepped onto the grass. 'Felix Draber? Could I have a chat?'

Felix positioned himself to put the next ball. 'What's it about? My tee offs in a few minutes.'

'I'm investigating the baby found on the beach.'

Felix didn't look up. 'What's that got to do with me?'

'Well, I'm a reporter and -.'

'You from The Gazette?' He putted. 'We advertise there.'

'No, it's called The Skeptic's Handbook. It's a membership-based magazine focussing on unexplained events.' The ball rattled the flagpole and dropped in. 'I've already spoken to your sister- '

'That thieving cow.' He lined up his last ball.

'We're just following up a lead relating to the waste collections at the hospital.'

'What's that got to do with a dead baby.'

'Probably nothing. But there's no harm in checking everything to be sure, wouldn't you agree?

Felix looked up. 'I guess so.'

'What can you tell me about your contract with the hospital?'

'Not much. It's waste collection. Twice a week. It was a good contract at the time. We've had it for a few years. It's not a core part of what we do anymore.' He paused to put. 'Why?'

'It's pretty different from digging up rocks.'

Felix Draber leant on the putter as he faced him. 'This is a small island. There's not a lot of choice for who can do what for whom. We already ran a fleet of trucks. It's not that different.' He checked the progress of his final ball. It had trickled past the hole. 'Bloody putter.'

'What happens to the waste after its collected?'

'It gets delivered to an incinerator in Portsmouth.'

'Is it checked?'

'What do you mean?'

'Well, would you know if there was anything in it that shouldn't be?'

Felix swung the club, catching the end in his other hand. 'Like what?'

'Babies.'

'Babies.' He rung the shaft. 'You've got to be kidding. Nothing like that should be coming to us. It should all be checked beforehand.'

'So, you don't check it?'

'Look, I don't what you're getting at. The hospital's boss signs of on everything. She might not check the bags herself, but she'd be the one copping it for anything illegal.'

Felix looked to the first tea, acknowledging someone waving.

'How well do you know the previous one? Rhodes. He must have signed the contract with your father.'

Felix started to collect his golf balls. 'I know who he is.'

'He was on this club's committee with your father.'

Felix approached Warren, pointing the putter him. 'What are you getting at? That my father got some sort of backhander?' Warren held up his hands. 'Dr Rhodes was close to our family but that doesn't prove anything.'

'No, no, you're right.' Felix lowered the club. 'Did you ever go with him to the committee meetings?'

Felix swung the club across the grass, brushing its surface. 'No. Once, maybe. It was a long time ago. I don't really remember.' Warren waited. 'Mother had had chemo that day and wasn't well enough to come home. Corinne was on a school trip, so I had to go with him.'

'How was it?'

Felix sighed. He waved at his playing partner. 'Well, they didn't hold it here, which was odd. We drove to a pub near Avebury. They sat round a table at the back. I remember being bored. I must have been eight or nine. Then we drove to Maiden Castle.'

'The hillfort?'

Felix Draber nodded. Warren had read about it. Maiden Castle sat several miles north of Weymouth and was one of the largest Iron Age structures in Britain. In its time, it protected hundreds of residents and towered over the surrounding landscape. The workers that built Avebury's stone circles had been thought to have lived there.

'I was told to stay in the car. Dad turned on the radio. He'd bought me a few comics. It was raining so I didn't mind. There were other cars nearby. People were getting out, but I couldn't see very much. But then I really needed to pee. I knew how upset he'd be if I wet myself, so I snuck out and went in some nearby bushes. When I'd finished, I was on the way back when I heard crying from inside one of the cars. I followed the sound and then I saw the woman. Her cheek was pressed against the glass. I didn't realise that there were tears running down her face. I thought it was the rain She held something to her cheek, I thought it was a handkerchief. But it was too big. It had some of animal print on it.' Felix's shoulders slumped. 'She saw see me staring at her, but she just looked straight through me. If I could go back, I'd…look I've got to go.'

Felix picked up the rest of the golf balls, striding to his golf bag. He pushed them into the top pocket.

'Would you recognise her now?'

'No,' he said, pulling the trolley towards his playing partner. 'I'm sorry.'

'If there's anything else, I'm at the Royal hotel in Weymouth.' Felix ignored him.

Warren returned to the clubhouse. He sat in a corner armchair, watching the cream in his coffee swirl on the surface. Parents hid things from the children. Awful things that they weren't mature enough to understand. But how could you look back on it and know whether they were right to do so when you didn't know what they were hiding.

Warren checked the GPS application. One of the dolls had come ashore. The other had drifted out of range or the tracker had stopped working. It was the one launched from Pulpit Rock.

Warren started the car. The doll hadn't landed on Chessil beach but a couple of miles further south. This effectively ruled out Ope Cove as the launch site. There was some uncertainty in the models Glade had got hold of, but they'd know for sure after they'd tried the other sites.

The traffic was heavy between Weymouth and Portland. It puzzled Warren. Now that he was familiar with the name Draber, he saw it everywhere: on their blue trucks in a traffic queue or on signs on construction sites. A blue truck loomed behind him, filling the rear-view mirror with its smiling grill.

He turned into a narrow slip road that should finish near to a cliff path, leading down to the doll's locations. It couldn't have been there more than an hour so should be untouched. The truck followed, scraping bushes on both sides.

Warren slowed as the lane dissipated at a bank of gorse bushes. To the right was a small sandy patch with room for a couple of cars. As he turned, there was a crunch of metal on metal, shoving the car forward into the vegetation. This wasn't going to help his relationship with the Draber's. He looked in the wing mirrors, but no one had got out of the cab. He leant across to pull out his insurance documents. The car leapt forward, crashing into the bushes. 'What the hell!' The car crept forward, the vegetation scraping against the windscreen, like hyenas. He pressed on the brake, slowing the car's progress, but it crept forward, branches crackling around the side windows, like a demented car wash. 'Hey!' He screamed repeatedly, straining to look over his shoulders, trying to release his seat belt. The cliff edge must be just in front. He applied the hand brake, but the car continued to slide forwards, pressing against the thick vegetation. It held the car in place.

The truck reversed with a grunt. He unlocked his seat belt and grabbed at the door handle. The door opened but only partially. He pushed the door, widening the gap. The truck struck again, and he hit his head on the steering wheel. The bonnet tipped downward, his legs dropping forwards. He held himself up using the steering wheel, pumping the door against the vegetation. He leant across but his prosthetic foot was stuck under the accelerator pedal. The car fell forwards and he threw himself towards the gap.

CHAPTER 19

He woke alone and in darkness.

When they'd removed most of his leg, he'd regained consciousness during the night. His mother was told he'd sleep straight through. As he did that night, he ran his hand down his left thigh, feeling for the limits of himself. There was no padding or bandages, just the smooth round stump. His eyes remained dry as the blackness took him.

Voices in his dreams became conversations outside it. He turned towards them, making his forehead pulse in retaliation. The room was full of light, and he squinted as he opened his eyes. DI Pale was talking to PC Matthews by the door. He handed her something large and left the room.

She approached the bed, dropping the object by his feet. 'It seems your prosthetic is a lot tougher than you or your car.'

'Carbon fibre,' he tried to say but the response was mumbled interpretations. He turned and began to push himself to a seated position. He winced with each centimetre gained.

'That'll be the two broken ribs.' She pointed at the prosthesis. 'The strapping's come loose so I've asked PC Matthews to find someone able to fix it.' She stood over him, surveying him like a building site. 'Your ribs will have to mend themselves.'

'They don't feel broken,' said Warren, running his hand over his chest. Pain shot through his left shoulder. 'They reckon you must have been holding onto something as the car went over the edge.'

He couldn't remember much more than trying to grab something outside the car. The palms of his hands felt tender. He'd grabbed at the vegetation as the back of the car headed swung towards him.

DI Pale sat on a plastic chair near the top of the bed. 'I spoke to Dr Halstead earlier. She says you're somewhat of a frequent visitor. It seems you have a thing for heights.'

'Just following lines of enquiry,' he croaked. He extended his arm towards a red plastic cup. If he slowed his movements, he could curtail the pain. He held the cup, but the jug was too far. 'Could you pour me some water?'

'What can you remember?' she said, pouring.

'Not much. A blue truck nearly pushed me off a cliff.' He drank the contents of the cup and held it on his midriff. 'It was one of Draber's.'

'Are you sure?'

'Very.'

'Did you see the number plate or the driver?' Warren shook his head as he drunk.

'Would there be any reason someone from there would want to harm you?'

'Kill me,' said Warren. DI Pale waited, her lips twisting. 'Nothing comes to mind.'

After DI Pale left, PC Matthews took a more detailed statement. Warren told him the facts they'd learnt but not the details. He didn't tell them anything about his late-night trip to the hospital or the doll. He knew it was lying by omission. But he'd had a near death experience and had been knocked unconscious. His memory was bound to be fuzzy.

A doctor was followed by a nurse. She re-dressed the cuts on his arm and face, leaving him some painkillers. He took them and drifted off.

He rose to consciousness to find his mother, sister, and nephew in the room. His sister sat on the same chair as DI Pale. His mother sat next to her, growing at Peter, sitting on the edge of the bed, swivelling the prosthesis in his hands. He watched them with one eye, the other shut, nestled in the soft pillow.

Faith caught his gaze and smiled. 'Be careful,' said their mother to Peter. Faith nudged her and realising Warren was awake, hissed at Peter, 'Stop playing with it.'

'What?' Said Peter, examining the direction both were facing. 'Oh,' he said, dropping it behind him. 'Hi, Uncle Warren.'

'You didn't all have to come,' said Warren, his words muffled.

Faith leant back, stretching the plastic seat to its limit. 'Of course, we did, you bloody idiot. I told you I needed to look after Peter because Mum wasn't willing to.'

'That's not strictly true, dear,' said Alison, resting her hand on Faith's upper arm. 'If he was at mine that would have been no problem. But at yours, it's all so complicated. I don't know where anything is or how anything works.'

'That's ridiculous,' said Faith. 'You've been to stay lots of times.'

'Could someone help me get upright?' said Warren, turning onto his back.

Faith sent Peter to the far side and the lifted him. Alison watched with her arms and legs crossed.

Warren told them what he remembered, Faith forcing him to fill in details. Their mother gazed painfully as Peter stared enraptured.

'You nearly died,' said Peter.

'Peter!' said Faith.

'If you had man in your life, he might pick up some better manners,' said Alison.

'Mother, for god's sake,' said Faith. 'This isn't about me, right now.'

'We need to collect the doll,' said Warren, moving his legs.

'You're not going anywhere,' said Faith, standing. Warren stopped. They sat in silence. When he'd been in hospital as a child, he'd been desperate to leave. He found restrictive and once he'd gotten through the pile of comics his father had brought him, intensely bored.

Peter picked up the prosthesis. 'If you did die, Uncle Warren, can I have this?'

'What on earth for?' said Alison.

'To take to school - it would be cool to show everyone,' Peter said.

'Of course, you could,' said Warren, 'unless I'm getting cremated and then it might have melted.'

'How do you not know if you're going to be cremated?' said Faith.

'Funerals aren't for the living. Why do I care, I'd be dead,' said Warren.

'DI Pale said you didn't see the driver,' said Faith.

'Too low down?' said Warren. 'I'd just spoken to the son.'

Faith nodded. 'Do you think it was him?'

'Possibly, but he'd have had to arrange it very quickly. Did you check the doll's location?' said Warren.

'Not today,' said Faith.

'I think that's enough work talk - Warren need his rest,' said Alison, letting go of the bar.

'I can't - the doll's come ashore,' said Warren. 'We need to pick it up.' He swung his right leg out of the bed and began to shuffle towards the prosthetic.

'You'll go nowhere, Warren,' said Alison, moving

towards him. 'Faith already told me this is the second time in a week you've fallen. You could get permanent brain damage.'

'How would we know?' said Faith. 'I'll go and pick it up. I've downloaded the app. I just need your login details.'

'We can get it,' said Peter, bouncing on the bed. 'Can't we Mum?'

Faith handed Warren her phone. 'Sure, we can.' Warren entered the login details.

Alison put her hand on Peter's shoulder. 'Let's leave him to get some rest. We'll be back in the morning.'

Peter jumped off the bed. 'Bye, Uncle Warren,' he said, heading for the door followed by Alison.

Warren handed Faith her phone. 'Go straight there,' said Warren. Faith nodded.

In the morning, things started to really hurt. Warren had asked for painkillers and was still waiting after they'd delivered breakfast. When the door opened, he turned in anticipation. It was the Seymour.

'I saw you were in here last night when I was making me final round,' he said, walking to the end of the bed. 'Had a quick look at your chart. All seems okay, you should be out today.'

'Thanks, Doc.'

'I heard you'd driven off a cliff.'

'Not out of choice.'

'So did you find out anything more about the baby?'

'We're working through a couple of theories.'

'What you gonna do next?'

'Once I get out of here, find more about Draber - the company collected the hospital's biological waste.'

'I'd be careful. They're not too picky on the type of people they employ.'

Warren drank from his cup of tea. It was cold. 'I don't suppose you've ever been to a home birth?'

'Where they use a paddling pool, and the baby pops out under water.' Warren nodded. 'Never.'

'Me neither. Yet it's really popular here.'

'You just never know what folks are really up to, do you? He walked to the door and glanced through the small window. 'Must be quite messy.'

'Must be.'

'I'd better be going. Look after yourself.'

The doctor did one final check and the nurse helped him to the shower. He'd had mild concussion and was told to rest for a few days. His phone had gone but his wallet had remained in his jacket.

Someone had repaired the strapping on the prosthesis. When Faith arrived with a carrier bag containing fresh clothes, he was attaching it.

'Did you find it?' said Warren.

'We didn't go.'

'What the hell do you mean?'

'It was too late to do it yesterday. Mum was tired and Peter was hungry.'

'Where are they now?'

'Mum's taken him to a museum. He's not happy.'

'He's not the only one. Check your phone.'

'I already did, there's no signal.'

'What?' Warren pulled the bag from her grip and shut the curtains.

Faith followed him out of the hospital. As they reached the exit, the janitor stopped him. 'What is it?' barked Warren.

'Warren, there's no need for that.' She turned to Seymour. 'I'm sorry about my brother, he's had a bump on the head.'

'Don't apologise for me,' said Warren. ' What is it?'

Seymour pulled out a slip of paper from a hip pocket in his overalls. 'This is Silvia's phone number. She and I used to go out, you know. Quite a looker. She used to do a bit of cleaning to make the pension go a bit further when her husband died. She used to clean these posh houses. They'd give her the keys and she'd just go in whenever. I told her about what you'd been saying. She said on one occasion, she'd come into this house as normal and found the living room carpet sodden. When they came back, they'd told her the washing machine had leaked but she didn't believe it.'

Warren smiled. 'Thank you,' he said, patting him on the shoulder.

CHAPTER 20

Warren sat in the passenger seat of Faith's hybrid as they filed away into the bright morning sunshine. He rested his head against the cool glass. Portland was heavy with holiday traffic. Cars queued on the the strip to-and-from Portland. They sat and waited.

'Where are you going?' said Warren.

'Back to the hotel,' said Faith. 'You need to rest.'

He twisted towards her. 'Turnaround. We need to speak to Silvia.'

The car edged forwards. 'You don't even know where she lives.'

The cars edged ahead in procession. Warren held out his open palm. 'Give me your phone.'

She shook her head. 'You need to take it easy. I've got some supplements for you when we get back.' They nudged further. 'You shouldn't have lost yours.'

'I'll try and remember to hold onto it next time I'm shoved off a cliff.'

They all went for dinner. Peter ate all his chips and most of his fish. Faith told him that meant he couldn't have any ice cream. Alison tried to intervene and there was an argument.

Warren said he was tired, and they left the restaurant in a welcome silence.

Warren slept poorly, waking several times. He took more painkillers over breakfast.

Afterwards, Alison took Peter back to Oxford. Alison had agreed to have him for him for the start of the week and Alison would take him if Faith hadn't returned.

The car would be picked and delivered to a garage near his mother's house for repair. It would get dropped off back at the house. His mother hugged him as Peter kicked his prosthesis.

After they'd gone, Faith went for a run. Warren checked his emails and ordered a new sim card. The quarry manager had said he'd drop off his old one if they found it. He assumed by this time; it was either buried or crushed by one of the trucks. The Prof and Harris had both emailed him after failing to get hold of him by phone. They'd started gathering copy for the next issue. They had a few freelancers who'd provide material. Harris had sent a bare draft of the crop circle piece. Warren would need to finish it. Harris had found a local independent financial advisor who'd let him use a desk on trial for six months. It wouldn't just be mortgages, so he'd have to do a bit of learning on the job. Warren replied to both.

Faith and Warren had a walk along the beach. Gusts blew spray into their faces. Faith was worried about Peter and Warren tried to reassure her. They headed into town. Warren bought another doll.

Warren shoved the box into Faith's hands as the young receptionist appeared from the back office. As they climbed the stairs, her eyes tracked the doll. As the stairs turned ninety degrees towards their rooms, they scuttled along the corridor giggling.

They flopped onto Faith's bed. 'You should have a real baby,' Faith said.

'I think I'll stick to the plastic ones,' he said, turning to face the box squashed between them.

'It would be good for you.'

'In what way?'

'It makes you think about life in a different way.'

'One where you wish for peace and quiet.'

Faith picked up the box and lifted it, so she faced it. 'I'd always wanted a second, you know?'

Warren looked at the ceiling. 'It could still happen.'

'I don't think I could go through it all again now. Peter's enough.'

'He's a good lad. Surprisingly bright.'

'Thanks,' she said, dropping the box onto Warren's chest.

He pushed himself up and put the box on the table, so it faced them. 'Some of the stuff he comes out with is so mature. When's not kicking or trying to steal my leg.'

'Once I was cleaning the oven and he said to me, "Dad didn't care if things were clean did, he?" No,' I said. 'Not really. "He should have, shouldn't he?"'

Faith flipped up to her feet and went to the table. She pushed the doll to one side and picked up a see-through bag.

'Jellybeans?' He said, sitting down. She shook her head. 'It was more in hope.'

'I've made you a selection of supplements to help your recovery.'

'I should say "Thank you".'

'Yes, you should.'

She dropped them into his lap. Warren winced and grabbed the bag. He got up and opened the door. 'I'll see you for dinner. Seven?' She nodded. 'Don't spoil your appetite,' he said, shaking the bag.'

CHAPTER 21

Warren directed Faith through the morning rush hour. The map was open on his thighs. Whenever he saw a Draber truck he felt his muscles tense. The sun shone through the dissipating dark clouds reflecting off mirrors on the pavement.

'What did she sound like on the phone?' said Faith.

'What do you mean?' said Warren, looking in the glove box.

'What are you looking for?'

'Nothing.'

'Did you get any sense of what she was like?'

'Not really.'

'Odd name.'

'Silvia?'

Faith tutted. 'Quiddles. For a cafe,' she said, leaning forward. 'Over here should be, okay?' He nodded as she pulled into a space.'

A stone staircase led down to an esplanade with Quiddles at the nearest end. The cafe curved around the cliff facing the sea. It's cream walls and pale blue piping made it look like a half-finished cake. Faith gripped the railing and stared out. Warren waited between her and the cafe.

'Do you think he was alive when he entered the water?' she asked.

'Where any of them?' He walked over.

'You really think there was more than one? That first one was just a photo. That woman might have been lying.'

Warren gripped the handrail and stared out. 'She might have but I don't think so. The policy autopsy should have determined how he died. We just need to find out.'

'Some part of you hopes it's more than one. It would make a better story.'

Warren turned to her. 'That's not fair.'

Facing him, she let go of the railing. 'I'm sorry, I didn't mean it.'

'Come on,' he said, 'Let's get a cup of tea.'

'They'd better do cake.'

Many the tables were empty. A few tables of pensioners were sat drinking pots of tea. A table of teenagers passed around their phones in their phones alongside shrieks of laughter.

Faith walked towards the counter looking around. 'Which one is she?'.

'I'm not sure. She said *she'd* recognise us.'

'What you having?' said the woman at the counter. Her hair sat high on her head exposing the large gold bangles that hung from her ears.

'Two teas, please,' said Warren, stepping to the counter.

'They have cakes,' said Faith, looking through the glass display.

'You must be them two detectives,' she said, keying in the order on the till. 'I'm Silvia. With an 'i' not a 'y'.'

'I'm Warren. We're not detectives. I'm a journalists and my sister's a PC.'

'Would you like a sticky bun?' said Silvia to Faith.

'They look good, don't they? Why not?'

Warren handed over a tenner. 'Will you be able to have a chat?'

'Sure, dear, take a seat and I'll be over in a bit.' She turned around. 'Harry, take over for us.' She turned back. 'My daughter's husband. His Dad owns the place. My daughter's normally here but she's having a bit of trouble with her pregnancy. Here's your change?'

Warren and Faith found a table. They watched the teenagers leave like a multicoloured octopus.

Silvia slid the tray onto their table. She sat down opposite them. She took off the tea pot, cups, and cake. Faith pulled the cake towards her.

'Do you still clean houses?' said Warren.

'Not any more - too much bending down,' said Silvia.

Faith cut the iced bun into quarters and moved it into the centre. She picked up a piece and ate it. 'Very good,' she said. Silvia smiled.

'So, we were told by...your ex-boyfriend about a time you found a water spillage in one of the houses you cleaned.'

'Seymour,' said Silvia.

'Yes, that's it, Seymour,' said Warren, looking at Faith, who'd picked up a second piece.

'Seymour's a bit of a slob but he was good to me. He took me to Bath for my birthday.' Faith offered the cake to both. Silvia shook her head. 'Need to look after me figure.'

'The house,' insisted Warren.

It was one of the bigger houses up in Weston. If it was at the weekend Seymour would drop me off and pick me up.'

'Do you know the name of the owners?' said Faith, biting into a third quarter.

'It was the Draber's. She was still alive at this point. Poor women. When she died, they didn't hire me no more.' Warren and Faith exchanged looks.

'Are you sure it was the Draber's?' asked Faith.

Silvia leant forwards. 'I'm sure.'

'Seymour said you'd found the carpet wet?' said Warren.

'It was soaking. They said the washing machine had leaked but the thing was, the bit of carpet nearest it were still dry,' said Silvia.

'DId you see anything or notice any other thing out of the ordinary?' said Warren, picking up the last segment.

'Not really. At the end of each clean, I take out the bin bag. Even if its half empty - it's just a thing we do. The bins were outside in the garden. I opened the first one, but it was already full.'

'Did you see what it was?' said Faith.

'Not clearly. It was something made from blue plastic. Maybe a paddling pool.' Faith looked at Warren as he pushed the last piece into his mouth.

'Did you say anything about it to them?' said Faith.

'No, you learn not to. You find all sorts of things when you're cleaning someone's house. Teenage boys' bedrooms are usually the worst. It's best to say nothing and leave it - usually by the following week, it's gone.'

'Could it have been a birthing pool?' said Warren, pouring the tea.

'I don't know what one of those looks like,' said Silvia. She looked over shoulder towards the counter. A queue had formed.

'Neither do I, really,' said Warren. 'Do you?' He looked at Faith - she shook her head.

'I'd better get back,' she said, standing up.

'Thanks for your help,' said Faith.

'I hope everything works out with the baby,' said Warren.

CHAPTER 22

A light rain fell as they parked near the hotel. Faith pulled on her raincoat as Warren opened the boot to retrieve the new doll. He pulled it out of the box.

Water dripped off the underside of the arch as they entered the square. A couple in matching lime green stood in the middle. Warren hid the doll under his coat and Faith tightened the cord around her face. The man and woman turned to face them. It was the Danish couple.

Warren attempted a smile. 'What shall we do?' said Faith.

'We'll have to wait until they're gone,' he said, smiling again at the woman as they walked close by. He raised his arm in greeting and the doll fell onto the ground. She grabbed her husband's arm, directing him to her viewpoint. He stared at the mutilated toy and pulled his wife towards the arch.

'It's okay,' said Warren, picking it up. 'Science experiment.'

The couple hurried up the steps, talking loudly. 'Well, that got rid of them,' said Faith.

'Let's get this over with,' said Warren, walking to the far edge and peering over. Faith joined him. 'Could we not throw it from here?'

'We could but we'd not know for sure where it had landed.' 'Let me go down this time.' Warren shrugged his shoulders. He placed the doll on the ground and helped Faith lower herself over.

'Be careful,' he said, 'there's not much space to turn around.'

Faith let go of his arms. She swivelled on the spot and looked over the edge. The bulge in the cliff stuck out like a splinter. The sea frothed underneath.

'Do you think you've got enough room?' he said.

'Pass it down.'

He held the doll by one of its legs and dangled it above her head. She grabbed it. 'I'll hold onto your hood,' he said, lowering himself to the ground. He lay on his front and gripped. Faith held the doll in both hands, bent her knees and launched it into the air. It clipped the edge and cartwheeled into the sea. She leant forward to see it enter the water, losing her balance, pitching forward. He yanked back on her hood, pulling her towards him. She gripped the edge, looking up at him. He let go of her hood and she adjusted her coat.

'Okay?' he asked.

'I'm fine.' He tilted his head. 'It should be fine too.'

'Come back up.' She pushed her body flat, and he shuffled backwards up onto his knees. He yanked her up and she stood upright, pulling him up.

'Check your phone,' he said. Faith let him go and pulled it out of her pocket. 'Looks fine,' she said, turning it around. A red dot blinked.

Faith pulled off her raincoat as they approached the car. She shook it out and dropped it onto the back seat. A police car stopped on the other side of the road. Two officers got out and crossed the road. The first was PC Matthews.

'Here we go,' said Warren, shutting the passenger door.

'Be polite,' said Faith, walking around the car.

'PC Matthews, lovely to see you. You've brought a friend with you.'

PC Matthews crossed the road with his colleague. 'This is PC Lyons. I briefed her on the way here. She was at the station for your interview.' PC Lyons smiled at Warren.

'What can we help you with?' Faith asked, standing next to Warren.

'We had a call from a rather excited woman on the phone saying something about a baby.'

'Didn't have a Danish accent by any chance?' PC Matthews looked at PC Lyons who shrugged.

'A doll. It was a toy doll,' said Faith.

PC Lyons turned as a car approached. PC Matthews ushered them onto the pavement.

'Can we see it?' said PC Matthews.

'If you come back to our hotel we can show you the empty box,' said Faith.

'Why are you throwing a doll off a cliff?' said PC Matthews. 'You could be done for littering.'

'It's a science experiment,' said Warren. Both PCs stood still.

Warren walked up a shallow grass bank and pointed over their head to the sea. 'Out there are thousands of currents. They push and pull in different directions at different times of the year. Or even the month. Some don't really go anywhere; they just swirl in circles. But they're consistent year to year and can be tracked.' Warren held up his right hand, palm forwards and motioned with his left. 'Let's say this is Portland. We know the flow of water around the island at any time.' We also have historical data for weather patterns. Like the body of an infant. It could still be from a ship, but that would create a lot more opportunities for detection. And however good modelling may be there's no substitute for experimentation.'

'Warren put a GPS tracker inside the body of a doll, and we throw it into the sea,' said Faith.

'Of course, it could have been left directly on the beach, but the autopsy should confirm that.'

'There was sea water in its lungs, and it may have died from- 'said PC Lyons. Warren dropped his hands.

'We can't say anymore as it's an active investigation,' said PC Matthews, snapping his head sharply at PC Lyons. She shrunk.

PC Matthews turned to Faith. 'Please don't repeat what we've told you. Even though you're a PC too - we can't say anymore.'

'I understand,' said Faith.

Warren raised his arms. 'Since we know where it was found, we can make predictions of where it entered the sea. The doll should tell us if we right. Now, you'd think that if you dropped an object close to the beach it would end up there. But that's not necessarily the case.'

'Wouldn't everything end up on the beach,' said PC Lyons.

'One disappered,' said Faith.

'How many have there been?' said PC Matthews.

'Two, so far,' said Faith. Warren waved his hand. 'Sorry, go on.'

'Something dropped here, near Hallelujah Bay for example, could easily be caught in a whirlpool and never make it out. Or it could it be dragged out to sea. But if we can find the entry point that might help determine if there's a ceremonial aspect to its burial.' Warren put his hands into his pockets.

'Ceremonial?' said PC Matthews.

'That the sort of thing Warren investigates,' said Faith.

'Oh,' said PC Lyons. 'Do you think that's what is going on?'

'Perhaps, said Warren, stepping back down onto the pavement.

'There are some sick people about,' said PC Matthews. 'You'll need to inform us if you find anything.'

'Of course,' said Faith. Warren nodded.

'How do you recover the dolls - you said something about GPS?' said PC Matthews.

Faith took out her phone and showed them the application.

'Have you identified the baby?' said Warren

PC Lyons opened her mouth. 'No official statement has been made yet,' said PC Matthews.

'What about an unofficial one?' said Faith.

'I've already said we can't say anything.' He stepped closer to them. 'I will say that there are no records of a baby being born, or due to be born, fitting its profile,' said PC Matthews.

PC Matthews turned towards the police car. 'Let's go,' PC Lyons followed. At the car, he turned around. 'I'll be giving DI Pale an update.' PC Lyons smiled.

'Of course,' said Faith.

Warren grimaced and got in the car. 'You know what this means?'

'That either the baby wasn't local, or its birth was hidden from the authorities. What do you think?'

'You know what I think.'

'The worst outcome.'

He nodded so subtly that anyone else would've missed it.

CHAPTER 23

Warren rung the doorbell at Corinne Draber's house. The driveway was empty, but it was worth a try. He slid back through the gravel and got back in the car.

'Off to the gym then?' Faith said.

'I guess so,' Warren said. Warren looked over his shoulder as they left. 'Is that your gym kit on the back seat.'

'Want to borrow it?' Warren smiled.

Warren sat in the gym's cafe working on his laptop. Blue armchairs surrounded low tables like gorillas around campfires. Faith slumped opposite him, dropping her bag.

He looked up. 'How was your taster session?'

'Not bad,' Faith said, 'running her hand through her damp hair.'

'What did you learn?'

A staff member cleared his coffee cup. 'Aren't you going to buy me lunch first?' Faith threw out her arms.

Warren picked up the menu and leant forward to drop it on her thighs. 'Just order me a veggie burger,' said Faith. 'And an orange juice.'

Warren got up and ordered, returning to find her checking her phone. 'Any news from home?'

'Not really. Peter's doing okay - they went to the zoo yesterday. Mum couldn't get the oven to work so they had pizza delivered.'

Warren sat down, closing the laptop. 'What about Corinne?'

'She doesn't remember anything about the wet carpet. But she had a lot of sleepovers. Often at short notice.'

'School friends?'

'Not always and sometime not even friends.'

'What about Felix?'

'Same for him - shipped out to his friend's or friends of their parents.'

'We've not got much to go on. If we can't find out what happened in these pools, we can't link it to the bodies.' Warren looked around the gym. Wet-haired men and women sat reading newspapers. 'Did she say anything more about this row with her brother?'

'That's mostly what she talked about. Sibling rivalry. Felix doesn't see why all his hard work should go to her getting a large Director's dividend each year. She says she doesn't interfere with the company but says they're keeping her in in the dark about what they're doing.'

'Them?'

'The board of directors. She's got no executive powers despite owning most of the shares.'

'Who owns the rest of the shares?'

'She didn't say.'

'You mean you didn't ask?'

'You do want my help, don't you?'

Warren began to speak as the food arrived then thought better of it. They ate in silence. After dinner, Warren looked up the split of shares. There was a single recipient that wasn't a Draber, Swift Services, with a residential address in Portland.

The street was quiet. Bungalows lined both sides like squashed beetles. Concrete driveways split them into pairs, front doors faced each other. Pairs of white rimmed windows faced the road.

Warren stood by the small garden as Faith locked the car. He traced the border with its clinical edges and started at the single rose bush in the middle of the lawn. 'What is it with roses?'

'People like them,' she said, nudging past him, 'Come on.'

A dog barked until the door opened. 'We're looking for the owner of Swift Services,' said Warren as a dog ran out.

'Mr Plowright, what an unexpected surprise,' Warren said as the dog ran around his legs. 'I hope Buster's a bit friendlier on home turf.'

'She'll be fine while I'm here,' he said, 'What do you want?'

'We'd like to speak to the owner of Swift Services,' said Faith.

'You'd better come in,' said Mr Plowright, opening the door. The dog followed Mr Plowright into the house. The hallway was decorated in pastel colours. Several watercolours of cricket grounds were visible.

'Do you play cricket?' said Warren.

'I used to umpire for the local club. I watch as much as I can.'

They turned right at the kitchen into the split lounge. The wallpaper had a rose motif. A dining room was at the back, separated by glass doors.

Mrs Plowright slid them open. 'Who was it?'

'That brother and sister we met at the church,' said her husband.

Mrs Plowright stood still, holding a small scissors-like tool. She put in her pocket and came out of the room, closing the doors. Through the glass was a vase of flowers, dead heads lying around it. 'Would you like some tea,' she said ushering them into the front room. 'You should have said you were coming.'

Warren and Faith sat in two armchairs in the bay overlooking the front garden. Mr and Mrs Plowright sat opposite on a sofa. Buster deposited himself by Mr Plowright's feet. Warren and Faith sat on the edge of their armchairs holding their teacups.

'When did you form Swift Services?' said Faith.

'A long time ago. Maybe ten years,' said Mrs Plowright.

'And you weren't involved at all?' said Faith, turning to Mr Plowright.

'No, it was just me,' said Mrs Plowright, putting her hand on her husband's knee. 'I'd trained as a bookkeeper. Worked for the Council most of my life but that ended. I worked at a few different places. Harold had a steady job so if I didn't have anything we could manage. But we had some difficult times. It made sense financially to form a company.'

'How did you acquire the shares in Draber's?' Warren asked.

'It's only a small percentage,' Mrs Plowright said. 'Would you like a top up of tea?'

'No, thanks,' said Warren.

'I will,' said Faith.

Mr Plowright stood up, waking the dog. He gripped the large tea pot and topped up Faith's cup. He put the pot down on the small table between them. Mrs Plowright pushed forward her cup. He lifted the pot, filled, and put down the tea pot, his hand shaking.

'So, how did you acquire the shares?' said Warren.

Mrs Plowright slipped her tea. 'I was doing the books after their last bookkeeper left on maternity. They were small back then and had some large loans. As I went through the books, I realised they'd underpaid their VAT. Looking back, it had been going on a number of years. If it had gone on any longer and then been discovered by HMRC, it might have force the company into bankruptcy.'

'Were Corinne and Felix's parents both alive at that point?'

'Yes. Julia, that's her mother, didn't have much to do with the business, she left it all to David. He'd started working in the quarry as a teenager. The previous bookkeeper decided not to come back after giving birth, so he asked me to stay on. The company has just signed a big contract with the Council, so they were happy with the continuity.'

'The shares were what, a bonus?' said Warren.

'I guess so, not that's it any of your business. It's a family company and I was treated like one of them, for a while. We used to get a good dividend,' said Mrs Plowright. 'But Felix has reduced it.'

'It's still good enough,' said Mr Plowright, 'We don't need a lot anymore.'

Warren looked at Faith who nodded. 'I think that's all.' Faith placed her cup on the table. Warren stood up and finished his tea, handing it to Mr Plowright. Buster stood between them wagging her tail.

'No, we're not going for our walk yet,' said Mr Plowright to the dog. He headed towards the kitchen, the dog following.

Mrs Plowright got up, 'I'll see you out.'

'One more thing,' said Warren, 'did you ever have children?'

'No,' she said, 'we thought about it but as it turned out, Harold wasn't able to.' Harold paused at the doorway; his mouth opened briefly before he continued into the kitchen.

The dog left the kitchen and stood by the door. Mrs Plowright yanked it back by its collar. It whined as she held it back as she opened the door.

CHAPTER 24

As they entered the hotel, the young receptionist turned to the owner before disappearing into the back office. Warren smiled as they approached.

The owner leant against the desk, his glasses swinging forward. 'Mr Stance, could I speak to for a moment?'

Warren taking his foot off the first step the staircase. Faith came back down from halfway up.

The manager turned a newspaper one hundred and eighty degrees around to face them. It was The Chronicle. On the front page was a photograph of the first doll. Above it ran the headline *Sick Hoax found on beach*. Faith leaned on his shoulder to read the article.

'Jasmine told me she'd seen you with a similar looking doll. Is this anything to do with you?'

'We can explain,' said Warren, tearing at the corner of the page. 'We're investigating the dead baby found on the beach.' He looked at Faith.

'That doll is an experiment to determine where the baby might have come from.'

The owner started at each of them in turn. 'I'll think you'll need to leave. Jasmine has been really upset by this. I think she already told you she'd had the same doll as child.'

'But-,' said Warren

Jasmine appeared in casual clothes and walked around the desk. She looked at them before hurrying out of the hotel.

'Could you check out of your rooms tomorrow.'

'You can't do that,' said Warren, tearing off a larger corner of the paper.

Faith put her hand on his, easing it off the newspaper. 'We'll find something else.'

'It's peak season,' said Warren as he clumped behind her upstairs.

Warren sat down heavily at the breakfast table. A slice of bacon slid off his plate, taking several baked beans with it.

'Got enough?' said Faith, sitting opposite.

'Might as well get my money's worth,' Warren said. 'The next place doesn't look so good.'

'They'll always have cornflakes.' Faith held a spoonful of cereal along with a tangerine segment. 'At least you found somewhere. Have you had any thoughts about yesterday?' She took the spoon into her mouth.

'Some. What do you think?'

'I feel sorry for Harold. And the dog.'

Warren flipped the slice of bacon back onto his plate. 'What about the story about the shares?'

'You said the accounts show five per cent. Seems like a very generous gift for a bookkeeper. Why not just a cash bonus?'

Warren finished his mouthful. 'That would be easier to hide too. But shares lock them in for the long term.'

'Shall I check how the doll's doing?'

'I checked on the laptop – it's still out at sea. I've given Glade access as well.'

'Did you get your SIM?'

'Arrived this morning. Let's pick up a phone on the way.'

'Where?' said Faith standing up to get some more food.

'The high street's bound to have some place. She also did some extra digging on Rhodes and his friend. Both served time in Verne prison. Rhodes was white collar crime, something financial, and Craig Samson was a former wrestler in for assault. They both overlapped by about six months.'

'So, the clean-cut Hospital Administrator is not so squeaky clean after all.

'We should we pay them another visit.'

'Materially speaking it doesn't change anything. You can't just keep turning up on people's doorsteps, asking them questions, hoping they'll confess to something.'

'Why not.'

Warren sat in the hotel's foyer with the luggage. The owner had done the checkout.

'I'll bring the car round,' said Faith, picking up the smallest of her bags and heading down the corridor.

The Danish couple came down the stairs a step at a time. Both saw Warren and then fixed their gaze on the breakfast room. Warren watched them go inside. As they entered, he said, 'Don't worry, we're leaving.'

His phone rang. 'Where are you?' he said, peering towards the exit.

'You'd better come round,' said Faith.

'What about the bags?'

'Leave them, they'll be safe enough. Bring your camera if it's handy.'

He walked into the shaded court behind the building. Faith stood with her back to the hotel, staring intermittently at the car's bonnet.

'Has someone scraped it?' He said, swinging the camera round to his chest and grabbing it.

She pointed to the front of the car. He walked alongside it and slowed to a stop beside her. On the bonnet of the car was a phallus, complete with testicles. It was about a foot in length, grey and positioned neatly in the centre.

'Lovely,' he said. 'What do you want me to do with it?'

'Whatever you like, just get it off my car.'

Warren took off the lens cap and began to take pictures. Someone approached them. 'Mr Stance. Could I have a word?'

It was young man, with neat fair hair that tilted over his black-rimmed glasses.

'Speak to my sister,' Warren said as he adjusted the camera.

The man walked towards Faith who remained leant against the wall. 'Could I speak to you about - what the hell is that?' he said.

'A phallus,' said Warren,' looking into the viewfinder. 'Horse or cow.'

'Whatever it is, I'm not touching it,' said Faith.

The man pulled a small camera from his small satchel and began to take pictures. Warren replaced his lens cap.

'I wonder what the Prof will make of these when I send them to her,' said Warren, 'I can't imagine she's been sent many dick pics.'

Warren placed his hand on the man's shoulder, 'Who are you, my friend?'

The man stopped taking pictures. 'I think I've got enough,' he said, putting the camera into his bag and pulling out a business card. 'James Horsey, Dorset Advertiser,' holding out the card. 'I wrote the baby hoax story.'

Faith took the card. 'That wasn't a hoax,' said Warren. 'It was science.'

'It was you,' said Horsey. He started to take pictures of Warren and Faith.

'Please stop,' she said. 'Or I'll arrest you for harassment.' Horsey continued to take pictures.

'If you stop, I'll tell you what this might be about,' said Warren.

Horsey lowered the camera. 'What is it?'

'It's most likely a warning. Or it might also be someone trying to help.' Faith scoffed. 'Come to the front.'

Horsey moved to the corner of the car as Warren pointed at the genitalia. 'If you look at it, you can see that it's been laid out with the head facing upwards.' Horsey tilted his head and nodded. 'Right, so what shape is that?' Both shook their heads. 'It's a cross.' Warren motioned with a finger. 'Admittedly, it's a crude one. But a cross nevertheless. In Christianity, it's the symbol for salvation.'

'You're saying that someone is trying to save us by putting that on my car?' said Faith.

Warren nodded. 'Leave now and you'll suffer no harm.'

'Really?' said Horsey. 'Will you?'

'Of course not,' said Warren.

'You might not be but I'm beginning to reconsider our stay here,' said Faith.

'Or it could refer to its pagan use as a fertility symbol.' Warren put his hands in his pockets.

'Which would mean?' said Horsey, writing in his notebook.

'Go fuck yourself,' said Warren.

'Warren!' said Faith.

'What?' said Warren.

'Can I quote you?' said Horsey.

'Sure, on one condition,' said Warren, holding one palm out. Horsey stopped scribbling and looked at Warren. 'You help me get this into a bag.'

CHAPTER 25

They checked in to the other hotel around noon. Warren was relieved that the hotel was at ground level. It's white banner had streaks of dirt under each dark letter. It was further out, and they had to park on the street.

The manager arrived at the ring of the door. She was a petite grey-haired woman in a faded blue gilet. Every wall was hung with artwork related to horses. The photographs had lost most of their colour. Without exception, each was of a horse in mid-flight ridden by a female rider. The resolution was too poor to confirm if it was her.

Warren checked his text messages in the lounge as Faith finished unpacking. She entered the lounge. Warren's brow was furrowed. 'What's happened?'

'A warning from Glade. Looks like the Prof has seen the news story about the doll.'

'What are you going to do?' said Faith as she was enveloped in the other armchair.

'I could go back for a bollocking, or I could just hide down here with you.'

'If you stayed sitting in on of these armchairs, they'd

never find you. They must breed them down here.' She stretched out her legs, sinking further inside.

Warren pushed and wriggled himself up and out. 'I'd rather go out fighting.' He picked up the large see-through bag from the table in front of them. 'We've got a severed penis to identify.'

Warren and Faith queued on a butchers on Fortuneswell Street. Warren curved his body around Faith to look at the meat counter.

'Fancy a steak later?' he said.

'Funny,' she said, sliding the phone out of her jeans. Warren stared at the families bustling past towards the sea front. 'It's moving south,' tilting it towards him. 'We should have given her a name.' Warren raised his eyebrows.

A man left the shop with a small white bag. That left a woman on a dark red overcoat with a trolly in front of them. The young man serving her picked minced beef off and on the weighing machine. She held her gaze on the black needle. She nodded and he spun the small bag, tied it off and handed it to her. She looked for a space for it in her trolley.

'How can I help you?' he said, turning to Faith.

'Ask him,' she said.

Warren stepped to the counter lifting the gruesome bag into the air. 'I'm looking for the owner of this.'

'Oh, dear,' said the woman. She flipped the lid over and hurried out.

'Are all your customers that sensitive?' Warren said.

The man forced a smile and took the bag. 'I don't think we sell this sort of thing. I'll get the boss.' He carried the bag in front of him, eyeing it at an angle as he walked toward the plastic curtains.

'We only want to know where it came from,' said Faith, leaning on the counter.

A man came through the barrier like a boxer entering the ring. His white overalls were freshly bloodied. His white hair net floated on his bald head. He dropped the bag onto the counter.

'Big fella - not anyone I know. What about you, Danny?' he said, swinging it around and laughing. Danny grinned.

'Could you tell where it might have come from?' said Faith.

The butcher looked at Warren. 'If you're asking what type of animal, most likely from a bull. In terms of getting this sort of thing - almost no chance.' He turned to face Faith. 'It's usually ground up and fed to pets.'

'Would someone cut off a living bull?' said Faith.

The butcher laughed. 'Not unless you're willing to get crushed by a ton of prime beef. You'd need to go to an abattoir. Even then, they'd not just hand you it - you'd need a man on the inside.'

'Is there one nearby?' said Warren, pulling the bag off the counter.

'There's only one in Portland. It's on the Southwell industrial estate. We get our meat from there.' Warren turned away. 'Could I interest you in some pork chops while you're here?'

'I'm vegetarian,' said Faith.

'And I'm considering it,' said Warren, pulling open the door.

The industrial state was on the outskirts of Weston. A board at the entrance listed the occupants, but they couldn't see anything that sounded like an abattoir. They drove past several anonymous warehouses before they found it.

The back and sides of it were hidden by opaque fencing with a single-track road each side. A single door faced the road at the front with no signage visible. Faith had spotted a wooden-slatted livestock lorry entering down the right-hand side. It hadn't come out.

Warren got out of the car and waited for Faith on the curb. She remained in the car. He bent over and looked through the window. 'Coming?' Faith shook her head.

Warren shook his head and turned towards the building. Next to the glass door above the buzzer a small plaque read *Draber Services*.

It took two attempts before someone came to the door. A man in black trousers and a white shirt unlocked an opened the door. His hair net covered his shiny black hair. He shielded his eyes from the bright sunshine. 'Do you have an appointment?'

'I just want to ask a few questions.'

'Are you a reporter?' he said, looking at Warren's camera. 'Where are you from?' He kept the door ajar.

'I work for a magazine called The Skeptic's Handbook.'

The man stared. 'Never heard of it. Look, mate, I can't be talking to you - you'll need to speak to head office.'

'I'm looking for the rest of this,' he said, holding up the bag.

'That's from a bull. Fresian most likely. I need to go.'

'Did it come from here?' said Warren. The man shut the door. 'I'm not a vegetarian. Yet.'

Warren turned towards the car, paused, and then moved away from the door to the left-hand side of the building.

The road was empty. When he got halfway a lorry approached. It didn't slow down and there wasn't time to go back. He flattened himself against the wall of the building. The truck rumbled past. He stepped back into the road - there was a tyre mark on his left shoe.

He strode to the corner and peered around it. The live animals were unloaded on the other side and the empty trucks exited the way he'd come in. The high fences hid everything. Men in white overalls unloaded the carcasses nearby.

He pulled himself onto the loading bay and crept between several trolleys packed with boxes of shrink-wrapped meat packages. The nearest man was stacking more of them. Warren held up the package. 'Excuse me, could this be yours?'

The man leant backwards and shook his hands. 'Sorry, no understand.'

'Do you have someone who does?' Warren looked inside. The interior was segregated into different sections, and he could only see a fraction of it. The nearest workers stood by conveyor belts as chunks of meat rolled past them in packages. A face he recognised turned towards him. It was Rhodes's sidekick. 'Hey, Samson,' shouted Warren heading towards them. He saw Warren and ducked out of sight. 'Stop!'

Warren pushed away the nearest pallet, upsetting the worker who tried to grab him. He shook him off and headed after his target. People turned towards him as he pushed past. It grew colder. Carcasses swung from hooks and there was gentle hum of the conveyors. 'You can't be in here,' someone shouted. He looked in its direction and saw the man who'd answered the door. He scanned from side-to-side went further inside. Moisture formed on his face. He slipped on the floor - he saw dozens of yellow boots turning his way. He grabbed the square edge of a metal and pulled himself up. A large cleaver came down besides his head into a carcass.

He wiped his face with his sleeve and pushed himself on. He saw Samson go through a door. Someone grabbed him but he shook them off. He pushed open the door and was inside a changing area. There were lockers against the walls and benches in the middle. Steam drifted out of a communal shower - a pair of yellow boots lay at the entrance. He checked inside. A force from behind knocked him against the edge of a locker and onto the floor. He held out his arms as he trying to brace his fall against a bench. His back spammed as he his side hit the edge. Samson ran out of the changing room in his socks.

Warren got up and followed him through a door into a small office. A man was on the phone and lowered it as Warren came through. Warren saw a figure through the glass of the exit and stumbled towards it, knocking into a clock cardboard pon the wall. He unlocked the door and yanked open the door.

The sun flashed yellow, and he shut them. He held up his arm and squinted under b it. Wherever Craig was he was no longer running. And he wasn't nearby.

Warren stepped outside and saw that there were two people near Faith's car. He ran towards it. Faith was knelt over Samson who was face down on the ground. She held his arm bent behind his back.

'Let go of me,' Craig said, wriggling.

'I'd tap out if I was you.' said Warren.

Warren dropped the packet by Craig - his neck stretching like a fish for air.

'Did you leave that on my car?' said Faith.

'What if I did - it ain't no major crime?' Craig said.

'It could be a hate crime,' said Warren. 'Why'd you do it?

Craig continued to wrestle against Faith's grip, saying nothing, so she pushed his arm higher. He yelped in pain.

'Tell us, 'said Warren.

'What's going on here?' said the man from the office. 'I've called the police.'

Faith let Craig go. He turned over and sat up rubbing his arm.

'We just want to know about that thing,' said Faith pointing to the ground.

The office manager picked it up and studied it. 'It's a bull's,' he said. 'It might be from here; I can't say and there's no way of knowing. The rest of it will be in tins or butchers by now.' He handed it back to Warren. 'Is that sufficient? If so, maybe you could let Craig get back to work.'

'Did you know he'd served time?' said Faith, looking up as sirens were heard.

Craig got to his feet, wiping his mouth, clearing blood from a cut lip. 'So, what if I did?'

'Quite a few of our employees have patchy employment history. That doesn't mean they can't do a good job.'

A police car pulled up. DI Pale and PC Matthews got out. 'Just our luck,' said Warren.

'How nice to see you DI Pale,' Warren said.

'Let's see if it is,' she replied. 'Who's Simon Elliot?' She looked at PC Matthews who nodded.

'That's me,' said the office manager.

'What's happened?'

'This man,' pointing at Warren, 'broke into the abattoir and then she assaults one of our employees here. Craig Samson.'

'Did he do any damage?' DI Pale said.

'Not really.'

'What about you, Sir, looking at Craig. Do you - Do I know you from somewhere?'

'I don't think so,' Craig said, shuffling.

PC Matthews leant towards DI Pale and said something inaudible. She nodded.

'I thought you looked familiar. The altercation at Denny's nightclub last year. The witness dropped his complaint.'

'I never done nothing,' Craig said.

'The bouncer was left with two black eyes,' said PC Matthews.

'He fell over,' Craig said.

'Funny how that happens everywhere,' said Faith.

DI Pale walked towards Faith. 'PC Matthews did a little digging for me. You're on indefinite leave, aren't you? It seems an undercover operation went wrong.'

'I'm not to blame,' said Faith.

'No, I'm sure you're not,' DI Pale said. 'Do you want to press charges?'

'I should,' he spat, holding his arm. 'But I don't want to deal with no more cops,' he said, shoving past PC Matthews. 'Enjoy the protein,' he said walking back to the abattoir.

'What about you, Mr Elliot?' DI Pale said.

'I'll leave it too,' he said, 'I'm all for the easy life. Enough blood has been spilt already.' He returned to work.

'Well, it looks like you two got lucky,' said DI Pale. PC Matthews put his notebook away. Warren and Faith headed for the car. 'One more thing. The island is spooked enough already by the body of the baby -

'Babies,' said Warren.

'We have no proof of more than one,' said DI Pale. 'Look, enough of the science experiments - this is your last warning. I'd have thought at least you'd have shown more sense, Faith. But I know how family ties can put pressure on people to do things they wouldn't otherwise.' Faith began to speak as DI Pale turned away. 'I look forward to reading the article, Mr Stance - there should be sufficient material now, don't you think?'

CHAPTER 26

Faith and Warren sat hypnotised by the car wash's brushes. They'd both loved it as children. Their father thought it was a waste of money, but mother was more persuadable. Even now, as they stared at the green fibres moving up the windscreen, they were smiling.

'Do you remember that time you opened the window?' said Faith.

'No,' he said, smirking.

'Liar,' she said, flicking her eyeballs at him. 'Soap suds ran down the inside of the window. Mum was furious.' She looked at the passenger footwell. 'What did you do with it?'

'There was a bin outside the shop.'

'If it was Samson who dumped it, they must be trying to warn us off.'

'But we don't know who they are? He could have been acting alone although he doesn't seem capable. He and Rhodes are close but serving time together doesn't make them buddies.'

'You'd be surprised - put two people in a cell together and-'

'Thanks, I get the idea. He works for the Draber's, driving trucks I think. I'm certain they're involved somehow.'

'Half the island works for them. Along with them and the Police we're not proving popular.'

'Welcome to my world, you'll get used to it. When you challenge people's beliefs and way of life - it undermines them.'

'You don't care about that though, do you?'

'It's not that I don't care - it's that I can't.'

Faith took a small box of raisins from her handbag and began to eat them. 'Have you checked where it is?'

'The doll? I had a quick look - it passed the tip of the island. Glade reckons this could be the one.'

'How is she?'

'She's okay. This is her last year. We're hoping she gets a job in town so she can train someone else up. The Prof says we couldn't afford to pay her to stay on once she graduates.' The brushes began their second sweep over the car. Soap glided down the glass in thick swathes like larva from a meringue volcano.

'I love this bit,' said Faith, leaning back in her seat.

'After this I think we should speak to Seymour. See what he remembers of his time in prison.' But Faith wasn't listening.

As they drove to the hospital, a squall hit the island. The rain ran in large droplets off the waxed surfaces of the car. Warren's phone rang. He heard only whimpering and the sound of the wind. He shrugged his shoulders and ended the call. Faith pulled into the hospital car park.

'Do you think he'll be here? Do you think he will speak to us?' She said, closing the door.

'Only one way to find out,' Warren said, catching his coat as the wind flipped it open.

His phone rang again. 'Hello,' he said. More white noise.

He held it away from his head. 'It's probably Harris wanting to come back but can't bring himself to say it.'

'Hello,' said a voice from the phone. Warren pulled it back to his ear.

'Hello,' he said, 'Who is it?'

'I got away,' said the female voice. 'But they'll find me, I know it. I don't want to let them have it.'

'Who are you? What do you want?' More static. 'Just tell me where you are - I'll come for you.'

'The lighthouse. Portland Bill.' The phone went dead.

'I'll come for you,' repeated Warren, walking around to Faith.

Faith handed him the keys. 'Who was it?' she said.

'I couldn't tell - maybe the girl from the tunnels,' he said. 'You find Seymour and I'll call once I've got her safe.'

'You can't go alone, what if it's some sort of trap.'

Maybe it was but wasn't it worth the risk. What if she was referring to another baby. 'I'm going.'

Warren stalled the car several times on the way to the lighthouse. He parked at an angle in the car park. The light was fading as he walked towards the white box building at its base. At the reception he searched the small shop.

'Can I help you?' said the woman behind the till, rolling up her flopping cardigan.

'I'm looking for someone - a woman?' The woman stared blankly. 'Probably quite young, maybe in distress.'

'There was someone who climbed up earlier, but I've been in and out of the storeroom so I can't say if she's still up there.'

'I'll chance it,' he said, heading for the steps.

'You need to pay, Sir,' she said, standing up.

Warren hurried back and handed over a twenty-pound note. Shouts of change echoed up the tight passage. At the top he stepped onto a platform that circled the large bulb encased in Fresnel lenses. There was no one inside. On the gallery, a dark object stood leaning on the railing. He stepped outside.

'Harold?' Warren said. He turned his head to face him and then returned to his gaze outwards. Warren scanned but saw nothing, only sea and an outcrop into the sea.

'Do you love your sister?' said Harold.

'I do.'

'Would you do anything for her?'

'Yes, I think so. Within reason.'

'What if there is no reason only belief.'

'I only *believe* in things proven through empirical evidence. I wouldn't believe in something just because I was told to.'

'But many people do.' He turned to Warren, tears in his eyes. 'It gives them meaning in their lives. An order to the chaos.'

'What's going on?' Warren grabbed Harold by the arm. 'Tell me.' Harold's blood-shot eyes just stared blankly into Warren's. 'Who is she?' Warren shook him but the man was frozen.

Warren let go and leaned over the railings. There was no one below. He looked out towards Pulpit Rock. A narrow path of rock led to a six-metre high cube surrounded by water. A thick slab leant againt the front-facing wall like a temptation even Evil Kneevil wouldn't attempt. A figure in white was shuffling towards the ramp. It was the young woman from the cave.

'Jesus,' he muttered and headed back down the spiral staircase.

He passed the woman at the till who tried to hand him his change. He ran up the gravel mound and slid down the other side. To the right were large amber blocks of stone like Scottish tablet. He stumbled down onto the rock path and headed right. Spray flashed over the wall on his left blinding him. He saw the figure, likely a woman, backed against the rock wall. Someone approached her but he couldn't see more than a bundle of waterproofs. Another jet of spray covered him followed by a scream. There was no one on the outcrop.

He ran along a sandy narrow path towards it. As the sand turned to rock it shimmered with sea water. He slipped and fell. Winded, he looked at the sea to his left as he recovered. Pushing himself up he limped forward. He reached the outcrop and looked down on both sides into the white sea but could see no one. Cracks ran across its width. At the slab of rock, he noticed a small bracelet. It's pink and white charms bring against the grey. He turned and walked back. To the left he caught sight of the other person scampering along the other perimeter path. In a another second, they'd stepped off it and were gone. The observation panel was empty too.

CHAPTER 27

Torch beams swept through the grey mist. PCs Matthews and Lyons tracked up and down either side of the corridor peering over the edge. DI Pale examined the bracelet through the side of the transparent bag.

Warren clenched his fists, pushing the grit into the cuts. 'Let me have a look,' said Faith, holding out her hands.

He turned away, 'They should be calling for a helicopter. Or a rescue boat.'

'You said yourself you couldn't be sure what you saw. Are you sure there were two people and not one?'

'You saw the bracelet.'

'You know that could have been left at any time.' She approached him. 'Let me see.'

He turned towards her and flung out an arm at Pulpit Rock. 'She was there - I saw her. They found out and probably killed her.'

'Well, if they find the body then they can do something about it.' She held his open hand and looked at it. 'Let's get back to the hotel and clean this up. Did they say anything more about the baby?'

'Nothing's been reported missing. They're still checking

records at all the health centres to check if anyone's missed a recent appointment. It could take weeks. She even said they were considering taking DNA swabs from everyone on island. They won't do that; they're just trying to flush someone out.'

Warren pulled away his hand and put both in his hands and walked away.

He sat on the bed while she wiped his hands with a wet wipe. His gaze tracked the contours of the room. Three of the four corners had cobwebs. *What was wrong with that one? What made a spider pick one corner over another?*

'Warren. Warren. Are you listening?'

He snapped back. 'Sorry?'

'I was telling you about Seymour,' she said, screwing up the tissue and throwing it into the metal bin by the door.

'Uh huh,' he said. 'What did he tell you.'

'He wasn't happy about having his criminal record being brought up. I thought I'd messed up. But I explained it wasn't about him and I wouldn't tell anyone else.'

'Go on,' he said.

'Wait a minute,' she said, getting up and going into the bathroom. She came out with a small tube of body lotion. 'This might be soothing,' she said, studying the writing.

'Anyway,' she said unscrewing the lid, 'He does remember Rhodes - he helped get him the job at the hospital when he was released.'

'What else? Did he say anything about his time in prison? About Samson?'

Faith dabbed a drop onto his hand and began to rub it in. 'How does that feel?'

'Fine. So did he?'

'He said he remembered the two of them but that was all.'

Warren pulled away his hand and got up, the open bottle falling off the bed. 'Let's go.'

'Warren!' she said, picking it up.

The floodlights lit the hanging moisture as they drove into the hospital car park. A man walked towards his car. As Faith picked her spot, Warren grabbed the steering wheel and pulled it towards the man's car. Faith hit the brakes, throwing stones into its bumper. The man shut the semi-open door and walked towards them, the lights shining into his eyes.

Warren got out and approached Seymour. 'What the hell are you doing?' said Seymour, shielding his eyes.

'Tell me about about what went on in the prison?' Warren said.

'Who's that?' said Seymour, squinting. Faith turned off the car's engine and lights. 'It's you. I've already spoken to your sister.' He turned back to his car, opening the door.

'You didn't tell her everything, did you?'

'I told her enough,' said Seymour.

'Enough for her but not for me.' Warren shut the door.

'Now see here, mate, I don't need no more trouble.'

'It wasn't too much earlier. Your conscience was heavy enough to tell us about the time in the incinerator room. What's changed?' Warren said.

'I told you. I didn't see nothing,' said Seymour.

'But you knew something wasn't right, didn't you?' Warren grabbed the man's sleeve. 'Now tell us what was going on there?'

She approached them both. 'Warren, let go of him.'

Warren let go of Seymour and stepped back. Seymour shrugged and opened the door.

'My sister said she'd not bring up your criminal record, but I didn't make any promises,' said Warren. 'I doubt Dr Halstead would likely keep you on knowing you'd beaten your wife close to death. The papers might also be interested in knowing how you'd colluded with Rhodes to get the job.'

Seymour closed the door and leant against the car. He looked around. Faith walked up to Warren, 'Don't make him.'

'I'd done about two years when Rhodes came in. He didn't

have any sort of reputation, but he had this way of looking at you. It made you feel that you were being judged. Anyway, I'd been in charge of the garden. To be honest, I hated it, but it gave me several extra hours a week out of the cell. Rhodes offered to help, and I could do with some company. He knew what he was doing all right. Totally transformed it. Trellises and all sorts. Filled it with roses. More people came in on different days to help out.'

'Was Craig Samson one of them?' said Faith. Seymour nodded.

'Go on,' said Warren.

'Well, I got sort of sidelined. I didn't mind, I still got the time outside. We even won a competition. Rhodes was given more time out there and more helpers. He even got the warden to buy a greenhouse so he could start breeding his own roses. Then it got a little strange. By this point, Rhodes had almost complete freedom to go there when he liked.' Seymour looked at his feet. 'Then they started meeting. I didn't know he'd recruited so many. They'd been rumours - there always are in a prison, there's so little else to talk about. They'd meet in the garden, between the climbing roses. I'd be just keeping a look out. The men would stand in the garden and listen to Rhodes. I didn't catch much of what they were saying. It went on for months. Then Rhodes got early parole and it all stopped.'

'Can you remember anything? Who else was there, maybe?' said Faith.

'I could write you some names,' Seymour said.

Warren took out his notebook and tore out a sheet. 'Do you have a pen?' he said to Faith. Faith delved into her handbag and pulled one out. He took it from her and handed it to Seymour.

Seymour began to write. 'What do you think?' said Faith. Warren shrugged. 'Perhaps they were planning to do a robbery when they came out. Or commit some fraud related to the hospital.'

'They certainly weren't meeting for their love of gardening,' said Warren.

'Perhaps Glade can find out where they are now?' said Faith.

'Let's hope so,' said Warren.

Seymour handed Warren the list and he scanned it. 'There was one word that kept coming up: proof. They kept referring to it. Either to finding the proof or proving something to someone.'

Other than Samson, Warren didn't recognise any of the names. He handed it to Faith. 'Did they say who to?' Warren said. Seymour shook his head.

'Thank you,' said Faith.

'Now, would you move your car,' Seymour said, getting in.

Faith pulled Warren away as he studied the list. They got in the car and returned to the hotel.

CHAPTER 28

Warren sat in the café writing as Faith jogged. He'd spoken to their mother who'd seemed quite distracted when he spoke to her. He finished his part of the crop circle article and sent it to Harris, who added pictures and further elements related to the drone footage. Warren had also given him an update on what had happened in Portland: the doll experiments, the phallus in the shape of a cross, the missing girl and the rose cult. Harris's baby had smiled for the first time. He'd also told Warren that before being a sign of Christianity, the cross symbolised the gallows of a criminal.

Warren entered Faith's room as she was drying her hair with a towel.

'Not using the hairdryer?' He spoke.

'Broken,' she said, looking down at it on the table. 'What do you want to do now?'

'I want to ring Harold Plowright's neck.'

'Then he definitely won't tell us a he anything?'

'I don't care - it would be worth it.'

'Well, you know you can't see him. DI Pale will be questioning him after your statement.'

'I know. I shouldn't have said anything. Then we could have had him to ourselves.'

Faith returned the towel to the bathroom. 'What's the progress with the doll?'

'The doll? It's nearly opposite Chessil Beach. We should know soon whether it will come onto the beach sometime today or bypass the island all together.'

The phone rang in the room. They looked at each other. Faith answered the phone while Warren changed channels on the television.

'It's that reporter - he's downstairs,' Faith said.

'You go,' Warren said, 'I'll probably be rude.'

Faith tied her back and pushed him towards the door. 'Let's go.'

At the bottom of the stairs Warren looked about. The owner, a squat man who always seemed to be polishing brassware, pointed to the breakfast room. Faith and Warren went inside.

Horsey stood up and shook their hands. 'Thanks for seeing me. I heard about the incident at Pulpit's Rock. I was hoping I could get your take on it.'

'Someone's killed a girl - probably a pregnant one,' said Warren.

'Really,' said Horsey, flicking quickly through his notebook for an empty page, 'I didn't get that from the police.'

'No body has been found but that's what my brother thinks he saw.'

'I don't think it, I know it,' said Horsey, holding his pen steady on an empty page.

'Why don't we all sit down,' said Faith doing so. Warren and Horsey followed. 'Perhaps the media could help us find out if there's anyone out there with any information. Perhaps we might flush out another girl?'

Warren nodded. 'I found a bracelet. It had pink and white - what are they called?' He looked at Faith.

'Charms,' she said.

'Yes. It might have belonged to the girl.'

'The police said that there are no reports of any missing girls,' said Horsey.

'It's still early,' said Warren. 'She might be an illegal immigrant.'

Horsey looked down at his notepad. 'Do you have any evidence of that?'

'No, I don't. Look, if you're not going to be helpful,' said Warren.

Horsey turned over to a new page in his book and twisted in his seat.

'You're a serving police officer, am I right?' said Horsey, pushing his glasses back up his nose.

'Yes, that's right,' said Faith.

'But you're on sick leave?' Horsey said. Faith nodded. 'But you're not actually sick, are you?'

'Now hold on,' said Warren, lifting out of his chair. Faith pushed him back down with her arm.

'It will help me to start talking about it,' she said. 'I am on sick leave but I'm not ill, exactly. It's PTSD.'

'Post-traumatic stress disorder?' Horsey said. Faith nodded.

'I was seconded to the Exploitation Unit. That's the unit that deals organised crime gangs and traffickers. They'd identified a group of men who were grooming women and migrant workers into the sex trade. They'd charm them first, buy them stuff, sleep with them and try to get them to take drugs - try to get them hooked. They'd found one of the women overdosed the week before - her child was found next to her.'

'I remember the leaked picture,' Horsey said.

'There was a lot of pressure to make some sort of impact. The team were up against it. Everyone was on overtime. We'd nicked someone for dealing and he'd given us a name. I'd been given a cover story and began working in a cafe they frequented. One of them hit on me and after a few dates, he said he'd take me to a party.'

'You don't need to tell him,' said Warren, leaning back.

Faith smiled at him. 'I was mic'd up, and my colleagues waited outside. The house looked like all the others from the front. But we went round and used the back door. They had someone standing behind it who let us in. All the curtains were closed, and it was hot. There were only a few men but lots of girls - most in their underwear. Most of them young and either drunk or high. They didn't pay me any attention.'

'What were their nationalities?' Horsey said.

'The women were mostly East European. The men: all types but all of the low variety. All much older than the women. I knew this would've been enough to trigger the raid, but my chaperone said more girls were coming, so I thought I'd wait. Maybe I could help those too. He offered me a drink and I took it but just sipped it. We went upstairs. People were having sex in the rooms - I can still smell it. One of the doors was open a little so I pushed it further. There was a middle-aged woman feeding a baby with a bottle. There were others in cots or just crawling on the floor. One boy sat in the middle, puke down his bib, crying. The woman shut the door and he pulled me down the corridor.'

'Jesus,' said Horsey, who'd stopped writing. Warren turned away.

'He went into the final room. I'd avoided being alone with him until that point. Even so, I'd felt confident I could handle myself. But I didn't expect there to be other men in the room. Before I had a chance to use the alert code, he had a hand over my mouth. I tried to fight him off, but another man was on top of me and then another, pulling at my clothes. They pulled a scarf across my mouth and pushed me down onto a mattress. I can still remember the shapes of the stains on it. The button pushed into my cheek.'

'You don't need to,' said Warren, jumping up and walking away.

'As they tore at my clothes, the mic must have become detached. That triggers a failsafe. If the connection is lost, that's a signal to come in.'

'Thank God,' said Horsey.

'God had nothing to do with it,' said Warren, turning back.

'We train for this sort of thing. They can get through a house in less than a minute. It was the longest of my life.'

CHAPTER 29

Faith sat on the sand, staring at the sea, daring it cover her. Warren shuffled behind her, holding his new phone.

'Is there any pressure on you to go back?' said Warren.

'Nothing's been said but after six months my pay drops. A few colleagues have started to make jokes.' Faith brushed sand from the tops of her thighs. 'Is it any closer?'

'According to this, it should be here.'

Their eyes flitted from breaking wave to the beach, expecting to see the pink body. Two black labradors sniffed at them before moving on. A couple followed hand in hand.

'You going in?' said the taller of the two men, holding the retractable dog lead.

'What?' said Warren. Warren followed the man's gaze down to the towel under his arm. 'Oh, this. Maybe later.'

'I've been thinking about the cross,' said Warren. Faith looked up from her feet. 'And water. Have you ever been to a baptism?'

'Gerry and I went to see his sister's son being baptised. It was somewhere in the Lake District. We stayed longer as it was our wedding anniversary.'

Warren sighed. 'You know the ritual. Holy water is poured over the child's head from a font.'

'At which point they burst into tears.'

'Must be a family trait. I remember Peter after his first game for the school. He scored an own goal losing them the game.'

'You're not such a good loser. Every time I beat you at badminton in the garden, you'd say I cheated.'

'I'm sure of it and it's about time you own up to it.' Faith stood up, brushing sand from the back of jeans. 'Anyway, the wetting of the baby's head signals a new beginning as you become part of God's family. But being baptised is also an act of obedience and strictly, should be by full immersion.'

'You couldn't do that to a baby.'

'You can if you throw them into the sea.'

Warren stared at his screen then thrust an arm at the sea. 'There!' Faith attempted to follow the line of his arm, but Warren had set off down the beach. 'I'll get it,' he said, stepping onto the wet sand. 'I'm semi-waterproof.'

Faith jumped down and grabbed his arm. 'No, I'll get it.' The next wave brought the doll closer. As the water receded, it rocked several times before sticking to the sand on its back. She leapt towards it and scooped it into her arms. She stared at it as a wave washed over her feet.

Warren unfurled the towel over his forearms as she walked onto the dry sand. She placed the doll in the middle and wrapped the cloth around it. She held the bundle close to her chest as they made their way to the car. 'So we know where it came from then – the place we found the cigarettes. Do you think it will help?'

'I think so.'

At the hotel, Faith received a text message from Felix. Faith carried the doll upstairs while Warren looked at it. He stood at the bottom step.

'The police have found a body near the lighthouse. It's most likely the woman from the tunnels,' he said.

In Faith's room, she'd put the doll on the bed. 'What shall I do with it?'

'Leave it to dry it. We might use it again.'

'Really? If it is her, the police will wrap up the case or are you just guessing again. She was clearly distressed and threw her baby into the sea. She was still distraught, perhaps even more so after what she'd done and threw herself from the viewing platform.'

Warren sat on the bed and placed a hand on the doll's stomach. Faith received another text. Warren handed her the phone.

'It's PC Lyons. They want us to come in tomorrow.'

After breakfast, they drove to the police station. PC Lyons walked into the reception with two takeaway cups of coffee.

'That's kind of you,' said Warren. PC Lyons hesitated. She gave him a smile before swiping through the security door.

She reappeared almost immediately. A dab of chocolate was above her top lip. 'You can come in now.' Faith pushed passed him and handed PC Lyons a tissue.

She left them in the interview room. When PC Matthews entered a few minutes later, his coffee was balanced on a small tower of plastic and paper.

'We know what this's about,' said Warren. PC Matthews gave a forced smile before the door opened.

DI Pale pulled out the remaining chair. 'Thanks for coming in.'

'That's no problem - what's it about?' said Faith.

Warren sat up in his chair. 'You've found her.'

'Not yet. We've called off the search,' said DI Pale

'You can't,' said Warren, scraping his chairs back along the floor.

DI Pale was static. 'There's been no missing person's report filed. You didn't see her fall in and we've no evidence she was even there.'

'You have the bracelet,' said Warren.

'You said yourself you were too far to be sure it was hers,'

'But-' said Warren.

'The janitor at Portland Hospital has been found dead.'

'Seymour?' said Faith.

PC Matthews looked at the top of his notes. 'Seymour Griffiths. He'd worked there nearly twenty years.'

Warren crossed his arms. 'What's that got to do with us?'

'Warren,' said Faith, snapping her head towards him. She rotated owllike forwards. 'We spoke to him.'

'We'd like to know that too,' said DI Pale, leaning forward.

DI Pale held out her open hand next to the evidence. 'He had an interest in your magazine.' PC Matthews pulled out a slim bag from near the top and placed it in her palm. It was copy of the Skeptics Handbook.

'It's always good to meet another fan. Would you like me to sign it?' said Warren.

'Warren, that's enough,' said Faith.

'It was found next to him,' said DI Pale.

'How did he die?' said Warren, pulling his chair forward.

'Blood trauma from multiple knife injuries,' said DI Pale.

'Do you know what sort of knife?' said Faith.

'Not yet,' said DI Pale.

'Any defensive wounds?' said Faith.

DI Pale looked at PC Matthews who shook his head. 'None. He was attacked from behind.'

'Can I see the photographs?' said Warren.

DI Pale considered the request. 'On condition you cooperate fully with the enquiry and try not to interfere.'

'Sure, sure,' said Warren. 'Let's see them.'

DI Pale nodded at PC Matthews who flicked through the folder. 'Here they are,' he said, pulling them free.

DI Pale spread the prints on the table. Faith and Warren leaned forward. His body was face down; his blue overalls soaked with blood. Close-ups revealed the entry points. Faith leant back as Warren picked up each in turn.

'Have you had a chance to speak to Harold Plowright?' said Faith.

'PCs Matthews and Lyons spoke to him. He volunteers at the lighthouse, so he had a good reason to be there,' said DI Pale.

'He was a decoy. Why else would he have been so upset?' said Warren, not looking up.

'He said his dog had died,' said PC Matthews.

'It was fine when we saw it,' said Faith, 'Wasn't it Warren?'

'What?' said Warren. Faith shook her head. 'Does anyone have a pen?' said Warren. PC Matthews pulled a biro from the spiralled edge of his notepad. 'Something thicker.'

PC Matthews shrugged his shoulders and DI Pale shook her head, pursing her lips. Faith scrummaged in her handbag. Warren peered in then dived inside. 'This will do,' he said, pulling off the top of the lipstick.

'That's expensive,' said Faith. Warren held her gaze long enough to force her to turn away, putting her handbag on the floor.

Warren pushed away all the prints except one. It showed the whole of Seymour's back. Warren pressed the lipstick into the top of the print and ran it downwards, leaving a jagged red line. He drew a second across the first. Each line covered the stab wounds in Seymour's back. They formed a cross.

CHAPTER 30

In the morning, Faith retrieved the GPS device from the doll. She poured any of the remaining contents of the toiletry bottles into the sink. She tried to to clean it. Wisps of seaweed from between its toes and fingers came away easily. But its skin had taken a grey pallor that wouldn't shift.

PC Lyons phoned Faith. The autopsy had confirmed the crossed pattern of markings on his back. He'd died from blood loss. None of the injuries had hit a vital organ. The knife was small. Marks on his wrists and ankles suggested that he'd been tied. His nose had been recently broken.

'We should have told them we'd seen him again,' said Faith, after she'd relayed the news.

'They'd have thrown us off the island,' said Warren, lying on the bed with his laptop on his thighs.

'Maybe that'd be for the best,' said Faith, sitting sideways on the chair.

Warren shut the lid. 'Do you want to go home?'

'Yes, but that's not why I said it. I just don't think we're getting anywhere. Sure, you'll get an article out of it, but someone has died, and it could be because of us.'

'You don't know that?'

'But what if it was?'

Warren dropped the laptop onto the mattress. 'Then there's all the more reason to find out what's happening?'

'At what cost? For someone else to get hurt or lose their life?'

They sat in silence. Warren swung his legs onto the floor. 'Look, if you want to leave, I'll be all right.'

'No, I don't want that. I want to finish this without anyone else getting...' Faith held her hand to her face. Warren walked over and put his hand on her shoulder.

'The best thing we can do is help the police. We'll try to be more careful, but I can't guarantee anything. This has taken a turn no one was expecting. Its show's there's more at stake than even we thought.'

Faith wiped her eyes. 'I am okay,' she said, turning her head towards him. 'What do you want to do now?'

'Go back to Pulpit's Rock,' said Warren.

'We'll not find anything,' said Faith. 'They did a complete sweep of the outcrop and pathways.'

'That's not what I want us to check.'

The sun had baked the rock to pigeon grey. The sandy perimeter path flicked sand over the thick stone slabs running out to sea.

'What are we looking for?' said Faith, scanning the ground.

'Clarity,' said Warren, stopping by the edge. 'This is where I fell.'

'How long do you think you were unsighted?'

'Twenty to thirty seconds at most.'

'Did you hear anything?'

'I might have heard a scream.'

'You didn't mention that before.'

'Because I only just remembered. With the sound of the waves, I can't really be sure if it was a scream or something else.'

They walked to then end of the outcrop. 'How long do you think it would take for someone to go from here back to the rocks behind the path?' said Warren.

'Why don't we try,' said Faith. 'How far from the end were they?'

'About ten metres.' Warren walked away. 'I'll go back to where I fell.'

Warren readied his watch then waved his hand. Faith walked back and onto the path, going out of sight. He walked the dozen metres of the curve and joined her.

'Well?' she said.

'About forty seconds.'

'Too long, then?'

'Unless someone was pulling you along.'

'What do you mean?'

Warren looked over the rocks. 'What if someone ran out from here and pulled you back.'

'But you'd still have seen her with them running in the other direction down the path.'

'What if they went straight through the rocks. They gazed at them. They resembled an upturned bowl of brown sugar cubes. It was up to four metres high.

'Let's see,' said Faith. She slid between the front two and clambered over another. She was invisible.

'Faith?' Warren called out. A hand waved. Then her head as she jumped up.

She climbed up onto a rock. 'There's a small gap down here - enough for two people to hide.' She swivelled around. 'You'd need to pretty agile, but you could make it to the car park.'

'Or just come from it, got the girl and then waited till I'd gone.'

In the car park, Faith opened the car. She opened the driver's side door then shut it slowly.

'I want to go up,' said Faith.

Warren stretched his hand over the roof. 'Give me the keys. I'll make a few calls.'

He spoke to the Prof who'd told him the copy had gone to press. She needed two articles for the next one. Now that Harris had gone. She'd told him that some of Glade's recent work was good enough for publication and that she'd signed off his recent expenses. He'd used all of this and half of next month's budget.

When she'd asked him why they'd needed more GPS trackers and dolls, he told her he had to go.

Warren left the car and walked into the gift shop. *Did tourists really buy all this stuff: miniature lighthouses, polished stones, stripy tea towels and bouncy balls?* Warren smiled at the woman; the arms of her cardigan appeared longer. 'Just waiting for my sister,' he said, approaching.

Behind her head hung a photograph celebrating the opening of the lighthouse's new gift shop. The mayor and other dignitaries were stood outside it. He leaned in, resting his arms on the counter. She leant back, pressing her finger-tips into her open magazine.

'Is that Corinne and Felix Draber?' asked Warren

She twisted her head back. 'That's right - they made a private donation.'

'The Draber's get everywhere.'

'Sorry?' She rolled up her sleeves.

'The Draber's. You see their trucks all over the place.'

'I guess. Their father made the decision after his wife died - she used to come here a lot.'

'They don't look particularly thrilled to be there.'

'I was surprised Corinne attended at all after what happened?'

'Losing a parent is not something you ever really get over.' Warren turned to face the postcard racks.

'Perhaps that as well.' She turned a page. 'But she'd only just lost the baby which must have been awful the way it happened.'

Warren spun around. 'Yes…that must be a difficult thing for anyone to go through. But it's quite common isn't it for new mothers, especially for the first few attempts.'

'Oh, it didn't' happen like that. This was stillborn. She'd known for weeks before she had to gave birth to it. Can you imagine having to carry it inside you, knowing it's dead but still developing- then have to give birth to it?'

Faith came down the stairs. Warren pulled Faith out by the arm.'No, I can't.'

At the Draber's house, Corinne's car wasn't in the drive. Felix was outside cleaning his own. Warren approached with Faith.

'No golf today?' said Warren.

'Played earlier,' he said. 'Stableford tournament, came third.'

'Well done,' said Faith. 'We were hoping to speak to your sister.'

'She's not here, probably at the health club. Or shopping,' said Felix.

'I'm surprised Draber's runs at all with the amount of time you both spend *not* working,' said Warren.

Felix dropped the sponge in the bucket. 'Now look here. How I run the business has nothing to do with either of you.'

'Let's go, Warren. We can go to the health club,' said Faith.

'One second. I want to know about Corinne's still born baby?' said Warren.

'That's a private,' said Felix.

'Seems like half the island know about it. Were you present at the birth?' said Faith.

'Of course not,' said Felix. 'She had a private ward at the hospital. Ken Rhodes arranged it all.'

'You didn't see the body?' said Warren.

'No, why does that matter? We were given a small urn,' said Felix.

'Let's go,' said Warren to Faith. They turned away.

'Wait. What's this all about?' said Felix, knocking over the bucket. Warren and Faith crossed the road.

Felix stopped as a car drove between them. 'I want to know. Tell me.'

Faith shut the car door as Warren stood with one leg inside. 'I think you need to speak to your sister,' said Warren, dropping to the seat and shutting the door.

The health club told them she'd not been in for several days. They drove past a few of the nearby shops. No luck. They'd been sent to the dog grooming shop but Fiffy, as that was the dog's name, hadn't been brought in for months.

They sat in their café, as they'd grown to call it. Warren opened an envelope.

'What's that?' said Faith, sipping a green tea.

'Something from Glade. Couriered to the hotel, so must be important.' Warren shuffled the top few papers. 'Financial records of some sort. Portland Council from at least a decade ago. It seems to be lists of contracts or planning approvals awarded by the Council.' He squared and passed them over.

'Is this legal?'

'Maybe.' Warren unfolded the single piece of paper he'd retained. 'They're from Harris.'

'I thought he'd left the magazine.'

'I think he's bored already', as he read the text.

'Come on. What does it say?' said Faith, spreading the rest of the papers in front of them.

Warren scanned through the first few lines. 'Since he had

some spare time, he thought he'd help us out. He's used Freedom of Information requests to gather a list of Portland Council's external contracts. He cross-referenced them with Draber's annual accounts and those of any other contractor that won repeat business.' Warren looked at the papers. 'He's highlighted sections. There's one.' Warren pointed at a section in yellow. 'From what he can tell, every time a new contract or planning approval was given to Draber's, a sum of ninety thousand was paid out.'

'Who to?' said Faith.

'Kaylin Enterprises,' said Warren. 'Interesting choice of name. And according to Glade's research, Kaylin Enterprises had two directors: Patrick Dutton, ex-leader of the Council, now deceased and a Kaylin Plowright.'

'Who's that?' said Faith, looking up. 'Is that Mrs Plowright?'

'In a place this small, there must be a connection.'

'It could be a coincidence.'

'At the beginning of the eighteenth century, an astronomer was looking through old records of comets when he noticed a coincidence. Several comets had the same orbits and appeared every seventy-five years. He concluded they were actually the same comet. To prove it, he predicted when it would next appear. On the night of Christmas day in 1758, Halley's comet lit up the sky.' Warren shuffled the papers back together. 'Corrine has a pregnancy that goes to full term but is stillborn. She's a healthy young woman, the statistics of that happening must be incredibly low.'

Faith parked the car at the end of the road. As they approached the Plowright's house, they passed Corinne's car. Harold was stood in the bay window as they approached. He turned inside as they walked up the drive.

Harold answered the door. 'What do you want?'

'We want to see your wife. And since Corinne Draber is here, we might as well talk to her too,' said Warren.

'They're not here,' said Harold, closing the door. 'Go away,' Warren put his left foot in the gap. Harold tried closing it again, harder.

'That's not going to work,' said Warren, pushing open the door.

'You don't have a warrant,' said Harold, stumbling back into the hallway. 'She said you can't come in.'

Warren and Faith brushed past him and entered the living room. Mrs Plowright and Corinne were sat next to each other on the sofa. Corrine's dog sat on her lap and bared its teeth as Warren approached.

'Well, isn't this cosy?'

Harold came into the room. 'I'm sorry, Miriam, they forced their way in.'

Mrs Plowright stood up and pointed at the two armchairs in front of her. 'Why don't you both take a seat since you're here.'

'I think we'll stand,' said Faith. 'We've just been with your brother. He told us about the child you lost. It must have been quite traumatic?'

'He shouldn't have told you,' said Corrine.

'I think something like that is hard to hide, isn't it?'

The doorbell rung and Harold, watching from the doorway, scuttled to get it, closing the door behind him.

'I read that some mother's like to wash and dress the body before it's taken away. Many even have a burial service,' said Faith. 'What did you do?'

'That's none of your business,' said Mrs Plowright. Corrine held the dog tight against her chest. 'Can't you see you're upsetting her.'

'It wasn't stillborn, was it?' said Warren, pointing at her. 'You let it be taken away, didn't you?' The dog growled.

'No. No,' said Corinne, starting to cry.

'I think you should leave,' said Mrs Plowright. 'Now.'

Felix flung open the door. 'What's going on here?' Felix

scanned the room and fixed his eyes on Corinne. 'What have you done to my sister?' He barged through Faith and Warren and pulled her out of the seat. 'Let's go. Out of my way.'

The house shuddered as the front door shut. Harold had moved to his wife's side. They sat down in unison.

'What was the baby for, was it for you?' said Warren. 'Because you don't have your own, do you?'

Harold began to speak as his wife put a hand on his forearm. 'No, we don't,' she said. 'We tried but it didn't happen. When we were younger, they didn't have the tests they have now. But we've made the best of it, haven't we Harold?' He nodded.

'We wanted to ask you some more about your work as a bookkeeper. You worked both for the Council and Draber's, didn't you?' said Faith

'Yes, that's correct.'

'You were able to witness the awarding of contracts from both sides,' said Faith. Her eyes bore into Faith, making her hesitate.

'Draber's won a lot of contracts,' said Warren.

'They submitted the best proposals,' said Mrs Plowright.

'I bet they did,' said Warren.

'If there'd been any unusual or irregular payments, would you have noticed?' said Faith.

'Not necessarily. I wasn't responsible for checking every payment or contract. I was just a bookkeeper,' said Mrs Plowright.

'There were payments made to a Kaylin Enterprises,' said Faith. 'Who is that?'

'Kaylin?' said Mr Plowright.

'You have to leave now,' said Mrs Plowright, getting up. 'You're beginning to upset him.' Harold stared into the distance.

'The accounts showed -,' said Warren

'That's enough. Get out or I'll phone the *real* police,'

'Let's go,' said Faith, pulling Warren by the arm. Warren stood still; his hands clenched by his thigh. He stared at Harold who remained impassive.

'Warren,' said Faith, 'Let's go.'

As they walked down the path, Warren saw that the rose bush in the middle of the lawn had gone. In its place, a rectangular, dog-sized mound of earth.

CHAPTER 31

n the morning, Faith went for a run. They'd argued over calling the RSPCA. Warren didn't want to give Mrs Plowright a reason to contact DI Pale. Peter had had called in the evening asking when Faith would return. Warren had asked the same question when she left the hotel but got no answer.

Warren sat in the lounge with his laptop. He called Glade. She'd completed some research on the names Seymour had given them. Two had moved away, one had died and two were back in prison. All the rest were employed at one of Draber's businesses so had probably been warned against speaking to him. All except one.

The taxi didn't know the name of the shop, so dropped him at the entrance to the marina. It sat inside a periphery road that itself was behind an undeveloped patch of ground, half a mile from Chessil Beach. Warren had checked the large white board that listed each business by lot number. The Diver's Store was unit ten.

Warren had never been in a shop where he understood so little of what they sold. Except the time he'd gone with his mother and sister to buy Faith a dress for graduation.

Including underwear. He felt queasy at the memory. Everything here was either black, yellow, or orange. And waterproof.

A young man with a flop of blond hair over a pale blue polo shirt stood next to him. 'Can I help you find something?

'Perhaps,' said Warren. 'I'm looking for Jonathan Wheeler.'

'That's me.' He gave a quick smile.

Warren looked towards the older man behind the counter, his identical top stretched over his stomach. 'Does he know about your previous line of work?'

'What are you talking about?' said Jonathan, his forehead furrowed.

Warren lifted two fingers to his lips as if to taking a drag. Jonathan waved him down. 'I don't do that anymore. They know about it. Most of it. Who are you?'

'I'm investigating the discovery of the baby on Chessil Beach.'

'I don't know anything about that.'

'But you do know Ken Rhodes?' Jonathan rocked on his heels. 'You served time with him.'

'I don't want to discuss it. You'll have to go.'

'I can't do that. Someone is in danger.'

'I'm sorry, I can't help you,' said Jonathan, turning his head.

Jonathan turned and walked away. Warren flicked a yellow float onto the floor. The man at the till looked up. Another float joined the first. Jonathan turned briefly then spoke to his boss. He returned to Warren and headed out of the shop, indicating that Warren should follow.

Jonathan pulled out a packet of cigarettes from the back of his tight jeans. He turned around, his head down, looking at the packet. 'I heard about the baby being found over there,' he said, lighting one. 'Who do your think's involved?'

'I was hoping you might tell me?'

'I don't know anything about it.' He blew a white cloud of pungent smoke to the side.

'Do you remember Ken Rhodes? Or Samson?'

'Yes, but I've not seen them since.' He took another drag.

'You'd meet in the garden - '

'Those bloody roses. I hated them. I had scratches up and down my arms for months. But it was the one job that gave me a break from all the stuff going on inside.'

'Why aren't you working for Draber's like the rest of them?'

'I did. It was part of the deal for working in the garden and listening to him.'

Warren sat down on a large Portland stone boulder and stretched out his left leg. 'Who got you the job?'

'I don't know. Samson was out and he got me started.'

'Who got him the job?'

'I don't know. But I think it was someone he and Mr Rhodes both knew.'

'What did Mr Rhodes say in the meetings?

Jonathan dragged on his cigarette and dropped it to the floor. 'Most of them happened inside and I found excuses not to attend. Those outside were mostly about the tasks that had to be done.' Jonathan ground the butt into the gravel. 'he said we were God's children and we had to prove we were worthy. If we did, we'd be taken care of.'

'What do you think he meant?'

Jonathan shrugged. 'Look, I'm not into religion, so didn't pay much attention.'

'What about Samson. Did he listen?'

'He'd pretend to. I used to dye his hair. But he paid attention when it came to the gardening. If he thought you were slacking, he'd let us know. He put a spade through someone's foot for forgetting to water over a hot weekend.'

Warren pulled in his leg. 'Why job did you have at Draber's?'

'The same as everybody, driving a truck.'

'Why did you stop?'

'I didn't like it.' Jonathan looked back at the shop. 'I need to get back.'

'Tell me the real reason first.'

'We were told to be on the look out for a girl and call if we saw anything. It was winter. I came round the corner, and something ran out of in front of me. I stopped. I didn't think I'd hit here but those trucks were so solid, you'd probably have no idea.'

'Go on.'

'She was just stood there, bang in the middle of the road, staring into the headlights. I got out to check she was okay, but she didn't say a word. She just stood there.'

'What was she wearing?'

'It was sort of a long nightie. It was mostly white but had yellow stains down the front. She had no shoes and in one hand, she was holding a doll by its arm.'

'What did you do?'

'It was cold, so I thought I'd better bring her back to the quarry rather than wait for Samson to come and get her. Once she was in the truck, she became much more talkative. She kept telling me about her doll. When we got back to the quarry, we waited in the main cabin with a few of the others.'

'Is that it?' said Warren, hands on knees.

'Well, I was expecting Felix Draber to arrive. But instead, it was Samson with Mr Rhodes. He told Samson to get her in the car. Once they'd gone, Mr Rhodes told us not to say anything about what happened. I didn't even get a word of thanks. The next day, Samson handed me some cash and told me not to come to work again.'

Warren stood up. 'Did the meetings continue outside?'

'I heard they did, but I didn't go.' Jonathan began to walk back.

'One more thing,' said Warren, holding out his hand. Jonathan shook it. 'Thanks.'

White Stones cafe had taken down the photographs. In their place were watercolours of the local flora. Warren squinted at the labels: liverwort, Portland Hawkweed, lichen, and Feathermoss. They still served Bakewell tart.

Warren sat down, placing two glasses of water in the middle.

'What do you think?' said Warren, flicking his head towards the nearest picture.

'I've never liked watercolours after trying it at school,' said Faith.

'How's Mum coping with Peter?'

'I think she's finding it tough. Gerry is going to pick him up in two days so that will give her a break. I miss him. I've not been apart from him for this long for a while.' She sipped her smoothie through a straw. 'Do you think you'll need me much longer?'

'If you want to go, you can go.'

'I don't want to go. I mean I want to be back with my son, but I want to help you finish this.' She smiled. 'You're my little brother after all.'

'Funny. It shouldn't take - '

A waiter arrived with their food. 'Cheese and ham toastie?'

'That's mine,' said Warren, holding out his hand.

The waiter gave it to him and place a salad in front of Faith. 'Aren't you starving after your run?' said Warren, frowning as he examined her leaf-dominated meal.

'I had a protein shakes. The hotel's been keeping them in their fridge. I'll need to drop some more at yours when we get back. I'm due a new batch.'

'I can't wait,' he said, biting into his toastie, the cheese stretching as he pulled it away. 'What do you think we should do next?'

'I'm not sure. I can't think clearly after Seymour.'

'That's exactly why we need to keep going. They know we're close, so we need to act before they do anything more drastic.'

'I know, I know.' Faith poked at her salad.

Warren lifted then put down his sandwich. 'I'd say we need to speak to Rhodes and Samson again. Samson should be a prime suspect for the police - having a record of GBH. They must have spoken to him by now.' He pushed away his plate. 'The autopsy on Seymour should've been done although I doubt, we'll learn any more. Maybe you persuade Lyons to give us the results.'

'Or you could try Lyons.' Faith forked several leaves and a cherry tomato into her mouth.

'What about the reporter? He seems well informed.'

'He did, didn't he? I'll head down to his office. What about you?'

'We need to find the woman. If someone took her, she's in danger. The Plowrights are not telling us anything, Corinne is too scared, and her brother says he knows nothing. I'd say we try Rhodes and Samson again and risk being thrown off the island. I'm way over budget anyway. If we go, it would have to be decisive. I know there's a story here, something the magazine needs. We need to find the woman. I'm sure she's the key to all this.'

Faith started the car. 'So where should I drop you?'

'I have no idea. Who'd have thought on an island it would be so easy to hide someone, assuming she's still here and that they have her.'

'What if they're not hiding her at all.'

'I don't understand.'

'If she's over eighteen, she might be in sheltered housing.

If there's any owned by Portland Council, they should be able to provide you with the details.'

'The council office is round the corner. Drop me off there'.

Warren watched the gears of government grind. This was the second office he'd been sat in. He hoped he'd been sent to the right place this time. A bearded man in brown corduroys and a green checked shirt approached him.

'Mr Stance, I believe you want to enquire about sheltered housing. I'm Paul Jessop.' He held out his hand and Warren stood up and shook it. 'Would you follow me?'

The meeting room had two chairs either side of a small table. An empty Portsmouth Football Club mug sat on the table. 'Sorry about this,' he said, pushing it to the side and laying down his pad and biro. 'So how can I help you? Are you looking for something for a family member?' He moved through his notebook to a blank page.

'Not exactly. I'm looking for a woman that may already be in sheltered housing.'

'Oh, well, I'm not sure how I can help you with that.' He began to fidget.

'If I described her to you, would you be able to tell me where she lived?'

'No, I couldn't do that.'

'What about if she'd escaped?' said Warren, leaning forward.

'Escaped? They're free to come and go as they please. Most of them have some form of additional assistance but it varies. Some get meals delivered or have help doing their washing or cleaning. Most of them have family members who look in on them regularly. They don't escape. They're free to go when-ever they want unless a curfew has been set. Most of them are no different from you or me: they have jobs, bank accounts, friends.'

'Do any of them have children?'

'Not many of them. There's a couple with Down's syndrome who have a child but they're on the mainland.'

'How many of these places do you have?'

'Three run by the Council.'

'Where are they?'

'I'm not sure I should tell you that. Some of the residents are vulnerable.'

'They're publicly-funded services, aren't they?' Warren poked his finger at the table. 'It's probably on your website or at least it should be.'

'I don't think it is.' Jessop closed his notebook.

'Look, I think this woman may be in danger.'

'Aren't the police involved, then?'

'They're focussed on the murder of the hospital janitor and the baby.'

'On the beach?' Warren nodded. 'They've still not made any arrests.'

'That's why its so important. If you just gave me the places where she might be.'

Jessop picked up the pen. 'I don't want this coming back to me.' He opened his notebook. 'Do you really think she might be in danger?'

'I do.' Jessop began to write.

As Warren left the building, he unfolded the paper, smiling.

The Olympic Rings, sculpted in stone, celebrated Portland hosting the sailing events in 2012. It had originally been positioned in the town centre but was moved near the cenotaph, overlooking Chessil Beach a year later.

Faith balanced the two cups on the lower rings. Occasional gusts yanked steam from them. Warren gazed at the beach, following its gentle curve, braced against the cobalt sea. The waves appeared static, like the fringe of a Turkish rug.

Warren described his encounter with the Council man.

'So how will we know which one she's in?' said Faith, studying the list. Warren took out a Bakewell tart from the paper packet, balanced on one of the upper rings.

'Couldn't we get Glade find a list of residents?'

'The Prof's got her on something else. We'll have to try each one. Do you want yours now?' He held out the packet.

'Let me tell you how I got on first.' Faith supped from the cup before putting it back. 'When I got to the office, they said he was out for lunch but didn't know where. I tried Horsey's number but got his voicemail. So, I took a chance and went to a few of the nearest pubs.' She took a gulp of tea. 'Guess what?'

Warren swallowed. 'Go on.'

'He was having lunch with PC Lyons. In fact, it looked like they knew each other quite well - I'd swear they'd been holding hands before I went in.'

Warren chuckled, 'We know where he gets his, now.'

'Anyway, she left straight away. He looked pretty embarrassed and didn't take much persuasion to give me an update. They've made no progress with the missing woman. They've interviewed a few of the ex-cons from Seymour's list but not are talking.'

'Anything on Seymour?'

'The autopsy provided little more than what we knew already. He was conscious or semi-conscious from a blow to the head, but he died from blood loss from multiple stab wounds. A closer look at them found they'd been caused by a curved blade.'

'There are all sorts of curved blades. Karambits are a curved blade used in Asia, originally thought to be used in agriculture. What happened with their interviews of Rhodes and Samson?'

'Nothing, from what I could tell. Mr Rhodes said little. He'd reminded them about his position in the community. Samson was taken to the station. He punched Lyons in the ribs although he claimed it was accidental. They both said they'd remembered Seymour from their time in prison but hadn't seen him since.'

'We know that's a lie.'

'Even so, all of their movements were accounted for.' Faith took the remaining tart from the packet. She folded the wax paper and slipped it into her handbag. 'They finished the autopsy on the baby. He was suffocated not drowned. The cause of the brain damage was inconclusive. It could have been prior to death - the damage was similar to shaken baby syndrome - but it could equally have occurred during or even after the body had entered the water.'

'I suppose the fact that he'd died before going into the water is something to be thankful for.'

'Is it? It shouldn't have happened at all. How can you say that?'

'I didn't mean it's okay. Just that it's better than it being alive when it went into the sea?'

'He. It was he,' Faith turned away, putting the tart down.

'I know. I know.' Warren approached her. 'What's wrong? You've been -'

'Sensitive? Maybe *you* should be a bit more sensitive.' Faith walked towards the car.

Warren stared at Faith as she walked away. He threw the rest of his cake away and picked up hers. He poured the remaining tea from both cups onto the ground and stacked them together.

Faith leant against the bonnet. 'I'm sorry,' she said, as Warren approached.

'So am I. This is the first time we've had anything really serious. The most horrific thing we've ever had was a few dead mice. 'I think I knew deep down that if I stopped to think how sick and dangerous this was becoming, I'd have given up. So, I've treated it like all the others.'

'Often that's the best way.'

CHAPTER 32

This morning felt colder than the rest as they got in the car. The first housing complex was six houses in Castletown.

Warren and Faith walked to each house or flat together, hands in pockets. Glade had finished her work for the Prof so was able to provide them with information on some of the residents. They visited everyone. Some stood behind half-opened doors. Others didn't open them at all but stared through the glass. Any that did answer, Faith spoke to them first. They got nothing.

The second complex was larger, so they split up. It was on the edge of Grove. After nearly two hours, they'd gone though it. Several of the properties had been empty.

'This is hopeless,' said Warren, getting into the car.

'This is just how it is,' said Faith.

'Well, I can't take much more of it. Even the ones you think understand what we're asking give answers that usually bear no relation.'

'Don't be mean.'

'It's not mean, it's honest.'

'It's both.'

Grove House was a single, Victorian large building over two stories. Roses snaked up each pillar either side of the entrance. The Duty Manager was a squat woman. She wore a tightly fitting shirt under a blue suit. Her tights rubbed together as she led them around the building.

'Are you looking for yourself or a family member,' she said, half-looking over her shoulder as she began to climb a wide staircase.

Faith looked at Warren. 'Our mother,' said Warren. 'She used to visit Portland as a girl.' Faith scowled at Warren as he quickened his climb.

'Grove House has twenty-two en-suite units, five studio flats and twelve one-bedroom flats. Each flat is fitted with a kitchenette area, microwave, and storage, fitted carpets and curtains and a video door entry system. We provide a family atmosphere based on a balance of independence, support, companionship, and privacy. Residents furnish their own rooms to create a home from home.'

'Privacy is important,' said Faith, running her hand up the bannister.

'Cooked meals are provided twice a day. Ingredients are provided for breakfast.'

'Can residents come and go as they please?' said Warren.

'Yes, but we ask them to be back by ten. After that there's no onsite cover.'

'How many of the residents are young?' said Faith. 'Perhaps in their twenties.'

'We have just the two at the moment although one recently left.'

'I don't suppose you'd tell us who that is?' said Warren.

The Duty Manager, stood at the top of the stairs, shook her head. 'Its not something we discuss - privacy is a priority for us here. We don't give out the names of our residents.'

Faith overtook Warren and stood next to her. 'Does that happen often?' Faith said, 'Residents being taken out.'

'It's unusual,' the Manager said.

'Did they say why?' Faith said.

'No, but they said it wasn't related to the standard of care.'

As Warren reached the top step, he noticed that someone was watching them along the corridor. It was a young man with dark hair and darker glasses. He was ducking his head out of one the rooms. Each time Warren caught his eye, he'd disappear.

The Duty Manager turned and walked the other way, not noticing the interchange. She opened one of the last doors. 'This flat is currently unoccupied. You can take a look to get a sense of what they look like before a resident moves in.' Faith followed her into the room.

'Could I use your toilet?' said Warren.

'I suppose so. There's one just down the hall,' said the Manager pointing along the corridor.

Warren walked towards the young man, who reversed quickly, slamming his door shut. Warren entered. The man, in jeans and a t-shirt, was sat on the edge of his bed. He held a Rubik's cube. Sunshine from the single window left dark shadows on his face. Warren closed the door.

'I never managed to finish one of those,' said Warren, leaning against the wall besides the door. 'My name is Warren, what's yours?'

'Michael. You can call me Mikey.'

'Mikey, maybe you can help me. I'm looking for a young woman called Kaylin. She might have had a doll.'

'This is really hard,' he said, twisting and turning it. Several of the small cubes were missing.

'Can you remember her?' said Warren.

'You have to match the colours.'

Warren grabbed the Rubik's cube and Mikey screamed,

holding it tighter. Warren let go. He took out his phone and scrolled through it. Heavy footsteps came down the hall. He showed Mikey the screen as the door swung open.

'What's going on here?' said the Duty Manager. She bent down by Mikey. 'Are you okay, Michael.' He nodded several times.

'I was trying to help Mikey with the puzzle,' said Warren.

'He tried to take it,' mumbled Michael.

'I'm sure he didn't mean anything by it,' said Faith, stepping between Warren and the Duty Manager. 'Did you, Warren?'

'I didn't mean to upset him,' said Warren.

'I think you should go,' said the Duty Manager. 'If you have any further question, you can ring me tomorrow.'

'Let's go, Warren,' said Faith, moving him towards the door.

Mikey stared out of the window, letting the puzzle drop from his hands. 'Kaylin liked babies. And pink. One charm for every baby. She liked babies. She's gone again but not come back. A man with no hair came. I saw him. He scared me.'

'How many charms?' said Warren, tugged by Faith.

The Duty Manager picked up the Rubik's cube and placed it in his hands. She got up and faced them. 'I think you've upset him enough,' ushering them out of the room and then the building.

'Six,' echoed from his room as the exited.

Faith and Warren sat on the steps for several minutes. Rose petals fell to the ground. Faith sighed. 'Door to door. I can't say I've missed it. It's so frustrating.'

'We know she was here,' said Warren, standing up.

'Even if we believe him, we don't know where she is now.'

Warren held his plan against the brickwork, his fingers beside a main stem. 'I hate roses.'

'They're just flowers.'

'I can't explain it.' Warren slid his hand over, pressing down on the stalk. 'Roses don't have thorns. Everyone thinks they do but that's not what they are. They're prickles - a modification of the skin. If you break one off, the skin stays intact, protecting the rest of the plant. The only way to kill it is to dig it up from the roots.

CHAPTER 33

Faith and Warren sat in the Crab Pot underneath Portland Bill lighthouse. Warren straightened the square piece of green glass over table. Faith starred outside the only window on their side of the restaurant. A chef sat outside smoking on top of a picnic bench, his feet on the seat. He finished his cigarette and swung himself onto the ground.

Faith nudged her half-finished plate of food forwards. 'If Kaylin has anything to do with Rhodes or Samson, we should speak to them again.'

'Would they tell us anything?' said Warren.

'What about the Plowrights, then? Could we find out if Kaylin has a legal guardian?'

'We don't know for sure it's her real name and without her surname, we'd don't have much of a chance.'

'We could ask around. If she'd run off more than once, other people might have spoken to her.'

'I don't think we have the time. What do you think of the residents we met today?'

'What do you mean?'

'Do you think they're happy?'

'I think so. They're safe. They've got their own rooms or flats. They have activities and someone to help them.'

'So why would you leave in the middle of the night?'

'Perhaps she was confused.'

'Maybe.' Warren put his cutlery onto the plate. 'I'm done.'

'Although it was pretty irresponsible to let her get into that state in the first place. Covered in urine.'

Warren watched the waves dissipate over the rocks. Below the window, concrete blended into the pale, grey rock that lifted them from the sea's clutches. As the layers of rocks, stepped downwards like tiers of a wedding cake, they became darker. Each one still had patches of white but also patches of grey, black and yellow. 'If that's what it was.'

'What do you mean?'

Warren leapt up, looking at his watch. 'Let's go.'

'Wait, I haven't finished.'

There weren't any parking spaces near White Stones cafe, so Faith paused outside to let Warren out.

'I'll only be a minute,' he said, getting out.

She switched on the hazard lights then called their mother. Her mother became agitated when Faith told her about the Seymour's death. 'Be careful,' she said as Faith rung off as Warren opened the car door. He had a paper packet under his free arm.

'More Bakewell tarts?' said Faith.

'Not this time,' he said.

Faith drove off and stopped next to the square. Warren pulled two framed photographs from the parcel.

Faith leaned over. 'When did you become an art lover?'

The first was of a group of large rocks by the sea and the other the roof of a house. The only thing she could see in common was that they were both covered in lichen. Bright yellow lichen.

On the way to their hotel, Warren described his theory that the yellow marks on Kaylin's night dress were not urine but lichen. If they could identify the lichen, them might be able to determine where she'd been heading when she'd left Grove House.

At the hotel, Felix was waiting in the lounge. Faith saw him and took the pictures. 'I'll send them to Glade,' she said, proceeding up the stairs. 'You can deal with him.'

Warren turned to his right as Felix lowered his newspaper. 'Wait,' he said, throwing it down. 'I want to know what's going on?' He jumped up, approaching Warren at the bottom of the stairs, grabbing his arm. As the hotel manager, entered the foyer, Felix released his grip.

'Why don't we go back in there,' said Warren, moving past Felix towards the lounge.

They sat in the armchairs either side of an electric fire. Unlit, it sat there like a stubborn child unwilling to dress for school.

'What did you find out?' said Warren.

'I never knew, I want you to know that.' Warren nodded. 'I asked her about the pregnancy. She'd lied about it. They all had - everyone knew except me.' He lowered his gaze. 'It was born alive but given away.'

Warren leant forward, aiming his words. 'By whom? What for?'

'It made no sense. She said it was part of a tradition that had gone on for years. She called it 'the proving'. I'd never heard of it.'

'Did she say what it was?' He leant forward. 'What is it?'

'It made no sense.'

'Tell me.'

Felix looked up and catching Warren's glare, pushed himself into the back of the seat. 'Each woman, when she comes of age, has to give up her first child.'

'Comes of age. It's archaic. Did she what they were for? What happens to the babies?'

Felix turned his head towards the door. 'Sacrifice.'

Warren sunk back into his seat, gripping the armrest. 'To what?' he bellowed.

'What do you mean?'

'Sacrifices are usually to something or someone. To God to bring a good harvest or to a ruler who wants a demonstration of loyalty. Like Herod in the bible.'

'She didn't say.'

'You should have asked her. How could you not know about this?'

'After that night at Avebury, I heard things - secret meetings and rituals but when I asked it was always something to with the golf club or a rotary club meeting at the council. It can't still be going on, can it?'

'Maybe someone started it again. Take a few impressionable minds, promise them something if they follow a set of rules, however illogical and you've got yourself a group of people that will do what you want. Did she say who's responsible?'

'She wouldn't say, she was too scared.'

'Where did the birth happen?'

'At the hospital. In a private ward.'

'Did she say who was with here?'

'Anyone who came in or out wore masks.'

'What about the father of the baby? Was he not there?'

'No. It was a French ski instructor she'd met as a chalet girl. I only met him once. I think my father paid him off - we never saw him again.' Felix stood up and walked towards the reception. 'Look, I have to get back home. My sister is by herself.'

'Did she know what happened to the baby?'

Felix stopped. 'She was just glad it was gone.' Warren

stared at the dead fire. When he turned back to the doorway, Felix had gone.

CHAPTER 34

n the morning, Faith spoke to her son. Warren spoke to the Prof - she wanted to know when Warren would be back. Without Harris, she'd had to try to find new writers to fill the next issue which was impacting the supervision of her research team. When he asked to speak to Glade, he felt the chill of disapproval.

Faith ended her call. 'Glade's ready,' said Warren, spinning around the laptop. Glade shuffled beside him on the bed.

'Hey,' said Glade.

'Hi,' said Faith.

'What have you got for us?' said Warren.

Glade peered around her laptop then began. 'There are two types of yellow lichen on the island, and one is unique. However, I couldn't find any geodata on their locations.'

'Well, that's disappointing,' said Faith.

'Did you try someone at the Uni?' said Warren.

'I spoke to Dr Bover in Botanical Sciences.'

'And?' said Warren.

'She said it is something that's mapped but only if it's an indicator species. Like the Antarctic where the increase or decrease of lichen can tell them if the hole in the ozone layer is widening or shrinking.'

'Interesting,' said Warren.

'Well, that's it then,' said Faith. 'We'll have to try searching in the vicinity of where we saw first her. Near the batteries.'

'We don't have time. If they find out that Corinne has told Felix or that he told us, they might kill her,' said Warren, grabbing the top of the laptop.

'Wait,' said Glade. Warren let go. 'After I spoke to Dr Bover, I accessed the satellite data. The higher resolution images were behind a NASA firewall, but I spoke to a college friend working there who got me in. Let me get the printouts.'

Warren turned to Faith. 'The Antarctic and Artic reflect sun's radiation, keeping the earth cool. Anything that's not white, like lichen, will reflect less.' Warren turned back to the screen as Glade reappeared. 'So, where are you going with this?'

'They don't only map the poles,' said Glade.

Faith shook her head. 'I don't get it.'

'They've mapped the world,' said Warren.

'That's right,' said Glade. 'I downloaded the images of Portland. You can see the patches of lichen but only if you zoom right in.' She held up a printout. 'I needed a quicker way to map the whole island, so I found some software. It's normally used to search for child abuse images as it can be set to scan the internet for skin tones. I changed the settings to scan for yellow.'

'You did all of this yesterday afternoon?' said Faith.

'I started last night, after she'd gone,' said Glade. 'Warren had texted me to say how important it was after you'd emailed me the images. I'll send you the locations now.'

'They're lucky to have you,' said Faith.

'If only she'd stay,' said Warren.

'I need to go,' said Glade.

'Thanks,' said Faith as Warren shut the laptop. 'You didn't give her a chance to say goodbye.'

'Americans never say goodbye.'

In White Stones cafe, Faith and Warren opened the map of Portland on a table. The edges hung over the sides. Faith opened each of the images sent by Glade one by one. Together they sketched each area of lichen onto the map.

The map now had five circles. Faith and Warren stood over it in thought together. The owner approached with two mugs of tea.

'Where do you want them,' he said.

'Put them on the other table,' said Warren.

'Righto,' he said, putting them down with clunk. He dried his hands on the tea hanging from the string of his pinky. 'You two were here with Seymour, weren't you?'

'Yes,' said Faith. 'Is Sylvie okay? We looked for her when we came in.'

'She's upset all right. But she's got a granddaughter to think about now. It's keeping her busy.'

'Boy or girl?' said Faith.

'Boy. Named him Roger.'

'Did you know Seymour?' said Warren.

'Not really. He'd come in quite a lot when he was dating her and I did that whole big brother thing and quizzed him a bit. But before that, not a lot. Maybe once a month. They'd sit over there,' he said, waving the tea towel towards the back corner.

'They?' said Warren.

'He'd be there on his own for a while. Then this bald guy'd come in. Broad like.'

'Did you hear what they were talking about?' said Faith.

He shook his head. 'Baldie never even ordered anything. He just handed over a magazine and left.'

'Do you remember what it was?' said Faith.

'Something to do with golf, I think. Seymour never read it. Always left it behind. As soon as baldie had gone, he'd wait a few minutes then leave.'

'When was the last time you saw them in here?' said Warren.

'Not for months. I figured they'd just been meeting somewhere else.' A shout from the kitchen forced him around. 'I'd better get back.'

'What do you think that was about?' said Warren.

'Money,' said Faith. 'Hidden in the pages - I've seen it before. Useful for small drug exchanges. If you slip a few £50 notes between the pages of a book, you can carry it around and look perfectly innocent.'

'To keep him quiet, I bet. He never worked for Draber's, so they found another way to keep him quiet.' Warren sat down. 'But he couldn't keep quiet anymore. When he met us, it gave him the chance.'

Faith studied the map. 'Where's the quarry?' Warren stared at the table in the corner. 'Warren, where's the quarry?'

Warren returned her gaze and then looked at the map. 'Here,' he said, picking up the pen. He drew a square.

Faith ran her finger across the map. 'This is the sheltered accommodation Kaylin was in. So, if she left to go somewhere that required crossing a patch of lichen and being found on the road to the quarry, this is where she was going.' She drew her finger to the edge of the map. 'Church Ope Cove, below Rufus Castle.'

CHAPTER 35

The first recorded Viking attack on Britain occurred at Church Ope Cove. Rufus Castle was built in response. Its remains sit on a cliff-top above the curved beach. Quarry debris lies on the sand, worn into soft pebbles like bars of soap. Neapolitan-coloured beach huts face the sea. The rocks behind them are dusted bright yellow.

Faith pulled the balaclava over her head. 'Is this really necessary?' Warren checked the two long metal torches. 'They killed Seymour.'

'We don't know that, and I still think you were wrong not to tell the police what we're doing.' Faith pulled at the arms and hem of her tight black jumper.

'DI Pale has told us we're on our last life. You said yourself, they're probably looking for a reason to get you off the force.' Faith began to to speak but stopped. 'We're only having a look. If we find anything, we'll call them.'

There were two paths leading to the beach. They parked by the least direct of the two which ran through a wood. A car slowed nearby as they entered. Warren pulled down his mask and they turned on the torches.

'Itchy,' said Warren. Faith shushed him from behind.

A brisk wind shook the branches. The torch beams flicked across trunks. Warren stopped at the stone steps. He shone the light downwards and two green eyes shone back. The animal's claws scrapped as they made the final steps towards him. It was a dog, probably a black Labrador. It flicked past his legs and circled around Faith.

'Hold on,' said Warren.

A man followed up the stairs. He wore a cap, blue raincoat and held a dog lead. Warren lifted his mask and indicated to Faith to do the same.

The man arrived at the top. 'All right?' he said, pausing to take a few breaths. 'My wife says I should swap him for a cat.'

Warren smiled as the man shuffled past, ushering his dog from Faith's circumference.

'We might as well leave them off,' he said, pulling off the balaclava and wiping the sweat from his forehead.

'Hallelujah,' said Faith, handing him hers. 'Take mine.'

At the base of the staircase Warren leant against one of the nearest rocks that formed the bottom of the cliff face. There were at least a dozen huts following its curvature, two or three deep in places. Most were small but several were caravan sized. Moonlight added frosting to the breaking waves.

Warren pulled away his hand and shone the torch on it. A yellow powder covered his palm. He held it towards Faith. She nodded.

They planned their route. Warren shone the torch at his feet - the oval stones ran all the way to their first waypoint. His forehead frowned as he stepped forwards.

At their target, Faith had overtaken Warren. Faith stood on tiptoes and looked through the window. It had blinds but it was clear there was no light on inside. She shook her head.

They repeated the procedure at each beach hut. None emitted any light. At the fifth, Faith found there was light from somewhere inside, but she couldn't see anyone there.

'This is a problem,' whispered Faith. Warren nodded, resting his cheek against the cooling wooden surface. 'What do we do now?'

'Follow me.'

At each hut, he leant his head and palms against it as Faith checked the window. After each manoeuvre, they conferred.

Two-thirds of the way around, they found a hut with both light and movement. Warren climbed the small flight of wooden steps and knocked on the door. There was no response. He tried again. Nothing.

Faith pushed past him and knocked on the door, 'This is the police, open the door.'

Rhodes opened the door. 'What do you want?'

'We want to look inside?' said Faith.

'Do you have a warrant?' Faith looked at Warren. 'I didn't think so,' shutting the door. A baby's cry escaped before the door clicked shut. A key turned in the lock. Warren pulled back Faith and kicked the door, sending Rhodes backwards towards the sink. His arms flailed out behind him, rattling into crockery. Faith followed Warren inside. 'You'd better be right,' she said.

On the far side of the hut stood Mrs Plowright, eyes fixed on them. Kaylin sat upright in a small armchair by her side feeding a baby with a bottle. She rocked back and forth. 'Gently,' said Mrs Plowright without looking down.

'You've got another,' said Warren.

'You're under arrest,' said Faith, sweeping her voice from left to right.

'For what?' said Rhodes.

'You've kidnapped this woman,' said Faith.

Mrs Plowright put her hand on Kaylin's shoulder. 'This is our daughter.' Faith looked at Warren who tilted his head towards the baby.

'What about the baby?' said Faith.

'My baby,' said Kaylin. 'A girl for Kaylin. I had a boy. Now I have a girl again. Girls are prettier, aren't they mummy?'

Warren turned to Mrs Plowright. 'How many have there been?' Her eyes narrowed. 'How many?' shouted Warren.

Mrs Plowright kneaded Kaylin's shoulder. 'It's what makes her happy.'

Faith moved towards the women. 'At what cost?' said Faith. 'All those children taken just so she can be... entertained.'

'She does try, really she does,' said Mrs Plowright. 'Don't you Kaylin?'

Kaylin looked up and smiled, 'Yes, mum. I clean her and I wash her till she smells so fresh.' Kaylin pulled the bottle out of the baby's mouth. It began to cry. 'But sometimes she's naughty and makes me angry, doesn't she, mummy.'

'Yes, dear,' said Mrs Plowright. 'Give her the milk, she needs more.' Kaylin returned the bottle.

Warren turned to Rhodes. 'She shouldn't be allowed to have a baby. It's not a toy to be used up and thrown away. That's why you needed to bring back the proving, didn't you? An ancient tradition combined with a prison full of impressionable men.'

Rhodes smiled. 'It's true. My wife was killed in a car accident. She was pregnant. We met at the hospital. Janice told me she couldn't have children. Then one day, Kaylin came to us. We were at my house, sitting in my garden. Harold was at work. We could hear crying and I realised I'd left the back gate open. And there she was, sitting in corner, holding her doll. Her dress had been torn by the roses. She'd run away from her care home. We took her back. She'd been there her whole life, given away by her parents because of how she is. No one else wanted her. We did.'

'But I was still married, and we were too old to adopt,' said Mrs Plowright, stroking Kaylin's hair. 'We taught her to come to us. We look after the child when she's in the residential home.'

'But you took her out,' said Faith.

'We knew you were getting close, so we had someone pick her up,' said Rhodes. 'It's not difficult to forge papers to fool someone for a while but they'll realise soon enough.'

'What will you do now?' said Faith.

'We're going to leave,' said Mrs Plowright.

Warren braced himself in the doorway. 'Are you religious?' said Rhodes to Warren, who shook his head. He turned to Faith, causing her to stop her slow progress. 'What about you, do you believe in anything?'

'Not really,' she said.

'We do. Belief is powerful. They all wanted to believe, these young men. I just had to give them something. It didn't have to be real, it just had to sound it.' He shook a finger at Warren. 'You pride yourself on your scientific, rational worldview. But you're in the minority. Most of the world believes in gods - however cruel or barbaric they were. We gave them something better to believe. Look how happy she is. They are all in work. I saved them.'

'Salvation is for god alone,' said Warren.

Faith moved closer. 'You received secret payments from the Draber's didn't you?' Mrs Plowright took the empty bottle from Kaylin. 'Yes, I did. I uncovered the bribes they were paying the Council for planning approvals. If I hadn't worked for both of them, it would have gone unnoticed.'

'The money's been moved. It will allow the three of us to start somewhere else,' said Rhodes.

'What about Corinne's baby?' said Warren.

'Such a shame,' said Mrs Plowright. 'I'd only turned my back for a few seconds, and she'd got hold of some secateurs.'

'Baby was being naughty, mummy,' said Kaylin.

'I know, dear, but you have to be more careful,' said Mrs Plowright.

'We have a doll in the car,' said Faith, 'if you give me the baby, you can have it instead.'

'Is it pretty?' said Kaylin, loosening her grip.

'Yes, very,' said Faith. She leaned towards the baby. Kaylin pulled the baby to her chest. 'I don't trust you.'

Rhodes rattled the cutlery on the draining board. 'Corinne gets an income from Draber's for the rest of her life without having to lift a finger.'

'Why did you use the sea?' said Warren.

'When I left the hospital, I couldn't use the incinerator. Full moon sacrifices seemed a good way to keep their trust. The fact that some of the babies were already dead, made no difference. We'd find one a year was enough to keep the faithful in check. This baby's from a young Polish girl, moved her from London with her boyfriend, a local lad. The women can have more babies. We only have one daughter,' said Rhodes.

Faith lunged towards the baby and Warren followed. He saw something glimmer as Rhodes lunged at him. Warren threw his right arm at him and deflected a knife into his left shoulder. He dropped the torch as he grabbed Rhodes, pushing him backwards. Warren slammed Rhode's arm against a cupboard door, causing the steak knife to fall to the floor. He pushed Rhodes hard against against the edge of the work surface, knocking the wind from him. Warren picked up the knife, brandishing it at him. 'Stay there.'

He turned around. Mrs Plowright had leapt in front of Kaylin and was struggling with Faith, the torch gripped in her hand. They fought above Kaylin and the baby. Warren approached. Kaylin saw him, ducked between the two women and past Warren's free hand out of the hut.

'Are you okay?' said Warren to Faith.

She turned briefly. 'Go!'

Warren stumbled down the steps. He threw the knife to the side and placed his hand on his shoulder. Warm and wet.

He scanned back and forth but his vision was impaired by the huts in front. The baby cried. He stepped down onto the pebbles and pushed off, losing his balance. He slipped in a different direction with each forced step. As he emerged from the final gap between huts, he saw them. Kaylin was in the sea, holding the baby.

He stepped onto wet sand and stood in front of them, waves flicking over his shoes.

'Kaylin,' said Warren, 'give me the baby.'

Kaylin looked down. 'Baby's dirty. She needs to be cleaned.' Kaylin took off a white blanket, letting it drop into the water.

Warren moved towards her. The waves lapped at her thighs, making her sway. The baby's feet stuck out of the remaining blanket.

'Kaylin,' said Warren, 'the baby will get cold. You don't want the baby to get cold, do you?'

Kaylin glanced at Warren. 'I sent you a picture of my baby. They said my baby had the devil inside and had to be taken away. I don't want them to take my baby away. Harold said you'd help me. Why didn't you help me?'

'I'm sorry. I'm here now, aren't I, to help you?' Warren stretched his arms forwards and moved forwards. 'If you give me her, we'll get her clean.'

Kaylin turned to Warren and screamed. Warren felt a blow from behind and crashed into the water. He twisted around to face upwards. Someone was on his chest. He gasped for water, tasting salt. Moonlight lit half of Samson's face as he flung a fist round in an arc, hitting Warren on his right cheek. Warren lifted his right arm up, but his left was frozen. The next blow came from the left hitting his ear, compressing the sound of the baby's cry. He tried to pull himself up, but more blows forced him back down.

The weight from his chest lifted. Samson landed heavily next to him, unconscious. Warren lowered his arm. Faith stood above him, holding the torch. 'Makes a good truncheon, should've kept yours.'

She pulled Warren up and they dragged Samson a metre further in shore. The waves lapped at the side of his face.

They approached Kaylin. She had dropped the remaining blanket. and held the baby's white body just above the water.

'Give me the baby, Kaylin,' said Faith, pointing the torch.

Kaylin turned the baby away and tried to move further out, resisted by the sea. She held the baby against her the water splashing against the underside of her arms.

'Kaylin, come here,' said a man behind them. Warren and Faith turned. It was Harold, striding through the water, holding his tweed jacket. 'Kaylin.'

Kaylin turned around; the baby held to her chest. Harold moved past them, his grey slacks turning black. As he approached her, she moved towards him. He put his arm around her and helped her to wrap the baby in the jacket.

As the three moved ashore, Warren and Faith left the water. Blue lights shone from the cliff top. Horsey ran towards them, taking out his camera. As Harold and Kaylin exited the water with the baby, he began to take pictures.

'How did he get here?' said Warren.

'You didn't say I couldn't tell the papers where we were going?' said Faith. 'He must have called Lyons.'

Warren fell to his knees. Faith crouched beside him, 'Are you all right, Warren?'

'I just need a minute.'

Felix followed Harold, Kaylin, and the baby up the beach. More police arrived.

'What happened?' said PC Lyons, standing above them.

'Just give us a minute,' said Faith.

'I'm okay, help me up,' said Warren.

Faith and PC Lyons helped Warren to his feet, wincing as PC Lyons held his left arm. 'Wait,' he said to Harold. Warren followed them as they slowed.

'You sent the picture,' said Warren.

Harold nodded. 'I wanted to do more but I didn't know how.' He began to shake.

'It's okay,' said Warren. 'They'll be gone soon.'

Harold gave a brief smile and turned back to Kaylin. A paramedic arrived and began to check the baby. Felix headed for the beach hut as the police reached it. Light shone out of its open door. PC Lyons followed him.

Faith helped Warren to the first row of huts. He sat on the step, head in his hands.

'I distinctively remember saying *final warning*'

'You did?' said Warren, smiling. 'I don't remember.'

'He's had a knock to the head,' said Faith.

'You seem fine, though?' said DI Pale. Faith gave a brief smile. 'How many do you think there were?'

'Do you still have the charm bracelet? '

DI Pale nodded. 'My daughter has one just like it. She adds more charms using her pocket money.'

Warren leant back, taking a balaclava from his trouser pocket. He pushed it against his shoulder. 'You tell her, 'Looking at Faith.

'We think each charm represents a baby. There's nine.'

DI Pale's eyes flicked from side to side as she stood still. PC Matthews arrived beside her. 'Ma'am,' he said, nodding at Faith and Warren. 'We found this in one of the suspect's car.'

PC Matthews held the see-through bag from the top. Faith pointed the torch at it. Inside it, was a small, curved knife with a wooden handle.

'Pruning knife,' said Warren.

'You should get that seen to?' said DI Pale.

Faith helped Warren to his feet and headed towards the staircase. Mrs Plowright and Rhodes were stood at the bottom.

'Do you think they'll talk?' said DI Pale.

'I doubt it,' said Faith.

'Harold will be able to fill any gaps we've left,' said Warren.

PC Matthews stood beckoning to DI Pale from the hut. 'It looks like you've got your article,' she said.

'I hope so,' said Warren. Faith saw a paramedic and hurried over to them.

'We'll be in touch,' said DI Pale, walking towards PC Matthews. Warren stood alone. His left arm hung limply. He dropped the balaclava and used his right hand to squeeze water from the bottom of his top. He watched the small, frail figures of Mrs Plowright and Rhodes climb the steps. Samson followed, a towel over his shoulders.

After some treatment, they climbed together. Faith got in the car and started it. Warren had turned back to the boot. She watched him in the rear-view mirror.

Warren walked to a nearby police car and leant over. PC Lyons wound down the window. Kaylin sat next to her, crying, her white fingers interlocked. PC Lyons held up her hands, taking the box from Warren. She passed it to Kaylin who cradled it in her arms.

ABOUT THE AUTHOR

Merlin Goldman writes what takes his fancy. This might be plays, poems, screenplays, or novels - both fiction and non-fiction.